# Scorched

#1 NEW YORK TIMES AND USA TODAY BESTSELLING AUTHOR

# Jennifer L. Armentrout

Spencer Hill Contemporary, an imprint of Spencer Hill Press

Contact: Spencer Hill Press
27 West 20th Street, Suite 1102
New York, NY 10011

Please visit our website at www.spencerhillcontemporary.com

First Edition: June 2015.

Armentrout, Jennifer L. 1980
Scorched : a novel / by Jennifer L. Armentrout – 1st ed.
p. cm.
Summary:
A college student's blossoming relationship with an amazing guy is threatened by her personal demons.

The author acknowledges the copyrighted or trademarked status and trademark owners of the following wordmarks mentioned in this fiction: AA (Alcoholics Anonymous), Dinobot, *Dr. Phil*, Durango, Facebook, Folgers, Grindr, Holy Cross Hospital, Imodium, *Intervention*, iPhone, Lexus, Louis Vuitton, Lowe's, Mack truck, Mercedes-Benz, Miller Lite, My Little Pony, One Direction, Pepsi, Pepsi Max, Redd's Apple Ale, Sallie Mae, Snapchat, Sonata, Target, Thermos, Tinder, Titanic, Toaster Strudel, Tom Hardy, Transformers, Tumblr, Tums, *US Weekly, The Walking Dead*

Cover design by Sarah Hansen of Okay Creations

ISBN 978-1-63392-016-3 (e-book)
ISBN 978-1-63392-015-6 (paperback)

Printed in the United States of America

## Also by Jennifer L. Armentrout (J. Lynn)

**The Covenant Series**
(Spencer Hill Press)
*Daimon* (novella)
*Half-Blood*
*Pure*
*Deity*
*Elixir* (novella)
*Apollyon*
*Sentinel*

**The Titan Series**
(Spencer Hill Press)
*The Return*
*The Power* (2016)

**The Lux Series**
(Entangled Teen)
*Shadows* (novella)
*Obsidian*
*Onyx*
*Opal*
*Obsession* (Entangled Covet)
*Origin*
*Opposition*

**The Nephilim Rising Series**
(Entangled Edge)
*Unchained*

**The Dark Elements Series**
(Harlequin Teen)
*Bitter Sweet Love*
*White Hot Kiss*
*Stone Cold Touch*
*Every Last Breath*

**The Gamble Brothers Series**
(Entangled Brazen)
*Tempting the Best Man*
*Tempting the Player*
*Tempting the Bodyguard*

**The Wait For You Saga**
(HarperCollins)
*Wait for You*
*Trust In Me*
*Be With Me*
*Stay With Me*
*Fall With Me*
*Dream Of You* (novella)

**Standalone Titles**

*Cursed*
(Spencer Hill Press)

*Don't Look Back*
(Disney-Hyperion)

*Frigid*
(Spencer Hill Contemporary)

*This book is for you, the reader,
for making this story possible,
and for anyone who has pulled themselves
free of life's darkest moments.*

# Chapter 1

**Andrea**

This had to be the absolutely stupidest thing I'd ever seriously considered agreeing to take part in. That was admitting to something pretty epic, because I'd done a lot of stupid in my twenty-two years strutting around on planet Earth. And I mean, a *lot* of stupid.

At the ripe age of six, I'd shoved a fork in my pappy's toaster when my Toaster Strudel got stuck—though I'm pretty sure even back then I knew that wasn't a clever thing to do. That ended in a trip to the emergency room and a near heart attack for the dear old man, who, after that, refused to babysit me again. Then, when I was ten, I allowed my older brother—older by *barely* a year—Broderick to convince me that jumping from the porch roof into the pool down below was a totally cool idea and not dangerous at all. That also ended with a trip to the ER, a broken leg, and a summer-long grounding for Brody.

Not all my stupid actions resulted in hospital visits, but that didn't make them any less dumb. When I was fourteen, I was positive that I could take my parents' car around the block without them ever finding out. Unfortunately, in the excitement of doing something naughty, I'd forgotten to lift the garage door and ended up driving *through* it.

In their shiny, new Benz.

Then I'd dated Jonah Banks, all-star quarterback in high school, and while that didn't necessarily sound like a bad thing, he'd been under the impression—and probably still was—that the sun revolved around the Earth. And because everyone else was doing it, I'd given him my v-card, and had immediately wished I could grow that damn hymen back, because the awkward fumbling in the back of his truck and all that sweating *so* hadn't been worth the pain and weirdness.

I was also beginning to think changing my major at the start of the new year from pre-med to education hadn't been a smart choice, because *cheese and rice*, I was going to be in school forever and when I graduated, I'd be so far in debt that Sallie Mae would be the godmother of any children I had. Not to mention, my parents were still reeling from my latest string of decisions that they didn't necessarily approve of. Both were doctors, successful ones, and Brody was already in med school, continuing the family tradition like the good child that he was.

But becoming a doctor…well, it had been what *they* wanted. Not me. Seeing Kyler, my best friend's boyfriend, change his major last year had given me the courage to do the same. Not that I'd ever tell him that, though. Or really admit that to anyone.

However, one of my latest and greatest idiotic decisions to date, and probably the most painful, was allowing myself to be charmed by Tanner Hammond. Because I totally, *totally* knew better. From day one, I recognized Tanner for what he was—a player's player. After all, I'd grown up with a brother who'd had the attention span of a gnat when it came to girls. Tanner was no better.

Fucker.

But I was about to make another epic bad decision, because as I stared into Sydney Bell's bright blue eyes, I couldn't tell my best friend no.

Well, I *could* tell her no. I'd told her no a lot, but I couldn't in this situation, because telling her no meant that I would be stuck here by myself, and nothing drove me more crazy than being…well, alone.

"Please," she said, clapping her tiny hands together as she hopped, causing her thick black ponytail to bounce.

Everything about Syd was small. Standing next to her, I felt like Bigfoot—a redheaded Bigfoot. "Please. It will be so much fun. I promise you. And it's going to be the last time any of us really have a lot of time to get away. Summer is almost over. Kyler is doing the vet school stuff. My grad school classes are going to suck up all my time."

And I'd be puttering around, being lame and useless, still taking undergrad classes like the loser I was turning out to be.

Plopping down on the edge of the bed in the apartment she now shared with Kyler, I tried not to think about all the indecent things those two had done on said bed. Or think about the constant reminder that all my friends were either paired off, entering grad school, or starting their careers while I was…unchanged.

Stuck.

Even though I kept changing my mind about, well, everything, I was still *stuck.*

"But it's a cabin in the woods of West Virginia," I said, shaking off troublesome thoughts before they festered into something I couldn't ignore. "That's like the start of every horror movie featuring cannibals."

Syd narrowed her eyes. "You had no problem going to the cabin in Snowshoe."

"That's because that cabin is in a tourist town, and this cabin sounds like it's in the middle of the mountains," I pointed out. "And may I remind you what happened the last time you went to Snowshoe? You got snowed in and some crazy dude attacked you."

"That was a freak occurrence," she insisted, waving her hand. It had taken her a long time to be so flippant about the event, but I noted that for this trip she and Kyler had rented a different cabin, rather than going back to the one his family owned. I honestly wasn't sure if Syd would ever go back to that cabin. "And the house Kyler and I rented is actually near

Seneca Rocks, so it's not that remote. It isn't like you're going to run into the chupacabra or a pack of aliens."

I snorted like a little piglet. "I'm more worried about six-fingered hillbillies."

She folded her arms across her chest. "Andrea…"

Exhaling, I rolled my eyes. "Okay. I know there aren't six-fingered hillbillies running around." Truthfully, I'd found West Virginia to be very beautiful every time I'd visited.

"The cabin is fully loaded and gorgeous. It's huge. Six bedrooms. Has a hot tub and a pool." Moving over to the dark cherry dresser, she started arranging the bracelets sprinkled across the top, organizing them by color. What a little freak. "It will be a week in paradise."

I lifted a brow in doubt. To me, paradise was lounging on an island in the Caribbean with a margarita the size of a toddler in my hand, but hey, what did I know?

"And the house is big enough that you won't even know Tanner is there," she added as she cast a sly grin over her shoulder. "If that's what you want to do. Of course, you don't *have* to ignore him."

"You had to invite him, didn't you?" Needing to move, I popped up from the bed and stalked past her, heading into the bathroom—the ridiculously clutter-free bathroom with its deep-blue floor mats and matching toilet seat cover. Ugh. Couples. I leaned against the sink and stared into the mirror. Yikes. My eyeliner was trying to mate with my cheeks. How had Syd failed to mention that?

"*I* didn't invite him." Her voice carried from the bedroom. "Kyler did. And what's the big deal? I thought you two were getting along now."

Swiping my fingers under my eyes, I dropped my hands to the cool rim of the porcelain sink with a sigh. "Just because we're getting along *right now* doesn't mean we'll get along tomorrow or next week or an hour from now. He's…he's moody like that."

There was no answer from the bedroom.

Rising onto the tips of my toes, I peered into the mirror, and then cursed under my breath. Was that a zit forming on my chin? A huge one, too. I puckered my nude lips. At what point would my face outgrow the pimple phase? "And why would Kyler even invite him? Tanner is as interesting as getting my eyebrows plucked. Speaking of which…" I pulled back from the mirror, wrinkling my nose. "My eyebrows look like caterpillars, Syd. Hairy and bushy caterpillars."

Syd cleared her throat. "Um, Andrea—"

"Actually, let me rephrase that." Settling flat on my bare feet, I smoothed my hands over my shoulder-length ringlets. My hair was a deep auburn in normal light and much redder out in the sun. Syd thought I looked like old-school Little Orphan Annie since I also had the matching freckles. "Plucking the hair off my chin would be more interesting than spending a week with Tanner. And why *do* we get hair on our chins? Don't answer that. You'll probably have some kind of logical explanation, and I'm against all things logic right now."

"Andrea—"

"But plucking any piece of body hair would be less painful. *God.*" Yep. I was getting riled up, like I always did when I thought about Tanner. "Do you know what that dickhead told me after you and Kyler ditched me at the park the night of the fireworks? And I don't even need to guess what you two were doing behind those trees. Perverts," I went on, anger resurfacing as I remembered what Tanner had said. "He told me I drank too much. And he said this while holding a beer in his hand. What kind of fucked-up double standard is that? Plus, I need to drink so I don't want to punch him in the gonads."

"Nice."

I stiffened, eyes widening as I recognized a voice way too deep to belong to Syd, unless she had been keeping a major secret from me. Two pink splotches formed on my cheeks as I turned toward the open bathroom door.

That was definitely Kyler's voice, and if he was home, there was a good chance he wasn't alone, which meant…

Oh, for fuck's sake.

Face burning and most likely matching my hair, I briefly considered hiding behind the shower curtain, but that was weak and would be really weird. I walked out of the bathroom and quickly discovered that I'd just inserted foot and my entire leg into my mouth.

Kyler Quinn was in the bedroom with one well-defined arm draped over Syd's slim shoulders. Her cheeks were flushed pink, so I was assuming he'd given her a heck of a greeting with his mouth and hands. He was a multitasking kind of guy. Right then, he was grinning at me like a cat that had devoured an entire box of mice. Kyler was hot. With his messy brown hair and Prince Charming kind of smile, he was a perfect match for Sydney, who sort of reminded me of a living, breathing Snow White.

Sydney and Kyler? Gah, they made me want to puke rainbows of the My Little Pony variety.

Their whole story was a thing of fairytales, what little girls dreamed of—what I still kind of dreamed of in a really pathetically sad sort of way.

Growing up together, basically best friends for life, they both had been secretly in love with one another, and last year, while snowed in together at the cabin in Snowshoe, they'd finally fessed up to their feelings. They'd been together ever since, and even though I was a wee bit envious of their love for one another, I couldn't be any happier for them. Those two deserved their happy ending.

The walking penis leaning against the doorframe? Another story.

My gaze slid to Tanner Hammond. He wasn't hot. Oh no. *Hot* was too weak of a word to describe all six feet and four inches of sexiness packed into well-formed arms, tight abs, and a broad chest, complete with narrow hips and an ass one could ogle for days. His bright, crystal-blue eyes were legit bedroom eyes, always half-hooded, sleepy and sensual. His face was almost perfectly pieced together—high cheekbones and a lower lip slightly fuller than the top lip, his nose faintly crooked from a break he'd suffered long before I knew him.

I usually liked my guys with a bit more hair, but he rocked the buzzed-at-the-sides and cropped-at-the-top look. Once, when I'd been…well, drunk, I'd gotten the great idea to rub my palm across his head. Probably another dumb idea, but I'd about died over how the prickly softness of his hair felt against my palm.

It had felt *go-oo-od*.

The first time I'd seen Tanner had been in my packed English 101 class, and my tongue had practically lolled out of my mouth and smacked off the floor. He, of course, hadn't noticed me. Hell, Kyler and Syd thought we'd only met in the last two years or so. Not true. I'd known *of* Tanner since my freshman year. That year alone, he'd been in two of my classes, and I had crushed on him hard—super hard—right up to the end of spring semester.

Tanner lifted a brow. "I stand by my word. You do drink too much."

My hands clenched as I drew in a sharp, stinging breath. "I didn't ask for your opinion, Dr. Phil."

"All I'm saying is that I've seen you puke more times than I would hanging out in an emergency room during flu season," he added dryly.

The vein along my temple started to tick while Kyler tipped his chin down, not doing a good job at hiding his smile. "Oh. So roughly the same number of times you screwed random chicks this week?"

His lips curled into a half-smile—the kind of grin that would've been mind-numbingly sexy if I didn't want to smack it off his face. "Sounds about right—no, wait. There's probably been one more random chick than you puking, if we're keeping count."

"Guys…" Syd murmured.

My shoulders tensed as I readied for a verbal battle, round five million. "So that means you've probably caught chlamydia *and* gonorrhea this past weekend alone, then?"

He raised one shoulder as he eyed me lazily. "Probably the same likelihood of you vomiting in your date's lap."

Warmth crept over my cheeks. I'd done that before. Once. Wasn't pretty. "How about this? Why don't you go fu—"

Tanner pushed off the wall, turning to Kyler and Syd. "Is she going to the cabin? If so, I need to pack hazmat gear."

I was going to hit him. Seriously. Plant my fist in his solar plexus, right at the exact moment he inhaled.

Struggling to keep a straight face, Syd looked at me. "I don't know. I was trying to convince her before you two showed up, but now that seems like a giant waste of time." She shot a dark look at Tanner.

He smiled broadly. "Sounds good to me." Clapping his hand on Kyler's shoulder, he started to walk back into the hall. "I was thinking about inviting Brooke."

My jaw hit the floor. Brooke Page? Blonde and big boob-a-licious Brooke Page who needed a calculator to count to one hundred?

"You are *not* inviting Brooke," Syd said, sighing.

Tanner chuckled. "How about Mandie?"

A choking sound came from Kyler.

I rolled my eyes. Now he was just being silly. "You have such classy taste in women."

Casting a long look over his shoulder, he winked. "At least none of them are spoiled little rich girls who couldn't balance their own checking accounts without Daddy's help."

"I am not a spoiled little rich girl!" I shrieked, and Syd suddenly found something interesting on the ceiling. Okay. Being that both my parents were very successful plastic surgeons, they were well off. The apartment I lived in? Paid for by Mom and Dad. As was most everything inside said apartment and the car—an older Lexus—I drove, but just because I came from money didn't mean I was spoiled. My parents were never afraid to remind me of just how much they paid for and how quickly all of that could go away— they were making me pay my tuition, now that I'd switched majors, and the loans were already adding up. "And I know how to balance my checkbook, unlike Mandie and Brooke."

"So you say," he replied, walking down the hall.

I prowled after him, ignoring the exasperated noise coming from Syd. "What? Tanner-man, you don't want me to go to the cabin?"

"Do I really need to answer that question, Andy?" He headed for the galley kitchen.

My lip curled. I *hated* that nickname. Made me feel like a dude with big shoulders…and I kind of did have man shoulders. Before I could reply, Tanner said, "It's Friday night, shouldn't you be plastered by now?"

"Ha. Ha." Actually, I *was* usually a bit tipsy by this point on a Friday night, but Syd was staying in tonight with Kyler, and the rest of our friends were gone.

*I can't go to the cabin.*

The moment that thought finished, a slice of panic twisted my stomach and my throat dried. If I didn't go, I'd be…stuck here. I'd be alone. And if I were alone, I'd just sleep and be…be lame, and if I didn't sleep, then I'd spend all the time *thinking*.

Sometimes thinking didn't end well.

I had to go to the cabin.

Stopping in the entry to the kitchen, I looked down the hall, back to where Kyler and Syd lingered. "When are you guys planning to go to the cabin?"

"Next week." Syd appeared, her hair mussed and out of the ponytail. Jesus. Kyler was a man of opportunity *and* a fast worker. "We're going to leave on Monday morning."

"Hmm." I turned to Tanner and smiled sweetly. "Well, since I'm a spoiled little rich girl, it's not like I have to get time off from work. I'm free next week."

Tanner reached into Kyler's fridge and pulled out a beer. Screwing the top off the bottle, he raised it to me. Wisps of cold air rolled up from the neck of the bottle. "Well, since I don't have a drinking problem, I can have one of these."

"I don't have a drinking problem, asshole."

He took a long and slow drink from the bottle as he rested his hip against the counter. The half-grin was back in full force. "You know, I've always heard the first step to recovery is acceptance that you have a problem."

I drew in another cutting breath and felt the warmth spread across my face. Tanner and I gave each other a hard time, that much was obvious, but for some stupid reason, a knot exploded in the base of my throat and the back of my eyes burned as I watched him take another drink. Embarrassment seeded in my stomach, blossoming into a tree that only bloomed rotten fruit.

I *didn't* have a drinking problem.

Tanner lowered the bottle, and the moment our gazes collided, the grin faded slowly from his striking face. His brows knitted as his lips parted, and I quickly turned toward Sydney, my voice embarrassingly hoarse when I spoke. "Count me in."

## Tanner

Aw, *shit*.

I watched Andrea walk into the living room, the normal twitch of her hips absent. No one swayed ass like Andrea, and seeing it gone from her step was answer enough. Our normal whatever-the-fuck-it-was between us had gone further than I intended. No doubt what I'd said had cut her, but shit, it was no different than any other day.

My hand tightened on the neck of the bottle. For the life of me, I had no idea what the hell Andrea Walters's problem was. Honestly. No fucking clue. One minute, sweet and sugary words parted those pouty pink lips of hers. Next second, she was a fire-breathing dragon from hell—a *hot,* fire-breathing dragon, but still. Her moods flipped more quickly than cups did during a game of flip cup.

Maybe it was because she was a redhead?

I smirked.

She'd always been this way with me, and the most fucked-up thing about it, there was a part of me that actually looked forward to whatever was going to come out of her mouth. Twisted as fuck. It was like a game between us, to see who could hit the hardest without lifting a finger. If nothing else, it was damn entertaining—or at least, it had been until now. Now, I wasn't too sure about it.

Those pretty doe eyes of hers had looked suspiciously damp right before she'd looked away, and yeah...that didn't sit right with me.

Kyler shot me a look as he walked past me and grabbed a beer out of the fridge, but I watched Andrea sit on the edge of the couch, her posture unnaturally rigid.

Sydney leaned against the arm. "We're thinking about leaving early in the morning, around six."

My gaze flicked to Andrea, expecting her to make some kind of crack about not getting up that early, but she was abnormally quiet. My spine stiffened.

"That should put us at the cabin between nine and ten in the morning, depending on traffic." Kyler stood beside me as he screwed off the cap. "Then we'll be heading back the following Monday."

"Sounds good to me." I didn't take my eyes off Andrea as she fiddled with a strap on her sandals, slipping them onto her feet.

Sydney glanced at me, smiling softly. "You're definitely off from the fire department?"

I nodded. Kyler had mentioned weeks ago about wanting to hit up the cabin before everyone headed back to class, and I'd requested the time off then. Which had meant I'd pulled a lot of doubles, but I hadn't minded it. Wasn't too different from the twelve-hour shifts we worked in the first place, and

I'd only be there until February of next year, and then I was off to the academy. Not that I was in any hurry to leave the fire department, but being a cop was in my blood. Except I wanted to be a *good* cop. I'd probably still volunteer at the fire hall once I knew what kind of schedule I was looking at on the force.

"It makes sense if we drive up together." Sydney toyed with a strand of her hair. "Kyler and I can pick you two up."

Andrea had twisted toward Sydney and started to protest the whole idea of taking one car. I zoned out, staring at her as the bottle of beer dangled from the tips of my fingers.

Damn…she was a cute girl. Nah, she was more than cute, and it wasn't like this was the first time I'd noticed that. From the first time I'd seen her at the bar with Sydney, she'd done more than just poke my interest. Hell, anyone with eyes knew she was a very pretty girl. Lush lips. Freckled cheeks and thick, dark eyelashes. Come to think of it, she reminded me of a girl I'd had a crush on in middle school. Hell, couldn't remember that chick's name, but she'd had freckles and red hair. I think I used to pull on her braids or some annoying shit like that. My lips tipped up in a small grin as I lifted the bottle to my mouth. Andrea was a motherfucking firecracker, though, not the kind of girl who was easily tamed.

Hell, not the kind of girl you even *wanted* to tame.

I did know she dated, but she didn't stick with any guy for long. There weren't many who could handle her. There wasn't even one dude I could think of who could. Well, other than me. I could fucking handle her, if I wanted to.

I hadn't back then, when I'd first met her. Relationships hadn't been my thing, but life had a way of slowing down, changing. I wasn't as interested in random hookups as I was a year or so ago, even though Andrea seemed to think my bedroom was equivalent to the metro station. Shit. It had been months since I'd taken anyone home with me or woken up in someone else's bed.

The night I'd met Andrea I'd known immediately she wasn't going to be like most girls. I'd hit on her, more than willing to engage in some fun times with her, and she had looked me straight in the eye, laughed in my face, and told me to keep dreaming.

Of course, I'd only wanted her more after that.

At first, it was the challenge, but then I realized she wasn't playing any game with me. It hadn't diminished my attraction to her; however, I spent the vast majority of time utterly confused when it came to her feelings toward me.

At some point, I guessed Andrea had relented to common sense, because she was standing and tucking a gorgeous curl back behind her ear. "Well, I'm going to get out of here." Those damn brown eyes drifted toward me, lingering for a moment before moving on, and fuck me if they didn't look wounded. Hurt. She rounded the couch, grabbing a purse the size of a small car off the chair beside the front door. "You know, head back to my posh apartment paid for by my trust fund and drink until I get sloshed and end up puking my guts up all over my Louis Vuitton purses."

My brows flew up, and for some damn reason, I didn't fire back. Didn't say a damn word as she said goodbye to Kyler and Sydney, and then left. And maybe I should've. An odd burning sensation in my gut told me that would've been the right thing to do.

"I'm going to…uh, go talk to her real quick." Hurrying around the couch, Syd stopped long enough to give Kyler a quick kiss and to smack my arm, and then she blew past us. "Be right back."

When the door shut a second time, I looked at Kyler. He arched a brow at me. "Soooo," he drew the word out. "I think you really pissed off Andrea this time."

"This time." I shook my head, somewhat dumbfounded as my gaze drifted back to the door. Shit.

Kyler eyed me as he leaned against the wall, crossing his ankles. "What is the deal between you two? I mean, seriously?

If I didn't know better, I'd think you two had hooked up at some point and shit didn't end well."

I huffed out a short laugh. "Come on, you know nothing like that happened between us."

He lifted a brow and took another drink. "Maybe you just haven't told me about it."

I snorted.

"Syd swears that you two have done something, and y'all are just not sharing."

A frown pulled at my lips. "Did Andrea say something like that?"

He shook his head. "No. It's just Syd's theory."

"Her theory is wrong."

"I don't get her deal with you," he said after a few moments.

"Me neither. I really have no clue," I murmured, taking a swig of the beer as I stared at the door. "But you know what? I'm going to find out."

# Chapter 2

**Andrea**

The music beat overhead, a steady thrum that matched my pulse. My skin was damp and my throat was parched, but I felt good—no, *great*. I felt great—free and weightless, my head blissfully empty. Smiling, I lifted my arms up, tipped my head back and smiled.

I don't know what song was even playing and it was probably one I'd be too embarrassed to admit I had on my iPhone, but right now I didn't care. Tonight was perfect.

"Whoa," a male voice said from behind me. I think his name was Todd? Tim? Taylor? Tiny Tim? I giggled. The guy lowered my right arm. "You're going to dump this all over yourself."

Dangling from my fingers was a slender glass, still half-full. I'd forgotten all about my drink. It was something fruity and sugary and awesome. Wrapping my lips around the straw, I slurped happily as my hips swayed to the music. I closed my eyes again, letting myself get lost in the best possible way. God, I needed tonight because of…of *stuff*—because of what happened last night at Kyler and Syd's apartment, because of what Tanner had said and the ensuing pep talk from Syd that happened outside their apartment.

*"I don't think he meant anything by it," she'd said. "I think he's just worried. We all are worried…"*

A kernel of unease popped in the pit of my belly. Worried? Why were they worried? There was nothing going on, and I shook my head, sending the curls flying. I wasn't going to think about any of that.

But remnants of that conversation by my car floated through my clouded thoughts. *You spent an entire week last month not talking to anyone.*

I'd been busy.

*You got really sick the last time we went out. It was scary. I was scared.*

It hadn't been that scary.

*Do you even know who that guy was you left with?*

I didn't want to think about that guy or that night.

Large hands landed on my hips, and then I felt a warm and sticky breath against my cheek. The scent of beer washed over me, ramping up the unease. "You are so sexy."

I frowned, for a moment having no idea who the dude was, and then I realized I'd also forgotten about him. Turning my head to the side, away from his, I opened my eyes. "What's your name again?"

The question didn't offend the guy. He laughed as his hands squeezed my hips. "You can call me whatever you want," he said, and even as buzzed as I was, I knew what kind of guy this was. He didn't care if I could even spell his name. All he was interested in was the likelihood of me going home with him or not. It wouldn't even matter if I passed out on him. He probably didn't know my name, and he really didn't put any value to that. He wasn't here to meet a girl he saw a future with beyond a few sweaty minutes.

The hands on my hips slid forward and his thumbs hooked through the loops on my jeans. I brought the glass to my mouth, finding it empty. Lifting my gaze, I looked around the bar. Almost immediately, I saw him and the air leaked out of my lungs.

Tanner sat at one of the tall, round tables. Kyler and Syd were with him, but their heads were bent toward each other, gazes fastened together. Tanner...he was staring at me. His blue eyes weren't lazy-looking. They were narrowed and he looked angry—furious actually. Heat traveled across my cheeks, and I wanted to look away, but I couldn't.

A girl approached their table. I recognized her. I think. She was pretty, blonde with pink streaks in her hair, and it was obvious she worked hard to fit into those skinny jeans she wore. She went straight for Tanner, angling her body toward him. He looked up and the irritated look faded from his handsome face, replaced by an easy and welcoming smile—the kind of smile I was so rarely on the receiving end of.

"I need another drink," I said, looking away. But it was too late. I couldn't get that smile out of my mind. It was cute, a crooked type of grin, as if he hadn't fully committed to a smile yet, but was happy.

"Yeah?" What's-his-name hauled me against him, my back to his front. "I can get you a drink."

That sounded perfect for several reasons, mainly because I wanted another drink, but I also wanted my personal space back more. Except that's not what the guy did. He didn't let go. Dry lips brushed my cheek as his hips grinded against my rear, and I could feel him, like *really* feel him.

Okay. I was done with this. I wasn't *that* drunk yet.

Stepping forward, I yanked myself free—or at least tried to. I got a couple of inches between us before he pulled me back. I bounced off his chest, almost dropping my glass. "Where do you think you're going? We're having fun."

"I am *not* having fun." I twisted, grabbing his hand with my free one. I dug my nails in. "Let go."

"What?" Spittle flew from his mouth, and my stomach turned a little more. "We're just dancing. Come on. Let's have fun."

"I don't even know your name," I heard myself say, which sounded stupid to my own ears, because a handful of moments earlier, I hadn't cared if I knew his name or not. "And you don't even know my name."

"Do I need to?"

I jerked to the side as someone—another couple— knocked into us, but his words held me immobile, recycling around in my head. For some reason, I suddenly wanted him to say something different. That he wanted to know my name—know *me*. I bet Tanner knew the name of the girl who was talking to him.

Dumb.

This was so dumb.

### Tanner

My foot tapped off the sticky-ass floor at rocket speed. I didn't know how much longer I was going to be expected to sit here and watch Andrea do whatever the fuck she was doing.

Andrea had been in a weird mood when she showed up at the bar. Quiet—almost shy in the way she had kept stealing quick glances at me. Part of me wondered if she'd been drinking before she arrived, but I really wanted to give her the benefit of the doubt and believe that she wasn't stupid enough to drink and drive. Yeah, she liked to party and could get wild, but she wasn't dangerously stupid or irresponsible. However, she had started drinking the moment she'd gotten here, and she hadn't stopped. I'd lost count of how many empty glasses she had racked up.

It was going to be one of those nights.

Skin prickling like an army of fire ants was crawling all over me, I'd sat back and done nothing when she announced she wanted to dance. Syd had joined her for a while, but she had returned sans Andrea, who was turning the dance floor into her own personal showcase.

Jesus H. Christ, every pair of male eyes that weren't on their own girls was fastened on Andrea. We were like fucking heat-seeking missiles when it came to hot chicks, and she was one hell of a flesh-and-blood target.

Those deep-red curls swung in every direction as she raised her arms above her head and swayed her hips to some rock song. Her cheeks flushed prettily and glowed with a fine sheen of sweat. The black shirt she wore rode up, revealing a quick glimpse of pale skin above the band of her jeans—and those damn jeans…they were like a glove made perfectly for her heart-shaped ass. And I still sat there, doing nothing—unable to move or look away, just like the other guys in the bar couldn't look away. My jeans felt about five times tighter.

When some tall, goofy-looking son-of-a-bitch started grinding all up on her, I'd stayed in my chair, but I'd leaned forward and my attention had shifted. In that moment, I realized that the whole time I'd been sitting here, I'd been hardcore lusting after the girl who'd likely punch me in the nuts instead of grabbing them in a fun way. A different kind of feeling brewed inside of me. It had nothing to do with desire—more with the need to piss around Andrea like some kind of caveman. I had never, in my entire life, felt the need to do that, and I had no idea why I wanted to do it now.

Goofy SOB grabbed her hips.

My eyes narrowed as an irrational anger surfaced. Why in the *fuck* was she letting this guy climb all over her? He looked like a dumb motherfucker, and she deserved way better than that.

Something moved to my right, and I looked, surprised to see Lea Nacker walking toward me. She smiled as her gaze flickered over to Kyler and Sydney. "Hey," she said, her voice carrying the soft southern drawl that announced she was not local. "I haven't seen you all summer. I thought you'd left the city."

"Nah. Just busy working. You?"

She tucked a long strand of pink-and-blonde hair behind her ear. "Same here. I've got one more semester left at UMD. You graduated, right?"

"Yep." I glanced quickly back to where Andrea was and swallowed a curse. Goofy SOB's hands were in an area I *so* did not appreciate. Was Andrea too…buzzed to realize where his hands were? Because I knew she normally wouldn't be down with that kind of shit.

"Well, if you're still around, give me a call," Lea said, and my attention swung back to her. It took a moment to get what she was saying—what she was offering. "I'll answer," she added with a cute little smile.

Shit. Shit on a sundae.

Lea and I'd hooked up a few times over the years. Nothing serious, and normally I'd be filing that little offer away to act upon in the not too distant future, but right now, there wasn't even a speck of interest. If I hadn't been inappropriately hard a few moments earlier, I would've thought my dick had stopped working.

Feeling like an ass, I forced a smile, because I'd had a lot of fun with her and she was a good girl. "Sure."

Lea started to say something, but my attention wandered back to where Andrea was, and I was over this conversation and being polite. Goofy SOB was tugging on Andrea, and it was obvious she was not happy with the treatment. I didn't stop to think.

"I'll be right back," I announced, glancing at the couple sitting with me.

Kyler lifted a brow, but said nothing, and I kind of think he knew better. Standing, I nodded at Lea, and then didn't look back as I crossed the floor.

Nearing the cluster of dancers, I heard Andrea say, "And you don't even know my name." Her words slurred together a bit, and my shoulders tensed.

"Do I need to?" the guy replied.

My gut clenched and my entire body jerked. From behind, I smacked my hand down on the guy's shoulder. He let go of Andrea, and I saw her stumble to the side, catching herself before she lost her balance. Our eyes met briefly. Hers were glazed over, and my anger hit another level.

"Yeah, if you want to be touching her, you need to know her fucking name," I said, flattening my hand and shoving him back a good step. Before he could react, I got between him and Andrea. "But you don't need to know her name.

You don't even need to remember. You're not worth any of that."

Goofy SOB tried to step toward me, and I'm proof-fucking-positive the look on my face made him change his mind. His gaze shifted away from mine. "Who the hell are you? Her boyfriend?"

I almost laughed in his face, except Andrea had already been insulted enough for the evening, even if she had no clue. "Yeah. So get the fuck out of my face before I knock you through that goddamn door."

"Tanner." Andrea's hand pressed against my lower back, but I didn't take my eyes off the guy.

Tensing, I waited for the asshole to do anything, but he raised his hand and flipped me off before turning around and stalking away. All I could do was laugh at his retreating form. The guy might be a classless asshole, but he had common sense. By appearance alone, I had a good twenty or so pounds of muscle on his scrawny ass.

The hand on my back dropped away, and I drew in a deep breath before I turned around. That was a good idea, because that breath got stuck somewhere in my chest, and I had no idea what the hell was up with that. Did ovaries replace my balls at some point? Possibly.

Andrea stared up at me, her full pouty lips parted and brown eyes wide, full of such a potent sadness that an urge to sweep her into my arms hit me hard. I barely felt whoever it was that bumped into me as I moved toward Andrea. Her lips moved but I didn't hear her.

"What?" I asked.

"You don't smile at me," she said louder, and I blinked. Her shoulders rose with a heavy sigh, and that urge increased.

"Andy," I said, shaking my head. "I always smile at you."

"No. Not really." She lifted her empty glass, looking down at it. "That guy had grabby hands."

"Yeah, he did." I didn't want to talk about that asshole, and I wanted to change the forlorn quality to her words.

Folding my hand around her smaller one, I took the empty glass out of her hand. "Come on."

Of course, she dug her heels in. "I wanna dance."

I lifted a brow as I walked around her, stretching our arms out as I leaned over, placing her drink on the bar. "You sure about that?"

She cocked her head to the side, brows knitting. "Yeah." Slipping her hand free from mine, she threw her arms up and whirled around. Balance off, she stumbled to the side, right toward the group of guys waiting to get served at the bar. Oh, this was going to end badly. Shooting forward, I wrapped an arm around her waist, stopping her from face-planting some random dude's back.

Andrea's giggle was infectious and also concerning as she fell back against me. Placing her hands on my arm, she started to twist her hips against my groin. My jaw clenched as a jolt of lust slammed into my gut, fierce and fast.

Aaand back to the inappropriate hardness.

God, my cock freaking throbbed as I stepped back, trying to put some space between us. "Andy," I all but groaned. "What are you doing?"

Turning her head to the side, her eyes were closed as she smiled. "I'm dancing, and you're just standing there."

I *was* just standing there.

And roughly five seconds later, she turned me into her own personal stripper pole.

Turning around, she placed her hands on my chest as she slid down, her palms trailing over my abs. I jerked on reflex, mouth dry as she reached the belt on my jeans and smiled up at me, her eyes hidden behind thick lashes. The throbbing increased tenfold.

I wanted to let her go, to see how far she'd take this. A very huge part of me wanted that so damn badly, and she was so close, practically on her knees as she stared up at me, her fingers nearing my fly.

Good God, I grabbed her wrists before she went any further, and I ended up turning into one of those guys I hated. Hauling her up, I tried not to smile when she pouted at me. "I'm taking you home," I told her.

One coppery eyebrow lifted. "Wow, that...that escalated quickly."

I ignored how a certain part of me got all kinds of interested. "Knock it off."

"How about bang it off?" she said, and then tipped her head back and laughed like that made an ounce of sense. "I don't know if I want to go home with you."

"That's okay." I slipped an arm around her shoulder before she turned away from me. "Because I'm taking you back to your place, not mine."

Her lips turned down as if she was confused by what I was saying, and I used that distraction to my advantage, guiding her toward Kyler and Sydney. Both stared at us with a look of smug knowing. I glared at them and opened my mouth, but Andrea beat me to it.

"He's taking me hooome," she said, laughing as she started to dance away with me. "All the waaay hooome," she sung. "Oh yeah, we're gonna go hooome."

What the holy hell? My lips twitched as I caught her hand. Sydney's eyes widened with alarm. "We can take her back."

"You guys are having fun," I told them. "There's no reason for you to leave."

Sydney raised a brow. "Uh-huh."

"Yeah, because that's just weird." Andrea stopped dancing, but she swung our arms between us like she was two, and I tried not to find the act adorable. "I like you guys, but four is like more than a company. It's like some freaky swinger shit."

Sydney choked on her drink.

"Not that I'm saying being a swinger means anyone is a freak," Andrea chirped on blithely. "But I'm not in a relationship so it wouldn't be swinging. It would be an orgy, and I don't really want to see either of you naked."

All I could do was stare.

Kyler covered his mouth with his fingers and murmured, "Feeling is mutual."

Andrea nodded understandingly and rather somberly, and then looked up at me, still swinging our arms. "Are we leaving now? Because I would like another drink."

"We're leaving now," I said.

She sighed. "You're no fun, you party-pooper-pants-pooper."

"I really have no idea what to say to that," I admitted.

Andrea rolled her eyes.

Popping up from her seat, Sydney slid Andrea's purse over her shoulder and then gave her a quick hug. Looking up at me, she gave me her best serious face. "Anyone else, I would not let her leave, but I trust you. Don't make me regret that trust."

A bit of guilt burned, because it wasn't like I was having completely clean thoughts about Andrea, especially if she did another little dance. "I know. She'll make it home safely."

"She better," Sydney warned, fucking fierce for a pint-size thing.

"Y'all know, I'm like standing right here." Andrea flipped her curls with her free hand. "Maybe I don't want to be safe. Maybe I want to live dangerously."

Sydney sighed. "No you don't."

"Maybe I want to get on my Grindr account," she announced.

I frowned. "What?"

"You do *not* have a Grindr account," Sydney said.

Andrea narrowed her eyes, looking a bit cross-eyed. "Maybe I do."

"This is epic," Kyler said.

"Grindr is mostly for gay guys the last time I checked," Sydney explained, shaking her head. "And I just don't think you really qualify for that."

Andrea blinked. "I meant Tinder."

"You *so* do not have a Tinder account," I said.

She smiled at me, all innocence, and I suddenly wanted to burn her phone and the world down with gasoline and piss. It was time to get her home, and that process took a God-awful amount of time. She was like a drunk hummingbird, buzzing from one thing to the next, and by the time I got her inside her apartment, I was exhausted.

Apparently, Andrea had an endless supply of energy, because she dropped her purse on the floor, kicked off her heels, and immediately made a mad dash for her kitchen. I knew she was heading for something to drink, and that wouldn't be water. Picking up her purse, I placed it on a chair, dropped her house keys in the bag, and then intercepted her.

Placing my hands on her shoulders, I steered her toward the narrow hall. "Why don't you go get ready for bed?"

She rocked back on her bare feet, her smile crinkling the skin around her eyes. "Geez, Tanner-man, you move fast."

Again, inappropriate thoughts to the max. "Andy, come on. You know I'm not here for that."

"I don't know that," she said, dancing away from me. She started to walk backward down the hall, her hands fluttering to the hem of her shirt. I was more concerned with her tripping and breaking her neck. "I don't know why you're here at all."

My gaze dropped to where the swell of her breasts pushed against the material of her shirt as I followed her. With great effort, I managed to pull my gaze up. "I brought you home."

"Duh." She stopped at the entrance of her bedroom and leaned against the wall. A thin sliver of her belly was exposed as she toyed with her shirt. "Double duh." Then she moved.

My spine straightened like someone had poured steel down it.

Damn, the image she offered right there was almost too much to resist. Her back was arched slightly and her eyes heavily hooded as she toyed with the hem of her shirt. Each breath she took raised breasts I'd always known would be fucking glorious, because if they looked that good covered up, they'd have to be marvelous with nothing hiding them. She pressed the back of her head against the wall and wetted her lips.

My cock jerked in response. "Andy…"

"Tanner…" she mimicked.

I bit back a groan, and then tensed as she suddenly pushed off the wall. She swayed a little on her feet as she eyed me. "What are you doing?" I asked.

"Nuttin'."

No way did I believe her. Wariness and a whole different kind of emotion warred inside me as she sucked her bottom lip between her teeth. "Can I ask you a question?" she asked.

"Sure." My voice had thickened.

She tilted her head to the side, lashes lowering. "Why have we never hooked up?"

"What?" I really prayed that I heard something different.

"Are you being coy?" Andrea moved an inch closer. "Or are you just dumb?"

"Whoa. You really know how to come on to a guy."

Her grin flashed, and then disappeared quickly. "Don't you want—?"

"Don't finish that question," I cut her off, more roughly than I intended.

It was like watching air being let out of a balloon. She deflated that quickly. Shoulders lowering as her hands moved to her denim-clad thighs, she dipped her chin as she shrugged. "Yeah. Okay." She turned sideways, toward the door, lifting her chin slightly. "I'm home. Y-You can go now."

"Andy, I…" What could I say? That the idea of her coming on to me only when she was drunk filled me with the urge to punch something? And that when she was sober, she was more likely to stab me than smile at me?

She stopped, her lashes lifting as she looked up at me. Her smile was wan, so unlike the earlier ones. "It's okay."

My tongue felt glued to the roof of my mouth. I had no idea what to do with her, but then she placed her hands on my chest again. There was enough time to stop her, more than enough time, but I didn't, and I had no idea what that said about me, but then I wasn't thinking. She stretched up as her hands reached my shoulders and she pressed her lips against mine. It was soft and quick. Andrea tasted of sugar and liquor, but her mouth was warm and sweet as her lips moved over mine.

The single kiss hit me hard, jarred me and rattled me up. So much so that when she moved away, entering the bedroom and partly closing the door behind her, I didn't move for what felt like five minutes. No shit. There was a good chance I actually did stand there for five minutes, like some kind of dumbass with a hard-on for a girl who was so drunk I'd had to cart her sweet ass home.

But she'd kissed me.

But she'd kissed me while drunk, which canceled out the whole kissing part.

"Fuck," I muttered, rubbing my hand over my head as I stared at the door. Part of me wanted to run, the other half was still dumbstruck. I needed to check on her. That's what I told myself when I walked forward and pushed at her door.

The lamp was on, casting the room in a soft buttery glow. Andrea was on the bed, lying atop the covers, half on her side and half on her belly. I couldn't leave her like that. No way. Walking over to the bed, I carefully lifted her legs and managed to get them under the comforter, shifting her so that she was safely lying on her side. Then I grabbed one of her extra-long body pillows, shoving in behind her back so she couldn't roll over, just in case she got sick.

"You change your mind?" she mumbled.

I coughed out a laugh as I tugged up the comforter. "No, Andy."

She sighed heavily, and when I glanced down, thick coppery-brown lashes fanned her cheeks. "Stop calling me that…dick."

Another chuckle rumbled out of me. She was insulting me. That had to mean that I'd seen her far worse than this. "You have such a mouth on you."

There was no response, as she had fallen asleep. A strange, soft smile tugged at my mouth as I stared down at her.

"I'll lock up," I said, even though I knew she didn't hear me. I reached for the lamp, hesitating. This wasn't the first time I'd put her sweet ass to bed. First time she'd been a mess, drunk off her ass, but this…yeah, this was the same, except last time she hadn't said I never smiled at her, and she hadn't kissed me.

Rosy lips parted as she rocked a little, as if she was trying to roll onto her back but couldn't do it. Under the covers, her legs curled up, and something…something odd in my chest clenched. Kind of like a pressure clamping down. Not necessarily bad, but different, and I had no idea what to make of that.

I never had any idea of what to make of Andrea—not from the first time I'd met her at a bar outside of College Park, sitting next to Sydney. Immediately, I had been interested in her. Fuck. Those curls? The lips? That ass? But then she'd taken one look at me, opened her mouth, and I quickly learned the girl had a razor-sharp tongue.

And she did *not* like me.

Oh, she wanted me. I knew that for damn sure. I'd seen the way she'd looked at me when she didn't think I was paying attention, but I'd never let myself even think about going there. I didn't even know why I was letting myself do it now.

But fuck, I was.

Several curls had toppled across her freckled cheek, and without thinking, I reached down and carefully brushed them back. The contact with her silky soft cheek sent a jolt through me, and I yanked my hand back. Staring down at her, a rough breath punched out of me. Jesus Christ, I wanted to touch her again, really, in a very bad way. My fingers practically buzzed to pull that cover back, see if that swell of her breast was just as soft as her cheek, if her thighs were as sweet.

Cutting off those thoughts was harder than I ever imagined. Turning from the bed, I saw a tiny trashcan and grabbed it, positioning it by her bed. Then I went out to the kitchen, grabbed a glass of water and brought that back into the bedroom, placing it on the nightstand. She'd be thirsty when she woke up. She'd probably have one hell of a headache, too.

There was no real reason to linger any longer, but I worried about her—about how much she drank, if she'd be sick in the middle of the night when there'd be no one here to look after her. I thought about calling Kyler and getting Sydney on the phone, but I ended up planting my ass in a silver chair that was low to the floor but surprisingly comfortable. There was luggage beside the chair, zipped up.

I ended up sitting there for hours, until the first rays of dawn began to peek through the curtains over the large window, until I was sure that there was little chance she would be sick, and until I was so shocked with myself that I realized I'd spent the entire night like some kind of bedside nurse, something I'd never done before—never even considered doing before. Even though I was tired and my back ached when I stood like I was much older than my twenty-three years, I knew that meant something, that had to. But I wasn't sure what to make of it.

# Chapter 3

**Andrea**

Idly flipping through the pages of the latest *US Weekly*, I quickly gave up and tossed the magazine onto the beige cushion beside me. My attention wandered over the potted plants in front of the darkened window, to the TV, and I sighed heavily.

Sunday nights just weren't the same without *The Walking Dead*.

Bored out of my mind and beyond restless, I pushed myself off the comfy couch and walked the short distance to my bedroom. My apartment was more of a loft converted into a one-bedroom. The rooms were decent-sized, larger than most, and I was super grateful that my parents had hooked me up my junior year of college. I could stay here without worrying about that kind of expense. No matter what some people thought, I knew how incredibly lucky I was.

I stopped a few feet from my bed and stared at the gray and white comforter I hadn't straightened this afternoon when I'd peeled myself out of bed after spending most the day nursing one hell of a hangover. Last night was a blur of cocktails mixed with tequila and rum. I remembered dancing and grabby hands, and I also remembered Tanner intervening and driving me home, but after his truck pulled up in the parking lot, I honestly didn't remember a thing. I figured he'd gotten my butt into my apartment and bed, because there'd been a glass of water on my nightstand when I'd woken up that I doubted I'd gotten myself.

God, I needed to stop drinking.

I looked around my room. What was I doing? I had absolutely no idea why I'd even walked in here. My suitcase, already packed for the trip to the cabin in the morning, was sitting by the silver-cushioned papasan chair next to my dresser. I was one of those people—the ones that sometimes packed *days* before a trip.

Exhaling yet another deep sigh, I stood there for a couple of minutes and then spun around, walking into the kitchen. This time I stopped in front of my fridge. Stainless steel. Double sides. My parents had wanted updated appliances, only the best, but all I could see were my fingerprints all over the door and handle.

I yanked open the door and the ring of bottles clattering off one another sent a shiver down my spine. The jangling was like music—like *Jingle Bells*, if *Jingle Bells* was drunk. Six bottles of Redd's Apple Ale sat all by their lonesome.

A spasm caused my fingers to tighten on the handle, and I started to kneel down, my other hand flashing out, reaching for a bottle. *You do drink too much.* Sucking in a sharp breath, I closed my eyes. I didn't drink *that* much. Just every now and then, no different than half the population of the United States, so it wasn't like I had a problem.

*Not yet,* an insidious, annoying voice whispered.

Grabbing a can of soda, I shoved the fridge door shut, ignoring the enticing rattle that haunted my steps. I walked back into the living room, popping the top on the can. I leaned against the back of my couch, the soda dangling from my fingers. I tried to make sense of the blurred images from last night, even though I knew that was pointless. It wasn't like I blacked out or something, not really. I just couldn't remember all the fine details. That wasn't the same thing. I shifted my weight from one foot to the next, suddenly uncomfortable.

A band of pressure tightened around my chest. Tanner was never going to let me live last night down. Even though it wasn't the first time he'd escorted me home, somehow it felt different. I wondered if I'd cussed at him. Worse yet, I seriously hoped I hadn't hit on him. Or tried to rub his head again. Goodness, if so, that was going to be so embarrassing. Squeezing my eyes shut, I forced myself to take deep and slow breaths until the band had eased up.

Time crawled by, and I had no idea how long I stood there, but it wasn't even 9:30 when I glanced at the sparkly wall clock. Walking my butt back to the kitchen, I placed the soda on the counter and opened up the cabinet above the microwave.

A Target pharmacy had exploded inside.

Allergy pills. Imodium. Tums. Cold meds. Red plastic bottles were sprinkled among them. I reached for the closest one, Sonata. The little blue and green pills of sleepy happiness rattled as I picked up the bottle. They really didn't help me stay asleep longer, but less than thirty minutes or so after taking one, I was out cold or completely loopy. Wasn't like that for everyone—my doc told me once that every person responded differently to sleeping aids, but for me, after taking the dose I was more than ready to end the day and rush toward tomorrow.

*Always* rushing toward tomorrow.

I smiled wryly as I twisted the lid off and shook a pill out. Tossing it into my mouth, I washed it down with what I realized, after I swallowed, was a Pepsi Max. A startled laugh escaped me. Sleeping pills and caffeine? I was a walking oxymoron.

It had been my junior year in college when I'd developed a mean case of insomnia. All that studying and those weird hours had formed a routine of only sleeping a few hours—usually around four in the morning—and I hadn't been able to break it. I'd never meant to continue using them. God knows I knew these pills kicked off a whole different kind of habit, but now I had a hell of a time sleeping without them. Which was really lame when I thought about it, being that I was twenty-two and already popping sleeping pills at nine-thirty at night when I'd slept half the day away as it was.

Syd didn't like that I took them. She wanted me to try something more natural. She also didn't like the other pills sitting in my cabinet. And she *really* didn't like that I... whatever. Being that Syd was well on her way to becoming a psychologist, she had a lot of opinions about a lot of things.

I'd just screwed the cap back on the bottle when there was a knock on the door, startling me.

"What the hell?" I left the bottle on the counter, next to the Pepsi, and walked into the living room. I wasn't expecting anyone, so I had no idea who it could be since Syd would've texted or called before showing up.

What if it was a mass murderer? Or—or a neighbor who needed sugar, a sexy neighbor who was in the midst of baking cookies and needed a key ingredient?

Please be a hot dude who needed sugar.

Hurrying across the room, I placed my hands on the door and stretched up, peering through the peephole. "Holy shit."

I had to be hallucinating, which seemed possible since those pills sometimes made me see some weird crap. And what I was seeing was bizarre. I recognized the light brown buzz cut, the chiseled cut of a jaw in profile.

Tanner was here.

Of course, he knew where I lived, but he'd never, in the history of ever, shown up unannounced for any reason. My heart dropped as I rocked back. Concern blossomed in the pit of my stomach. Had something happened? Oh my God, as a firefighter, would he know if something had happened to Kyler or Syd or even my family? Was that why he was here? Reaching down, I unlocked the door and threw it open.

"Tanner..." Everything and anything I was about to say died on my lips.

He'd turned to me, and his brilliant azure gaze collided with mine for the briefest of seconds before dropping in a slow perusal that glided from my eyes down to the tips of my blue-polished toes. But that gaze…it lingered in some areas more than others, halted in a way that made his stare feel like an actual caress. The air hitched in my throat. I felt sort of dizzy.

Then I realized what I was wearing.

Since I hadn't planned on company, I wasn't dressed for it—wearing cotton shorts that really weren't much bigger than boy shorts and a cami that did nothing to hide anything.

Oh my God.

I was almost naked. Practically. Like, the entire length of my legs were visible and if he'd thought I was a proud owner of a thigh gap, he *so* knew differently now. There was no doubt in my mind that he knew how chilly I kept my apartment because of how thin my tank was, and I was *not* lacking in that department.

The longer he stared, the more conflicted I became about the whole thing. I wanted to dash back to my bedroom and layer up with clothing, but I also wanted him to look his fill.

But I didn't have a body like Sydney or Mandie or Brooke. Or Clara Hansen, my freshman year roommate. I wasn't tiny like any of them. I wasn't straight up and straight down. My waist wasn't miniscule and my stomach sure as hell wasn't flat. It kind of did this weird concave thing, and right then, that damn pooch under my navel was probably visible through this freaking shirt. My hips weren't slim. They were full, as was my ass. In other words, I would never strut around wearing *this* in front of a guy. Instead, I would strut with clothing strategically designed to hide all the flaws.

I'd sure as hell never caught Tanner's attention in the past, never in a good way at least, so this…this was different.

Warmth invaded my cheeks, warring with the unsettling heat that had lit up my veins. I cleared my throat. "Is…is everything okay? Nothing happened, right?"

He blinked, dragging his gaze back to mine. "Yeah. Why would you think something had happened?"

I glanced around the otherwise empty apartment. "Um, maybe because you don't usually just show up at my place?"

"Good point." He raised a hand, dragging it over his hair. Clasping the back of his neck, he angled his head to the side. "Can I come in for a moment? I'm not going to take up a lot of your time. I'm heading in for a swing shift tonight."

"Sure." Confused and a bit curious, I stepped aside, but then my stomach dropped a little bit more. Was he here because of last night? Oh no. Had I done something so stupid that it warranted an unexpected face-to-face visit?

I was *so* never going to drink again.

Tanner flashed a brief half-grin and walked in. As I closed the door behind him, he dropped his arm, and I couldn't help but watch the way his biceps stretched the shirt he wore.

I folded my arms across my chest as he turned toward me. "Can I get you something to drink?"

He shook his head and then turned, heading toward the couch. Sucked to admit this, but he looked damn good in nylon sweats. He sat on the edge and patted the cushion next to him. "Sit for a sec?"

Okay. The smidgen of curiosity expanded, as did the anxiety. The band around my chest was back. Walking past him, I tried to ignore the kernel of self-consciousness growing in my stomach. I really hoped my butt wasn't hanging out of my shorts. I sat beside him, sending him a quick side-glance. "So, what's going on?"

Blue eyes so bright they almost seemed unreal met mine, and his gaze snared mine, hooked me in. Unsure of why I couldn't look away, I tensed. "How are you feeling?"

"Huh?"

That grin appeared again, and was gone way too fast. "You were...a little out of it last night," he reminded me.

"Oh. Yeah." I felt my face heat as I shrugged. At least he hadn't said I was trashed. "I'm okay. Had a bit of a hangover this morning."

"I can imagine."

I pursed my lips. "Is that why you came by? To ask me how I was feeling? Because if so, I've got to say, you must be either really bored or high."

Tanner laughed, and my insides got all squishy at the deep sound. "I actually wanted to come by and make sure everything was going to be cool between us this week."

My arms relaxed, settling in my lap. I was relieved, but also wary. "Why wouldn't they be?"

One eyebrow lifted. "Is that a serious question?"

I yawned loudly as I leaned against the couch cushion. "Sure."

Another smile greeted me, and I thought he was smiling at me a lot tonight, which made a weird, fuzzy memory wiggle loose. Something about smiling? "You and I? Well, we don't exactly get along often." He paused, like he wanted to choose his words wisely. "And I just don't want to ruin it for Kyler and Sydney, you feel me?"

I jerked a little. "I would never ruin their time together."

He turned the unnerving, piercing stare toward the TV. "Not on purpose."

I started to frown, but ended up yawning again.

"I mean, it's not just you. It's me, too. I know I upset you a couple of days ago," he said, and my mouth sort of dropped open as he smoothed his palms over his bent knees. "I'm sorry if I…if I hurt your feelings."

All I could do was stare at him. Was I hallucinating?

"We joke around so much, and sometimes I think we both cross a line. So…yeah, I just wanted to make sure we're going to be cool." He looked at me then and his lips twitched. "You okay?"

I blinked, about to tell him that I was fine, but something totally different blurted out. "You don't even remember, do you? We had, like, two classes together my freshman year."

Now Tanner looked puzzled. "What?"

Shaking my head, I wished I'd kept my mouth shut, but my tongue was loose tonight. "Do you remember Clara Hansen?"

His lips tipped down at the corners. "Not really. I'm not following where this conversation is going."

He didn't remember Clara? Seriously? Wow. Part of me was pissed off on her behalf and the other part was disturbingly gleeful. "Never mind," I said after a moment. "Everything will be fine. I'll be on my best behavior."

Tanner eyed me. "I don't know if that's possible."

I snickered, not sure if that was possible either. I mean, expecting the two of us not to argue would be like expecting me not to chase after the ice cream truck.

"Who's Clara?" he persisted, and when I didn't answer immediately, he looked away again, his eyes squinting.

Tired, I felt like I was sinking further into the cushion. "You know, you could've just called or texted me."

"True," he murmured. "But I was on my way past here." There was a pause. "Did we really have two classes together?"

I nodded. "Yep."

"Are you sure? I would've remembered you."

The way he said that as he frowned didn't really leave me with the warm and fuzzies. I sighed. My thoughts were slowing down, but I was almost positive that the fire department he worked for was *not* on the way to my place. I didn't know what to make of that as I watched him.

Tanner opened his mouth as if he was about to say something, but then seemed to change his mind. A moment passed. "You kissed me last night."

My heart stopped. He dropped that little bomb like it was nothing, like he was telling me that it was almost ten o'clock. "What?"

"You kissed me last night, Andy."

I leaned forward and to the side, away from him. "First off, stop calling me that and finally—most importantly— you're so full of shit. I did *not* kiss you."

Even as I said those words, I knew there could be a horrifyingly embarrassing possibility that what he said was true, since I didn't remember everything.

His eyes took on that heavy hooded look that always made me want to squirm. "First off, I can't help myself. I have to call you Andy, because I know you secretly enjoy it and finally—most importantly—"

I was *so* going to hit him.

"You did kiss me." He leaned back, tossing an arm along the couch as he eyed me. "You stretched up, put your hands on my shoulders, and you kissed me."

"No. No way."

He nodded. "You also sort of used me as a pole at the bar. That was nice."

I shot up, swaying as a rush of dizziness came over me. I ignored it. "I did not!"

"Yeah, you did." One side of his lips kicked up. "You tasted of sugar and liquor. Not a bad mix."

"Shut up," I warned. "You're messing with me."

"Why would I mess with you over that?"

Good question. "Because you're evil. That sounds legit."

He arched a brow at that. "You also sort of invited me back to your bed."

"*What?*" I nearly shrieked. "How does one 'sort of' invite someone to their bed?"

"Oh, trust me, you can sort of do it. You did." He leaned forward, looking up at me. "Honestly, if you'd been able to walk a straight line and knew what you were doing, I'd have been all kinds of down for that."

For a second, my brain got hung up on him being down with hooking up with me. So much so, all I could do was stare at him. Over the last couple of years, I honestly hadn't believed Tanner thought about me in any way that would fall under the warm-and-fuzzy umbrella, let alone the sexy-and-fun umbrella.

"You also sang 'Story of My Life' over and over again," he added. "And I do mean, the entire drive to your apartment."

I folded my arms. "So what? It's a great song. One Direction is awesome." I paused. "Wait. How do you even know that song? You listening to One Direction when no one is around?"

He shrugged. "I'm man enough to admit it's a decent song."

Shaking my head, I bit back a grin. Then I realized he wasn't messing with me and that I really must've thrown myself at him. While drunk. While so drunk I couldn't remember doing it. My face was on fire as I backed up, nearly knocking into the coffee table. More denials formed on the tip of my tongue, but as I stared down at him—down at that wonderfully formed mouth of his—an odd memory surfaced. Me, standing in the hall, walking toward him and doing exactly what he claimed, stretching up and kissing him.

Oh. My. God.

Fuck my life.

He cocked his head to the side. "You seriously don't remember any of that?"

Without answering, I smacked my hands over my face and groaned. I let out a muffled, "Nooo."

There was silence, and I lowered my hands, peeking above my fingers. Tanner was staring at the floor, his jaw set hard and he looked kind of angry. I folded my hands under my chin. "I'm...I'm sorry?"

His gaze lifted. "You're sorry?"

"For...um, kissing you? And treating you like...a pole?"

A small grin tugged at the corners of his lips. "Andy, you never have to apologize for using me as a pole. Anytime you want to climb on, you let me know."

"Oh geez."

He chuckled. "Look, it's not a big deal."

"Sure it isn't." I plopped down beside him, suddenly exhausted.

"I didn't mind," he said, his tone light, but when I glanced at him, something was off about his expression. I couldn't put a finger on it. "It could've been worse."

"I'm having a hard time believing that," I muttered, feeling like I needed to hide my face for the next year. "I'm never going to drink again."

Tanner opened his mouth, but then snapped it shut, and I thought that might've been a wise decision. Another moment passed. "Well, I need to be getting out of here. You mind if I use your bathroom first?"

"Have at it." I raised a noodle-like arm and pointed toward the bathroom.

He hesitated as he started to rise, concern pinching his mouth. "Are you okay, Andrea?"

"Yeah," I laughed. "I took a sleeping pill, so I'm just tired."

His blue eyes sharpened and latched onto mine. "You take them often?"

I shrugged one shoulder. "Sometimes."

"You don't take them when you're drinking, right?"

A surprised laugh shook me. "Of course not," I said, and dammit, if that wasn't somewhat of a lie. Sometimes I did, but I was always careful. Always. "It's just sometimes I can't sleep. They're prescribed."

Tanner nodded, then stood after a moment and he started to turn, but twisted back to me. "Just an FYI, if you were dressed like that more often, I wouldn't argue with you as much. I'd be way too damn distracted."

My eyes widened in shock as a pleasant trill hummed through me. Maybe he needed glasses, but I was...I was thrilled nonetheless at what I thought was a compliment, especially after I'd apparently thrown myself at him last night. I struggled to keep it cool when all I wanted to do was giggle. "You perv."

He grinned. "And I'm a hundred percent behind you dressing like that more often, just so you know."

Something stupid in my chest fluttered. Wasn't my heart. Had to be indigestion. "Duly noted."

Tanner chuckled as he rounded the couch and headed toward the bathroom. When I heard the door shut, I let myself topple onto my side, smacking my hands over my face once more. Maybe…just maybe I had caught Tanner Hammond's attention.

Just two years later than when I'd tried.

### Tanner

Okay. My mind was fully in a place it shouldn't be, but I couldn't help it.

Holy shit, Andrea had a body that went on for fucking days—the kind of body that knocked a guy flat on his ass and made him want to do stupid shit to get all up in that. How in the world I hadn't noticed that before was beyond me.

Actually, I *had* noticed she had curves in all the right places before, but I had no idea it was that…yeah, *that*. None whatsoever. Sweet Jesus, those shorts? That shirt? My sweats suddenly felt tighter as the image of her formed in my mind, the thin material barely holding her breasts back.

And those breasts…sweet Jesus, God had blessed her in that department.

As I closed the bathroom door behind me, I realized I was a lucky man, because there was a pool at that damn cabin and that meant Andrea would be in a bathing suit. A smile pulled at my lips. Hopefully, a two-piece.

Though she'd seemed a little self-conscious when I first arrived, which blew my mind. Never would I have ever thought she lacked in the confidence department, not with that fiery attitude. But there had been that sadness I'd seen in her last night and that had haunted me most of the day, but I knew that sometimes when people drank, they could be happy or sad.

Glancing around her bathroom, I had to grin. Her personality was everywhere. The hot-pink-and-purple plaid shower curtain, a blue bath rug, and as I ended up at the sink, I noted a yellow toothbrush holder. Not a damn thing in there matched. I washed my hands and then dipped my head, splashing the cool water over my face.

Straightening, I turned off the water and let out a pent-up breath. She'd been right. I could've called or texted her, but I'd wanted to make sure she was okay after last night. I also needed to apologize for the shit I'd said at Kyler's place and I'd needed to do that to her face. And I also wanted to dig in a little, figure out what the hell she had against me. Except the moment I saw those little shorts, I fucking forgot what the hell I was doing there. It was like being fifteen all over again. Damn.

But she really had no memory of kissing me last night. Man, that was a kick to the nuts. I had to laugh. Good thing I had an ego on me the size of a mountain.

Maybe three minutes, if that, had passed by the time I walked back into the living room, but when I looked at the couch I didn't see her. Frowning, I came up behind it and my brows flew up.

She was curled on her side, her legs dangling over the couch and arms tucked under her chest. The frown slipped off my face as I leaned over the back of the couch. "Andrea?"

Nothing.

I started to grin. "Hey, Andy?" I raised my voice. "Babe?"

Her lips moved, murmuring something unintelligible. The girl was out cold. Shaking my head, I pushed off the couch and looked around, spying the bedroom door ajar. I could leave her on the couch, but that seemed fucking wrong. My momma didn't put a whole shit-ton of effort into raising me, but she'd drilled in the whole "gentleman" routine.

Spinning around, I walked into her bedroom, snapping on the small lamp beside her bed. Déjà vu slammed me, except Andrea wasn't drunk tonight. The shade looked like someone had taken a hot glue gun and stuck damn purple diamonds all over it. I hadn't noticed that last night. Seeing that the bed wasn't even made, I sighed and then straightened it up. Peaches. Shit. The comforter carried her scent as I flipped the corner back. Andrea always smelled like peaches and vanilla.

I didn't look around her bedroom. I don't even know why. Too fucking intimate after last night. She was still out cold when I returned, and when I knelt down beside her, she stirred a bit as I got my arms under her.

"This is becoming a habit," I said out loud.

"What…what are you doing?" she mumbled.

"Taking you to bed." I lifted her up, and as I cradled her close, her head lolled against my chest, and red curls spilled across my arm.

"Not…not in your lifetime, bud," she replied.

I had to laugh again, shaking my head. Even half-asleep, she was a firecracker. I carried her back to her bedroom and placed her in the bed. Since she wasn't passed out, she sort of helped me this time as I wrangled her legs under the comforter.

Although, she'd taken a sleeping pill, so I wasn't sure this was even the real Andrea. Hell, who knew the real girl? I knew I'd barely scraped the surface with her, even after two years. I hadn't even known she had problems sleeping. Never once had I heard her mention it, and Syd or Kyler had never said a thing to me about it.

It took everything in me to step back and to walk out of the damn bedroom, but there was no hiding the smile on my face or denying the swell of anticipation for this upcoming week.

Things…things were going to change between us.

# Chapter 4

**Andrea**

Well, this trip was starting off super-awkward.

Sitting in Kyler's Durango, I was seated right next to Tanner and I felt like we were the two annoying kids stuck in the backseat on a long trip. Which would make Kyler and Syd our parents. Weird.

An hour and a half into the drive, Syd's nose was deep in her eReader, Kyler's thumbs were thrumming along the steering wheel as he hummed to whatever song was playing, and I was doing my best not to think about the fact I'd drunkenly kissed Tanner. Biting down on my lip, I glanced at him.

Blue eyes fixed on mine.

Oh crap, he wasn't asleep anymore. I quickly focused on the window and stared at...rolling green hills everywhere.

Another thing I couldn't stop thinking about was his visit last night—the way he had looked at me when I'd opened the door, like he'd really liked what he'd seen. And what he'd said to me before he'd gone into the bathroom, and I'd embarrassingly fallen asleep in that short burst of time. He'd carried me to my bed—*carried me*. Good lord, I was *not* a small girl. So that was impressive...and hot.

Watching a Mack truck loaded up with logs zoom past our SUV, I tried not to think about one of those *Final Destination* movies. But that would probably be better than what was consuming my thoughts. I was unnerved by how much I was thinking about this. I shouldn't care. It was

Tanner, and he and I could barely call each other friends. He'd also had his chance with me before and had blown it.

Not that he seemed to remember any of that, or that I'd really given him a chance back then. Wasn't like I'd talked to him or expressed any inclination that I wanted to practice making babies with him, so…

Tanner tapped my knee, drawing my attention. My eyes met his. "What?"

Lifting his hand, he curled a long finger. "Come here."

My stomach dropped at the sound of his low, husky voice. Having no idea what he was up to, I leaned across the space between us, turning my head to the side.

"I haven't been sleeping for a while," he said, his breath dancing along my cheek, sending shivers down my spine. "So…"

"So what?" I had no idea why he felt the need to share that with me.

"You've been staring at me," he whispered, and I started to draw back, denials forming on my tongue, but his arm suddenly moved. His hand curled around the back of my neck, holding me in place. "I don't mind it."

My heart stuttered and then skipped a beat. What the…? I swallowed hard, my normal, what-I-liked-to-consider witty rapport was nowhere to be found. The only thing that came out of my mouth was a whispered, "You don't?"

"Yeah." His fingers tangled in my hair, tugging the curls in a delicious way that sent fiery awareness across my skin. "I just decided that I don't."

"Right now?" I breathed.

Tanner shifted his head slightly and when he spoke again, his breath caressed my lips. Muscles low in my belly tightened. "Yep. About two minutes ago, actually."

A soft, surprised laugh came out of me. "Really. Two whole minutes ago."

"Maybe five," he teased, and my stomach twisted pleasantly. "Ten minutes might be pushing it, though."

I almost laughed again, but his mouth was so close to mine that if I shifted a fraction of an inch, our lips would meet, and I really wanted to remember my drunken kiss. His fingers found their way through the tangle of curls. I had no idea what was happening. For the first time in my life, I couldn't speak.

"No sex in the backseat," Kyler announced. "I just cleaned this thing out."

Snapping out of our own little world, I jerked free, wincing when my hair caught in his hand. Cheeks burning, I glanced forward as he eased his fingers out of my curls.

In the rearview mirror, Kyler grinned at me.

I flipped him off.

Heart thumping unsteadily, I glanced at Tanner. Our gazes met again, and a slow smile pulled at his lips. Leaning back against the door, he tossed his arm over the back of our seat. The stare was intense, piercing, like he wasn't seeing me, but was seeing inside me, scoping out all my secrets. Flushed, I was the first to look away.

Syd had twisted around, peering into the back seat. Her gaze flitted from me to Tanner and then back. Her lips pursed. "Alrighty then."

I had absolutely nothing to say as she flipped back around, tapping the screen on her eReader. Nope. I wasn't even thinking anything. I stared at the back of Kyler's head, totally bewildered by—by everything. As my heart started to pound even harder, I did know one thing. This week was going to be really interesting.

After what felt like forever, the Durango's tires crunched over gravel and as soon as it rolled to a stop, I all but threw open the door and hopped out. Okay. All ignorant jokes about West Virginia aside, this little piece of the world was stunning and breathtaking.

Tall pine and elm scented the air, and although the August sun was oppressively strong, the trees blocked the harsh rays, providing much welcome shade. Above the leafy branches and green needles, I could see a giant sandstone structure bursting into the blue, cloudless sky. The mountain glimmered faintly, and each jagged point reminded me of a massive hand trying to grasp at the clouds.

Syd joined me, smiling as she followed my gaze. "Those are the Seneca Rocks. I think Kyler wants to check them out either Wednesday or Thursday. You're more than welcome to join us."

I laughed as I shook my head. "I don't know. I'm more of a lie-by-the-pool kind of girl versus getting all up into wildlife."

Syd nudged me with her hip as she glanced over her shoulder, to where the guys were grabbing the suitcases out of the back of the SUV. "Or maybe a check-out-what's-going-on-with-Tanner kind of girl?"

I smacked her arm. "I'm not that either, and you know that."

"Uh-huh." She bit down on her lower lip as she turned her gaze to mine. "You know, I've always thought he liked you."

"Stop," I sighed. Syd was forever playing the matchmaker since she'd settled down with Kyler. The night I'd left her place feeling all kinds of butt sore over what Tanner had said to me, she'd started in on how she truly believed we were secretly in love with one another.

"What?" she challenged. "It's like a typical playground love affair. Instead of you two pulling each other's hair and pushing each other down, you get on each other's nerves on purpose."

"I'd like to think I'm a bit more mature than that."

She arched a dark eyebrow.

I giggled. "Okay. Maybe not."

"Yeah," she dragged the word out. "You guys have hooked up before, right?"

Shooting her a look, I shook my head. "Um, no."

A look of doubt crossed her face. "You've made out, then—"

"No. No, we haven't." I laughed under my breath, because I was *so* not counting that kiss. "Why do you think that? He and I have never done anything. I would've told you."

The disbelief didn't fade from her face, and I wondered why in the world she'd still think that after all this time. Pushing the conversation out of my head, I dragged in a deep breath and smiled. I realized there wasn't a hint of fumes or body odor or any other nasty street smell that clung to the city, a kind of smell you got used to until you were out in a place like this. Clean air. Lord, I'd forgotten how nice that was to breathe.

"Let's go help them." Looping her arm through mine, she slipped her sunglasses down and then led me to the back of the SUV.

Tanner had a duffel bag slung over his shoulder, and it boggled my mind how guys could pack for a week in a bag I could easily double as a purse. In his other hand was my pink and purple polka-dotted suitcase.

Slipping free from Syd, I went to his side. "You don't have to carry that." I reached for my suitcase.

"I got it." Facing me, I could clearly see myself reflected in the silver aviator-style sunglasses he'd slipped on. Damn, he looked good in them. Air Force pilot hot.

"I can carry it," I insisted while Kyler headed around the SUV. Syd was behind him, carrying an armful of plastic bags.

Tanner grinned as he stepped back, holding the stuffed piece of luggage out of my grasp. "Grab the leftover bags. I'll carry this." He pivoted around.

We'd stopped at the grocery store in town and there was a load of groceries in the back, enough to feed an army. Grabbing two paper bags, I lifted them out, eyeing him warily. "Are you trying to get laid or something? Because I know going a whole week must be hard for you and all."

Tanner stopped and then turned back to me. One brow rose above the rim of his sunglasses. "Now, come on, Andy. There's no such thing as trying when it comes to this."

My eyes narrowed as I walked to where he stood. "What is that supposed to mean?"

He lowered his head so that we were almost eye level. His lips tipped up at the corners and he spoke in a voice only I could hear. "If I wanted you, I'd have you."

What in the holy hell hotcakes? My jaw hit the gravel as I barked out a short laugh. "Oh, wow. That's cocky."

One shoulder rose. "Nah, just confident."

I snorted. "Or really optimistic in a special kind of dumb way."

He laughed under his breath as I shifted the bags in my arms. "Let's make a bet, Andy."

"Stop calling me that," I ordered, but hated—absolutely loathed—the breathlessness of my voice. I wanted to punch it out of my chest. Or him. Yeah, punching him would be better. "And I'm not making any bets with you."

I walked around him, stomping on the gravel with my sandaled feet. I'd taken a few steps when he said, "That's because you know you'll lose."

Halting suddenly, I almost tripped over my own feet. I whipped around, facing him once more. He did *not* just say that. No way. "Excuse me?"

Tanner's grin and walk were full of swagger as he strolled on past me. "Yeah, it is. You know you'll be under me by the time we leave this cabin."

# Chapter 5

**Tanner**

Andrea's cheeks matched her hair, and that was…it was cute. I didn't do cute. Or at least I didn't until now. Now I was all about the cute—the Andrea kind of cute.

I knew I should've felt like an ass for saying what I did, but I didn't. No regrets. None whatsoever. Heading up the porch steps, I realized I had no idea what that said about me.

And I'd be lying to myself if I said I didn't know what I was starting, because I did. I fucking knew exactly what I was provoking, but I had no game plan when it came to how this was going to end—no clue. And I always had a game plan.

Or, in other words, an exit strategy.

I'd always been a "no relationship" kind of guy. Everyone knew that. It wasn't that I ruled them out completely, but I didn't go there unless I really wanted to go there. Something fucking bizarre had happened between Friday night and this morning, because I knew I wanted to go there with Andrea. I couldn't put a finger on what exactly had happened to cause that and I wasn't sure why it was even Andrea. Why not Brooke or Mandie? Or Lea? Never once had they made me want to slam my face into a wall, and Andrea had brought me to the edge of crazy many times over.

Shit. I knew enough, to be honest. Andrea gave as good as she got. She was smart, and when she wasn't pissing me off, she was funny. And there were moments she could be the sweetest thing, and not just when she was falling asleep. None of that was news, but why now?

I honestly didn't have an answer for that.

"Holy crap," Andrea breathed, staring up at the cabin as she walked up the steps to the wrap-around porch. "How did you guys end up with this place?"

I stepped aside as she stopped beside me. Looking at the wide wrought-iron entry door and the floor-to-ceiling window across the front, the cedar log cabin was a McMansion. Big enough for more than just the four of us, an entire soccer team could be housed comfortably in this place, but I was glad I wasn't going to have to fight a shit-ton of guys for Andrea's attention this week.

"My mom knows the owner," Kyler answered, shoving the key in the door. His mom ran a hugely successful bar restoration company, which afforded some hellish contacts. "So, we lucked out with this."

"I'll say." Andrea grinned as she glanced at me. I expected to be on the receiving end of one of her death glares, but the grin had reached her eyes, warming them. "I cannot wait to see what the inside looks like."

Kyler pushed open the doors and a rush of cold air greeted us. Letting Andrea head in before me earned me an arched look, which I returned with a grin. She shook her head as she crossed the threshold.

She came to a complete stop, and I nearly plowed into her back—definitely not in the fun way either.

"Sorry," she mumbled, stepping to the right. An awed look crossed her pretty face as she took in the high ceilings and the exposed rafters, the huge fans and skylights above the sitting room. I couldn't believe, with the kind of money she came from, that this was the first extremely nice home she'd seen.

I'd have bet she grew up in something like this.

"It's beautiful." She turned that grin to Sydney. "Wow."

"And you haven't seen the rest. Kyler's mom sent us pictures of it. There's a living room on the other side of the kitchen, then a sunroom. Five bedrooms upstairs—three of them have their own bathrooms."

"And there's a media room in the basement, fully loaded," Kyler added.

That caught my attention.

We crossed into a room I wasn't sure had a purpose other than to look nice. With its white wicker furniture and thick cushions in pristine condition, I would bet money no one had ever used it. The stairs leading up were to the left, just outside the kitchen, and Jesus, the kitchen was bigger than my mom's kitchen *and* living room back at home.

Andrea stared at the stainless-steel vent hanging from the ceiling above the gas grilltop stove. "I'm going to make this kitchen my bitch."

Sitting the luggage down, I pushed my sunglasses up. "You can cook?"

She shot me a long look. "Yes. I can do things other than drinking my weight in liquor."

Normally I would've fired back with something equally biting, but I managed not to. I deserved an award. "So what are you going to make me for dinner, then?"

"Ha!" she laughed, sitting the groceries on the counter. "Keep wishing for that. Never going to happen."

Sydney grinned as she joined Andrea, helping her unload the groceries. "That sucks for you, Tanner, because Andrea can really cook."

"Yep." She shoved a large pack of ground beef in the fridge. "Yep. I can."

Leaning against the counter, near the sink, Kyler grabbed a water bottle from the stash his girl was trying to put in the fridge. "Her lasagna is banging."

I frowned. "You've eaten her lasagna?"

Kyler flipped the water bottle in his hand. "Yes, sir."

"That's fucked up," I muttered, oddly...jealous.

Andrea giggled as she looked at me over her shoulder. "Maybe you should've been nicer to me, huh?" She turned back, picking up the case of beer and shoving it onto the bottom shelf of the fridge. "Then you'd be all up and familiar with my lasagna."

"That's not what I want to be all up in," I said under my breath.

She stiffened. "What?"

"Nothing. Just clearing my throat." I ignored Kyler's wide-eyed gaze as I picked up the luggage. "But guess what? I have your stuff and I'm going to pick your room for you."

She whipped around, arms at her side. "You are *not* picking my room."

"Oh, yes I am." I took a step back and waited as Sydney and Kyler exchanged looks.

Andrea's eyes narrowed.

Our gazes locked, and then I wheeled around, heading for the stairs, not even attempting to keep the grin off my face when I heard her curse. I was acting like a fourteen-year-old boy desperate for attention. And I was—desperate for her attention, that is. Like a kid with a new toy, I didn't want to share her with Kyler and Sydney. A second later, she was right behind me. "I'm picking my room," she insisted.

"So, you say." I climbed the steep stairs at a rapid clip.

She groaned. "You're a tool. And your legs are too long. And you walk too fast."

I laughed as I reached the landing. When I glanced down, Andrea was still several steps below me. "It's not my fault your legs are short."

"My legs are *not* short." She finally joined me at the top, her cheeks flushed pink. "Your legs are just abnormally long. You have freak legs."

"You know what they say about long legs…"

Her eyes rolled. "They do *not* say that about long legs."

"They do in my world." I stopped at the first door and elbowed it open, revealing a massive room with a bed big enough for the four of us to sleep comfortably in. Across from the bed, a huge-ass TV hung from the ceiling. "I think this must be the master."

"Let's leave that for Syd and Kyler." Andrea closed the door, and then strutted forward, opening the next door. I didn't see it, but she huffed and then closed the door. The same with the next, and I guessed the third time was a charm, because she squealed as she pushed the door open. "This is mine."

My brows rose as I followed her, and I had to give it to her. She had good taste. The bed was large, not as big as the master, but nice. The room was rustic—exposed beams in the ceiling, the wood-paneled walls painted grey.

She skipped into the room, placing a purse the size of a baby on a chair situated in the corner. Then she headed straight for a large white door. Thrusting it open, she clapped her hands together. "Oh my God. This bathroom. I could live in it."

Setting her suitcase on an old wooden trunk by the door, I dropped my duffel on the floor with a *thunk* and followed her over to the bathroom. "Damn." I leaned against the doorframe. "You could sleep in that tub."

"I could! I just might." She turned and looked up at me, smiling widely.

Something tugged in my chest, causing me to straighten as she whirled back around to the bathroom. "It's a claw-foot tub. I've never actually used one of them before or seen one this big. It's kind of…romantic," she said wistfully.

I said nothing as she opened another door. "Oh, this bathroom must share with these two bedrooms." Closing the door, she brushed past me, back into the bedroom. The peachy scent trailed after her, like a lure. "This place is really nice. Kyler's mom has good taste."

"Yeah." I watched her walk over to a standing mirror, and of course, that meant I watched the way the snug jeans hugged her shapely ass. Andrea definitely was not lacking in that department either.

Shaking my head, I turned and walked around the bench placed in front of the bed. I glanced at her. She raised her brows. I power-bombed the bed and stretched out across the center. I only had to wait maybe three seconds before Andrea responded.

"What are you doing?"

"Getting comfy." I folded my arms under my head as she froze in front of a dresser. "This bed is nice."

"And it's my bed."

"No, it's not. It belongs to whoever owns the house," I pointed out gamely.

"No shit, Sherlock, thanks for clarifying." She glanced at the open door and then whiskey-colored eyes met mine. "Thanks for carrying my luggage up."

I winked. "You're welcome."

Interestingly, she sucked her bottom lip in between her teeth for a moment. "That was kind of me saying nicely it's time for you to get the hell out of my room."

"I know."

Both brows flew up. "And you're still here."

"I am."

She took a step forward and then stopped. "Don't you have anything to do? Like go explore the rest of the house? Snapchat pictures of your dick to random chicks? Annoy someone else?"

"Not really." I paused. Needless to say, I'd never sent anyone pictures of my cock, but now I kind of wanted to send one to her. "Guess what?"

She eyed me as she shuffled closer to the bed. "You're a total chicken butt."

Chuckling, I rolled onto my side, facing her. "That was pretty lame."

"It was." She shrugged, moving closer. "I'm not ashamed. I excel at being lame."

"Nah, that's not what you excel at."

A frown creased her face. "If you say drinking is what I excel at, I won't be responsible for my actions."

"You excel at distracting me and driving me crazy. Not necessarily in a bad way. Sometimes, but not always," I admitted. Her eyes widened, and nothing that I was saying was a lie. "You also excel at being beautiful."

Her lips parted. "You…" She shook her head. "…are still not getting laid."

I laughed, but then my gaze dipped over the pale blue tank top she wore. The way her full breasts stretched the material snagged my attention. With great effort, I lifted my gaze. "I'm picking the room next door."

Color pinked her cheeks. "Of course you are."

"I think it's awesome we'll be sharing a bathroom. We can bond." I smiled at her, the kind of smile that drew girls from across the bar like bears to honey. "I think we need to bond."

"I…I don't agree," she quipped, and I realized my smile wasn't working on her. Figured.

"Yes, you do."

She folded her arms, and the swell above her top increased. Shit. I needed to stop staring at her breasts. "There are other bedrooms with their own bathrooms."

"I like that one."

"You haven't even seen the other bedroom, Tanner."

I grinned. "I know I'll like it."

Clearly exasperated, she stared at me and gave a quick shake of her head. Curls bounced everywhere. A moment passed. "What are you up to?"

"Nothing." I patted the spot next to me. "Come here."

One dark auburn brow rose. "Why?"

"Because I want to ask you something."

"And you can't ask me while I'm standing here?" She shifted her weight.

Sticking out my lower lip, I patted the bed again. "I can't. I need you here, close to me. It's the only way that it can be."

"You are ridiculous." Her voice was soft.

"Maybe."

A long moment stretched out between us and then with a heavy, obviously annoyed sigh, she walked to the bed and sat by my legs. "Happy now?"

"Nope." Reaching out, I grabbed her arm and tugged her down beside me before she could do anything. "*Now* I'm happy."

Part of me expected Andrea to pull away and bounce off the bed, but she did neither, and I took that as a positive sign. When her pink lips parted on a soft inhale, the need to taste those lips punched through me hard—a real kiss, not one she'd forget. It shocked me, the power behind that desire. I didn't get it, but I didn't want to question it in that moment. She was close. She smelled damn good. And we weren't at each other's throats.

"What did you want to tell me?" she asked.

My gaze followed the shape of her lips. "I didn't want to tell you anything. I wanted to ask you something."

The corners of her lips twitched as if she were fighting a smile. "What did you want to ask me?"

Our faces were inches apart when I looked up. "What are you making me for dinner?"

Andrea blinked and then she laughed—loudly and deeply, an infectious and rich laugh that warmed my skin. "I'm going to make these hamburgers I saw on *Kitchen Nightmares*. They used minced onions, breadcrumbs, and more. They're really good."

Ah, fuck me, another thing that was cute. She got recipes off of a reality TV show. "I'll grill them."

"You might have to fight Kyler for control of the grill."

"I can take him." Her top slipped down her arm, revealing the pale blue strap of her bra. I reached between us, slipping my finger under the edge of her tank top. As I drew it back up her shoulder, the backs of my fingers glided over her skin, causing her chest to rise with a deep breath.

Her eyes widened, and I swallowed a groan when the tip of her tongue darted out, wetting her lower lip. Neither of us spoke as I straightened her top. Emboldened by the lack of protest, I trailed my hand down her arm, reveling in the feel of her skin. I stopped where her hand rested on her hip.

"What…what are you doing, Tanner?" she asked again.

Such an important question, but truth was, I really didn't know, because it wasn't about what I was doing right that second. It was more than that, and as I'd realized earlier, something had shifted between Friday and today, and I really wasn't sure what the fuck that meant or why or any of that.

So I smacked her ass.

Seemed legit.

A shriek squeaked out of her as she jerked into a sitting position. The cutest damn glare fixed over her features. There it was again, the word cute. "You mother—"

"No, Andy, I'll be a *father* one day. I'm a boy. You're a girl." Rolling off the bed, I hopped to my feet and cast a grin in her direction. "But right now, I'm going to go check out this pool I haven't seen yet."

For a moment she didn't move or speak, and I wasn't sure she was even breathing, but then she flopped onto her back. Raising one arm, she extended her middle finger.

I laughed.

# Chapter 6

*Andrea*

The hamburgers were chilling in the fridge, gussied up and ready to go on the grill later, and I'd taken my time getting them set. Everyone was out in the pool, and I was hovering in the kitchen, wasting time watching the local news on TV, and the only thing I discovered was that someone had spray-painted a mustache on some statue in some town I'd never heard of.

Breaking news around these parts.

I moved to the kitchen door, nursing a bottle of hard lemonade. From my vantage point, I could see everyone. The deck connected to the pool in a very interesting design, with a wide bridge connecting the main deck to the pool deck, which was at a lower level since the pool was an in-ground one. Having grown up with a rather large pool in the backyard, landscaped to mimic a rocky beach, I knew the owners had to have paid a pretty penny just for the deck and pool.

Syd and Kyler were on one side of the pool, trying to drown each other, or at least that was how it appeared to me. My gaze drifted to the left, and I swore under my breath.

Tanner.

Dammit.

My lips parted. There might've been drool forming, but I honestly didn't think anyone would blame me for that.

Tanner currently looked like he was posing for a photo for one of those "hot guys" Tumblr pages, especially the one with the kittens. God, I loved the hot guys and kittens

Tumblr page. Whoever came up with that page deserved an award—a lifetime achievement award.

His arms were braced behind him on the side of the pool. Muscles bunched in his shoulders, and his biceps were flexed. My gaze traveled over his broad, defined chest and the tightly packed abs that rested underwater. His head was thrown back against the ledge of the pool, face tipped up, and the sun kissed his cheeks and well-formed lips. He was grinning, a private smile that made me feel like he knew I was hiding in here, watching him like some kind of lovesick girl.

But I wasn't lovesick.

And I *was* hiding.

Before I made the hamburgers, I'd changed into my bathing suit and had slipped my clothes back on over it. Why in the world I had thought it would be a good idea to wear a two-piece was beyond me. For some dumb-ass reason, I had reasoned that because it was black, it was slimming. Which was stupid, because honest to God there was truly no such thing as a slimming bathing suit no matter what the advertisements claimed.

At the moment, Syd hauled herself out of the pool, her hair glossy and black and her body... I sighed. She was a tiny girl, and she looked perfect in a bikini, completely at ease. I should've packed a one-piece, but I didn't think I owned one.

Clutching the bottle to my chest, I glanced at Tanner. He hadn't moved, and I felt like one of those cartoons where the character's tongue rolls out of its mouth. Both guys out there blew the hotness charts, but Tanner...he'd always caught my eye.

And I'd never caught his, until now.

What the hell was he up to? His behavior in the car? In the bedroom earlier? Yeah, it was weird that he'd come over last night to apologize and make sure we weren't going to ruin the trip for Kyler and Syd, but his impromptu visit hadn't prepared me for the way he was acting. And I seriously doubted "behaving ourselves" meant hooking up.

Could I hook up with Tanner?

Apparently I could kiss him when I was drunk.

He lowered his chin, his lips spreading wide as he laughed at something Kyler shouted from the other end of the pool. I couldn't hear it, but my tummy fluttered nonetheless.

Oh, yeah, I could totally hook up with him.

That moment, without warning, I felt *it*—the flutter in my stomach had moved to my chest. And it wasn't a pleasant, delicious feeling. Oh no, it was sudden and sharp, kicking my heart rate up.

*No. No. No. This is not going to happen.*

Turning away from the door, I leaned against the counter and closed my eyes. I tried to take a deep, even breath, but my chest squeezed in, cutting it off. *No.* My chest was not squeezing in. Nothing was happening. It was all in my head. It was always in my head and nothing more. Pressure clamped down, but that also wasn't real. I forced my lungs to expand, desperately ignoring the way my heart raced. My knuckles ached from how tightly I held the bottle. A wave of shivers rushed up my neck and over my scalp like an army of ants.

A sharp pain lanced across my chest, and I shook my head, clamping my lips together so fiercely my jaw ached. What if it was going to happen? What if I couldn't stop it? I would—

I cut those thoughts off as I opened my mouth wide, gulping air. Nothing was going to happen. Nothing *had* happened. The sudden violent anxiety wasn't really tied to anything. It was all in my head. A handful of seconds turned into a minute, and that minute turned into two. Eventually my pulse slowed and the tingling receded from the back of my neck. Hand shaking, I lifted the bottle and swallowed.

The sliding glass door opened, and I opened my eyes, breathing a sigh of relief when I saw that it was Syd. Hair twisted over one shoulder, she was securing a beach towel along her hips. "There you are," she said. "I've been wondering where you were."

My smile felt as weak as my knees. "I was just getting the hamburgers ready for later."

She glanced around the kitchen. "You were?"

"Yeah. Just finished," I lied, pushing off the counter. "They're in the fridge."

A knowing look crossed her face. "You're hiding."

"No. No, I am not."

She crossed her arms as she lifted a brow and waited. I sighed.

"Are you okay?" she asked.

Syd knew that sometimes…sometimes I *wasn't* okay. In the beginning, I'd tried to hide it from her, but being that Syd was going for a doctorate in psychology, there wasn't much she missed when it came to my weird behaviors. She was one of those people who always read you within five minutes of meeting you, and was dead-on in her observations.

"I'm okay." I took another drink and then set the bottle on the counter. Tugging the elastic band off my wrist, I swept my hair up in a quick, messy ponytail. "I *am* hiding. Kind of."

"Do tell." She headed to the fridge, grabbing a soda. She wasn't much of a drinker.

I glanced at the door. "Tanner…he's acting weird." I knew I had her full attention in that moment. "He actually came over last night."

"What?" Her eyes widened. "You didn't tell me."

"I didn't think it was a big deal. He wasn't there for long. He actually apologized for being a dick the other day." I stopped, pursing my lips. I *so* wasn't ready to vocalize the fact that I had kissed him Saturday night. "Well, I wasn't very nice either, but whatever. He stopped by to apologize. I didn't think much of it."

"I think a lot of it," she replied. "He could've called you. Or he could've said something here. He didn't need to stop by your place."

"I know." I picked up my bottle and then drifted toward the glass doors. Water sprayed out of the pool as Kyler and Tanner screwed around. "He's been really flirty. I mean, *really* flirty."

"I've noticed that. I'm not surprised."

I shot her a look.

"What? You two have been dancing around each other since you met."

My stomach dipped. "But why now? Why all of a sudden?"

"I don't know. Does there have to be a reason?"

I laughed. "Yes."

"There really wasn't a reason why Kyler and I finally moved from friends to more. Yeah, we were stuck in the cabin together, but it could've happened at any other point. It just did then. Maybe it's the same thing with you and Tanner," she explained. "Maybe you two *just* needed to be someplace—a place like this, all romantic and what not."

"I don't think he's looking for romance." I faced her. "I think he's looking to get laid."

She rolled her eyes. "How do you know that?"

"Um, let's see. He's pretty damn vocal about not doing relationships. Based on Tanner's dating history—or should I call it, hook-up history, because I don't think he really dates—I'm going to go with, he's looking to get laid."

"People change. Kyler did."

"That's because he was always in love with you."

Syd smiled brightly. "True. But maybe Tanner has always—"

"Oh my God, don't even finish that statement." I snickered. "Because that would just be absurd."

"Okay. Fine. Are you looking for a relationship?" she challenged.

I opened my mouth to say no, but I snapped my jaw shut. I had no idea if I was or not. I wasn't actively seeking one, but if a good thing fell in my lap, I wouldn't toss it away. And even though I probably wouldn't throw Tanner out of my lap either, I knew he wasn't a good thing. Well, that was a complete lie. He would be a great thing, but there was no way someone like him wouldn't grow tired of me—of my bullshit. Sometimes *I* was tired of it.

I shrugged as I glanced back outside. Tanner was standing next to the pool, hands on his hips. He was staring at the doors, and I stepped back, feeling my cheeks heat. Thank God he couldn't hear us. "I don't know. I mean, who wouldn't go slut-a-roo for him?"

Her laughter filled the kitchen. "Slut-a-roo? Hooking up with someone doesn't make you a slut."

"That I know for sure." I sent her a cheeky grin over my shoulder, and she laughed again. "I don't know. It's just weird. It's just..." I nibbled on my lower lip. "I've never told you this, because honestly, I never saw the point and it was before I knew you, but...I met Tanner my freshman year."

There was a pause and then, "*What*?"

Wincing, I swore she'd hit a decibel higher than normal. I watched Tanner dive into the pool. "Well, we didn't really *meet*. He had no idea who I was. He was just in two of my classes, but I had the biggest crush on him."

"Why did you never mention this before?"

I shrugged and then faced her. "When I say he had no idea who I was, I'm not kidding. After my freshman year, I didn't think I'd really see him again, just around campus, but then he turned up at the bar with Kyler that one night."

She eyed me closely. "Okay. Now your attitude toward him is starting to make sense, and I know it's more than just him not seeing you or paying attention. What did he do?"

My cheeks started to burn. "Remember Clara Hansen? She was my roommate my freshman and sophomore year."

"Um. Yeah. A little. She wasn't at your dorm a lot. That I remember." Syd joined me at the door.

"Well, she had one of those classes with me. Clara had to know that I had the hots for him, because I think I drooled on myself every time he walked into a lecture. I mean, I never told her that I did, but… Whatever, it doesn't matter." I took another drink, enjoying the burn it made cascading down my throat. "One night I was studying at the library and came back to the dorm late. Clara wasn't alone. She was in bed and she was most definitely having sex."

"Oh. Oh no." Syd groaned. "Let me guess. She was with Tanner?"

"Yep."

"What a bitch!"

"Like I said, I never told her that I liked him and I never even talked to him."

Anger pinched her pretty face. "Whatever. How in the world does he not remember you when you walked in on them?"

"He was um…he was busy, and the moment I saw who it was, I backed out of that room faster than I've ever moved." I finished off the bottle. "He had to have known someone had opened the door, but he doesn't know it was me. And I know it's stupid, but that whole situation has always bothered me."

"I can see why," she said quietly.

Walking over to the garbage can, I tossed the empty bottle. "But it's dumb. Because he didn't know me. I totally recognize that. I like to think I've matured a bit since then." I laughed when Syd raised her brows at me. "So, yeah, that's that."

"What are you going to do about it now?" she asked.

I shook my head. "I don't know."

A slow grin spread across her face. "Well, I think you'll figure it out. But only if you come outside and stop hiding."

**Tanner**

The hamburgers Andrea made were literally the best damn burgers I'd ever tasted, and I tried to tell her that, but she'd spent the better part of our little cookout up Syd's ass, and now that it was dusk, we hadn't exchanged more than a handful of words.

If I didn't know better, I'd think she was avoiding me.

And I wasn't down for that as I was feeling rather attention-seeking at the moment, especially since the lovebirds were plastered to each other in the shallow end of the pool. Syd was in Kyler's lap, and I really hoped there were no shenanigans going on.

Sitting on the ledge of the pool with my legs dangling into the water, I leaned forward as Andrea came back outside. Arms crossed under her chest, she came to the edge of the pool and looked at me.

I waved.

Her head tilted to the side, and in the fading sun, her hair was a burnt auburn, reminding me of the season not too far away. Lips pursed, she glanced in the direction of Kyler and Syd.

"Andy," I called before she interrupted them.

Her head swung toward me. "Tanner?"

"Come here." I smacked the spot beside me. Surprise shuttled through me when after a moment of hesitation she made her way over. After that afternoon, I figured I'd have to get down on my knees and beg her. As she sat down beside me, dipping pretty toes into the water, I could barely drag my gaze away from her shapely legs. "I've missed you."

She laughed as she folded her hands together. "You did *not* miss me."

"Yes, I did." I leaned back on my hands as she stared at the water. There was a freckle under her left ear. I wanted to taste it.

"I've been right here," she said, splashing the water with her feet.

What would she do if I ran my tongue along that little speck? "Still missed you."

"You are so full of shit," she replied, but she was smiling, so I figured that was a good thing. Not good enough for me to lick that freckle. She'd probably punch me in the balls if I did that. Glancing at me, she lifted a brow. "It's a good thing you're cute."

"You think I'm cute?" I reached up, tugging gently on the black string around her neck.

"Sometimes." She smacked my hand away.

Grinning, I tapped her fingers with mine. "That's because the other half of the time you think I'm a sexy beast."

"Sure." Her eyes flashed to mine. "If that's what helps you get on with your day."

I laughed deeply. "You know what will help me get on with my day?"

"What?"

"Seeing what's under this top and those shorts," I told her. "You're wearing a bathing suit, and seeing that is something that will definitely get me through the rest of my days."

Shaking her head, her attention returned to the pool, to where her feet paddled in the water. "You are just on a roll, aren't you?"

"I have no idea what you mean." I totally knew what she meant. Leaning my arm against hers, I savored the warmth of her skin and the way she bit down on her lower lip. "So… you changed your major, right?"

She nodded as she tipped her head in my direction. "That's right."

"What do you plan to do, then?" I asked, genuinely curious. "Live a life of leisure?" The moment that question came out of my mouth, I wanted to punch myself. It was supposed to be joke, but it was about as funny as an accident on the beltway.

Andrea twisted at the waist, facing me. Her brown eyes had darkened, turning stormy. "Contrary to popular belief, asshole, I don't sit around all day and have people wait on me hand and foot."

I pulled back. "Andrea—"

"I've changed my major to teaching, and as you know, teachers aren't living the life of Riley. And when I'm not in class, I'm not just hanging around, getting manicures and pedicures. I spend the bulk of my time volunteering at Holy Cross Hospital. And not as a candy striper, either." She pulled her feet from the water and stood briskly. Too quickly. "You don't—"

Her feet slipped in the puddle gathering on the deck and she went down, her knee cracking off the edge. My hand shot out, reaching for her arm as she started to pinwheel, but I wasn't fast enough. One minute she was standing next to me, and the next second she was in the pool, water spraying into the air.

"What the...?" Kyler broke away from Syd and turned toward us. Disbelief colored his tone. "Did you push her?"

Ignoring him, I jumped into the pool just as Andrea's head broke the surface. "You okay?"

Gasping from the cold shock, she treaded water, her eyes wide when they met mine. Anger flashed across her face, quickly followed by a red stain that seeped into her cheeks. I doubted that was anger. Oh no, that was a very different kind of emotion. With a little shake of her head, she turned from me and swam to the ladder. Soaked, her hair stuck to her cheeks as she climbed out of the pool, her clothing clinging to her curvy form.

I followed, but she stormed across the deck, not looking back. Cursing under my breath, I reached for the side and launched myself out of the pool.

"What happened?" Sydney asked, already starting toward the steps.

"She fell." I shot them a look. "I got this."

Sydney frowned. "But—"

"I *got* this," I repeated, and thank God she backed off, because Kyler would probably flip his shit if I had to repeat myself for a third time, because it would not be pretty.

"Tanner," Syd said.

Losing my patience, I faced her. "I—"

"She volunteers in the mental health part of the hospital," she said, letting me in on the fact that she'd heard a part of our conversation. "And she also volunteers at the suicide hotline center in Georgetown whenever they need her."

Stunned, I blinked. "What?"

Kyler was staring at Sydney like she'd sprouted a third tit. "Are you serious?"

She nodded. "It's not something she broadcasts, but I thought you should know."

For a moment, I didn't move as I absorbed that hidden piece of knowledge about Andrea—the girl I thought of as a rich girl, a little spoiled and definitely a party animal. Never once had it crossed my mind that she volunteered her time for anything, unless the volunteering involved drinking or shopping for purses.

"Shit. I had no idea," I said, but that wasn't an excuse.

Sydney didn't respond, and guilt exploded in my stomach like buckshot. Again, I was reminded of the fact that there was so little I knew of the real Andrea. I murmured a thanks and then made my way across the deck.

Tiny puddles led the way for me once I was inside the house. She'd gone upstairs, and I took the steps two at a time. I went straight to her room, ready to admit to being a complete dick.

"Andy, I'm—" I opened the door, and words left me, flew right out of my mouth and did a power dive out the window, head first. My brain shut the fuck down. I didn't blink. I'd never blink again, and there was no way I'd ever get this image of Andrea out of my head. I wouldn't want to, because standing in the middle of the bedroom, Andrea wore nothing but a towel— a small towel. A whole lot of pink skin was on display, sweetly curved and soft-looking, especially where the towel gaped.

Lust—a heated, insane kind of primitive lust slammed into me and I grunted out, "Fuck me."

# Chapter 7

**Andrea**

It was like someone had pressed the pause button on life. I stood a few feet from the bathroom, my arms at my sides as I stared at Tanner. Neither of us moved for a long moment, but my heart pounded as a flush raced across my cheeks, down my throat and under the towel. Pool water still clung to his bare chest, coursing down his abs, forming little rivers.

Tanner…he stared at me with a heat and intensity that was hard to mistake. My knees weakened for the first time in my life. In that moment, he didn't look at me like I'd just busted my ass right in front of him and fallen into the pool. Right now, he didn't look at me like he thought I was a useless party girl.

He looked at me like he saw a woman he wanted—he *needed*.

Then he moved.

Kicking the door shut behind him, he steadily advanced on me. The *thud* of the door closing snapped me out of my stupor. "What the hell?" I shrieked, clutching where I knotted the towel above my breasts as I took a step back. I was completely nude under the towel, and I'd never been this undressed in a room with Tanner before. It was too much. "What are you doing up here? Do you know how to knock?"

Tanner didn't look like he heard me. "I came up here for a reason, but hell if I remember now."

"W-what?" I sputtered. "You probably came to hurl more insults at me."

He lifted his gaze to mine then. Some of the heat evaporated from his eyes. "I'm sorry. I didn't mean to be insulting, but I was. That's why I came up here. To tell you I'm sorry."

For a second, I forgot I was in a towel and he had barged in on me. This was the second time he'd apologized. Never before had he *ever* apologized. Neither had I. I blinked slowly, having no idea what to say.

Tanner's gaze dipped again, and his lips parted. A rough sound emanated from him, causing my toes to curl against the hardwood floors and my tummy to twist. That was about the moment when I realized there was one hell of a gap in the towel.

Holy crap.

Since I wasn't a size 2 or even a size 10, a normal towel didn't cover me completely. The towel parted just below my left breast, exposing the side of my stomach, my hip and my entire upper thigh. I knew he could see the underswell of my breast, and if he looked hard enough, God only knew what else he could see. I couldn't even fool myself into thinking something different. If I moved too quickly, he'd definitely get an eyeful of my goods.

I almost laughed, because I'd been *so* against him seeing me in a bikini a few hours before, and now he saw pretty much just the same. But the back of my throat and my eyes burned, and if I laughed, it might've sounded a little crazed.

Tanner exhaled harshly, jarring me. "You're beautiful, Andrea."

Anger and pleasure warred inside me. He'd said that earlier, but I'd dismissed it. Buried it so deep in my thoughts that it was like hearing it for the first time. "Don't say things you don't mean. Not stuff like that."

He frowned as his eyes met mine. "I *do* mean it."

I swallowed hard as I shook my head. My fingers tightened on the knot. I didn't know what to say to that. "You shouldn't be in here."

"I know." But he made no effort to leave. "You hurt your knee."

Huh? I glanced down, and saw he was right. Tiny drops of blood beaded over my left knee. "I…I must have skinned it when I fell." As impossible as it sounded, my face burned even brighter.

"Let me take a look at it," he said.

"It's fine. Just a scratch."

Tanner's long legs ate up the remaining distance between us, and he was suddenly standing right in front of me. "I'm sure it's fine, but I'd feel better if I looked at it. I can't believe I'm actually saying this, but why don't you put some clothes on and let me check it out."

I wanted him to get the hell out of my room, but he was giving me the option to escape. Shuffling to the bed, I grabbed the clothes I'd laid out before Tanner burst into my room. I stopped at the bathroom door and glanced over my shoulder. He still stood there, his hands clenched at his sides. Something about his stance unsettled me.

Actually, everything about Tanner right then unnerved me.

I slipped into the bathroom, legs shaking. My reflection in the mirror confirmed that my face was only a shade lighter than my hair. God, tonight had gone just amazing. Slipped and fell into the pool like a dork and then caught standing in a towel. I was ready to crawl into bed and pull the covers over my head.

Or down half a bottle of tequila, because if there ever were some moments to get shitfaced, this was one of them.

Picking up my clothes, I realized I'd forgotten to grab a bra. Fuck me. Seriously. Maybe I'd get lucky and Tanner would fall into a black hole or something. I quickly changed into the cotton shorts and shirt, cringing when I could plainly see my nipples pressing against the material. God was not a fan of me right then. I was pretty sure he was smiting me.

My knee ached a little, and I grabbed some tissue. I'd just sat down on the rim of the bathtub when there was a knock on the door.

"Are you clothed?" asked Tanner.

"Yes." Immediately, I knew I should've said no, because the next second, the door was opening, and he was stepping into the bathroom. Still shirtless. Still wet. God, wet abs were hot. I shook my head in disgust as I scowled up at him. "I could've been peeing."

He lifted a brow as he stopped in front of me. "I'd hope you would've said that."

"Why would I tell you I was peeing?" I fired back. "I shouldn't have to tell you anything. You shouldn't walk willy-nilly into rooms."

"Willy-nilly?" His lips twitched, and I swore in that moment, if he laughed, I was going to kick him in the balls, total kung-fu style. He grabbed the tissues from my hand and knelt. "Are you okay?"

I didn't know what he was referencing at first. "I said I was okay."

He tilted his head as he wrapped his hand around my left calf, causing me to jump a little. Pausing, he peered up through thick, sooty lashes. "Did I hurt you?" His voice was low, thick like velvet.

There was a distinct impression he meant more than touching my leg. Before I could respond, he went back to staring at my knee. I tried to picture him doing this on calls when he worked. Unlike now, he'd be covered head to toe, but I bet with that uniform, he'd induced a lot of swoons.

Tanner gently swabbed at the skin, dabbing at the blood. Several moments passed and then he said, "I really didn't mean to say what I did out there. I don't think you sit around all day and do nothing."

I stared at the top of his head. Wet, his hair was a dark brown, and I could see the tiny droplets clinging to the short strands. "Are you sure about that? Because I honestly think you do believe that."

His hand froze a few inches from my knee and then he lifted his chin. Cobalt eyes pierced mine. "You know, you're right to ask that." Settling back on his haunches, he didn't look away. "And you do deserve my honesty. Up until a couple of days ago, I really didn't think you did anything with your spare time. I had no idea you volunteered at the hospital or the suicide hotline."

I sucked in a breath. "Syd opened her mouth?"

He nodded.

There was a tiny, black-haired girl who was going to get throttled. I could not fathom why she'd tell Tanner about that. Then again, she could've overheard our argument by the pool, which proved she could multitask while she sucked face with Kyler. I wasn't embarrassed by my volunteer activities. It just wasn't something I ever believed Tanner would care to know.

"I think that's pretty amazing," he said, flashing a quick smile. "Not a lot of people could do that."

"No." Most could not surround themselves with those who were ill, or listen to the calls from people who so desperately needed help. I honestly had no idea how *I* could do it, but I guessed it had something to do with…well, with who I was. "So, what? Now you think I put the 'awe' in awesome?"

He grinned wryly. "I always thought you were pretty awesome, despite my obviously incorrect assumptions about you."

I pursed my lips together. "I find that hard to believe."

"It's true." Leaning back, he tossed the used tissues in the little wicker trashbasket. "I always knew you were smart. You were taking pre-med when we met and it wasn't like you were failing at that. You've always been funny. No one can twist words quite like you. And I've seen some profound moments of sweetness from you."

Oh geez, the burn was in the back of my throat, and I had to look away. I ended up seeing our reflection in the mirror, and it was so strange, him kneeling in front of me, his head tilted back, staring up at me.

"And you have to know that I always thought you were hot," he added. "For fuck's sake, you're a redhead. That alone puts you into the sexy-as-hell category."

I coughed out a short laugh. "That's not what most people say about redheads."

"Fuck them." His hand slid up to the back of my knee, causing me to draw in a quick breath. A series of shivers traveled over me. "You probably already know you should put some peroxide on this, but you'll live."

My belly was fluttering as he ran his thumb along the back of my knee. Sensations rioted. I'd had no idea that area was so sensitive. "I know."

Curling his hand around the space just above my knee, he peered up at me again, a small half-grin on his handsome face. Then he rose, slipping his hand off my leg. Instead of straightening, he clasped my cheeks in a gentle grasp that sent my heart thundering. "Let's start over. Okay?" he suggested softly. "My name is Tanner Hammond."

I stared at him in what had to be an attractive, bug-eyed look. He was being serious. There was no ignoring the earnest touch to his expression. Could people ever truly start over? I didn't think so. The past didn't just simply vanish because we wanted it to, but what harm was there in pretending? That was something else that I excelled at. "My…my name is Andrea Walters."

There was a brief glimpse of his smile growing wider and then he kissed the tip of my nose. "It's good to finally meet you."

Tuesday night was different. Not bad or anything, but most definitely different. The four of us sat on the deck, under the stars, and chatted about everything and nothing in particular. All of us were drinking, but not to get sloshed, and I was okay with that. Maybe it was the peaceful scenery. Maybe it was the people I was with. Either way, I didn't feel like I needed more to have a good time or to relax.

Kyler was excited to start veterinary school, while Syd was eager to get done with grad school and she hadn't even started it yet. Tanner and I were the odd people out, both of us on hold until the spring.

Not once did we argue.

Okay. That wasn't entirely true. We bickered, but it wasn't a knock-down, drag-out argument that ended with me threatening his ability to reproduce in the future. I wasn't sure, even after starting over, we'd ever be able to not snap at one another.

We stayed up late, and I ended up pouring myself into bed, falling asleep without having to take a pill to get there, and on Wednesday morning, Kyler and Syd made breakfast before they headed off on their first hiking adventure.

I stayed behind, because, well, bears. And coyotes. And deer. And physical activity. Plus, I was pretty sure they'd be stopping every couple of minutes to make out, and I really didn't need to see all of that.

Tanner strolled by where I sat on the barstool in front of the kitchen island. He tugged a curl and then leaned against the island, angling his body toward mine. "So, what are we going to get into today?"

"Why didn't you go hiking with them?" I asked instead of answering. One just had to take a look at Tanner to know he was all about physical activity.

He shrugged one shoulder, causing the faded T-shirt he wore to stretch across his chest. "They didn't want me to go along with them, so you're stuck with me."

I thought it was a little strange that they would've said that, but knowing Syd, she probably purposely disinvited him the moment she realized I wasn't going with them, leaving him behind to babysit me. But after our little one-on-one in the bathroom yesterday, I wasn't sure being stuck with Tanner was a bad thing. "I guess I am."

"Yep. So why don't you go upstairs, put that bathing suit on and we'll spend the day being lazy and getting sunburnt."

I started to make up an excuse, but considering he'd seen me in a towel that barely covered anything the night before, it seemed stupid to not want to go out there in a swimsuit. Still, I hesitated.

"Come on, Andy." He caught my hand in his and drew me off the barstool. His other hand settled on my hip. "Spend time with me."

Staring into eyes that reminded me of the summer sky before a storm, I found myself nodding. His grin was easy and contagious as he tugged me against his chest. My heart stuttered at the contact, and he seemed to have no idea how he affected me as he swept his arms around me. Hugging me tight, he lifted me clear off my feet and gave me a little shake.

I squeaked like a dog toy. "Tanner!"

"Sorry." He didn't sound remorseful at all. "I get a little excited sometimes." He put me down and let go. "Hurry. I'll be waiting for you outside."

I did just that before I changed my mind. Dashing up the stairs, I changed into the bikini and then tugged a tube dress made out of terry cloth over it. I didn't stop to check myself out or take time to really think about the fact that it felt like we'd paired off. Kyler and Syd and Tanner and me. Of course, the four of us went out a lot, but it never felt like we were coupling.

Coupling?

I giggled out loud as I ran a hand through my hair, brushing it back from my face. Back downstairs, I stopped in the kitchen and before I knew what I was doing, I was standing in front of the fridge, reaching for a bottle of Miller Lite. I figured one could help me relax, so I started to kneel to grab one.

I stopped and drew in a shallow breath. What was I doing?

Clutching the door handle, I pressed my lips together in dismay. Did I really need a drink to relax? No. I didn't. I didn't need one. I *wanted* one. Big difference there. Drawing in a deeper breath this time, I shut the door and took a step back. Turning around, I gasped.

Tanner stood next to the sliding glass door. I hadn't even heard him come in and I had no idea how long he'd been standing there, but I knew he'd seen me.

He smiled at me, giving me no indication that he was judging me, but he probably was. I was judging myself. "You ready?"

Leaving the fridge, I went to him and smiled weakly when he opened the glass door. I stepped into the bright and warm sunlight, sort of feeling like a different person. Like I'd stripped away a layer that had been itchy and uncomfortable.

Tanner prowled past me, peeling the shirt over his head as he walked. Dear mama, those blue swim trunks, a shade or two lighter than his eyes, hung indecently low on his hips. How in the world did they stay on him? When he turned to me, I couldn't stop staring at those V-shaped indentations at his hips. Good Lord, his body was downright distracting.

He winked at me and then turned, diving into the pool like a damn pro. My eyes narrowed as I sighed. Even that was graceful.

I approached the edge of the deck, on the other end of the pool where there were steps, careful not to slip and fall again like a total turd. Tanner swam to the other side of the pool. With his back to me, he called out, "Are you getting in?"

Expecting him to turn around, I waited a second, but realized that he was...goodness, he was giving me time to get the dress off, and that was…that was sweet. Oh wow, that really *was* actually kind of sweet. Fingers trembling, I gripped the dress and tugged it over my head. I scanned the water, finding him swimming under it. Heart pounding, I dropped the dress within easy reach and had just reached the first step in the pool, water licking at my ankles, when Tanner's head broke the surface.

I froze.

He'd made his way to where he could stand, bringing his chest out of the water. Sunlight glinted off his glistening skin, but it was the way he stared at me that tugged my breath right out of my chest.

His gaze was like a physical touch, and my body hummed in response. "Andy," he murmured, voice deep and low. "I have a secret to admit."

Feeling breathless and foolish, I resisted the urge to fold my arms across my stomach. "Is it an interesting secret?"

"Oh yeah." His lips curled slowly. "Kyler actually invited me to go with them today."

My brows rose. "He did?"

Tanner nodded. "I told him no. I'd rather spend the day with you."

# Chapter 8

**Tanner**

Snow could have started falling out of the sky, and I wouldn't be able to pull my gaze away from Andrea. The glimpse I'd gotten of those curves the night before had been just a sweet hint and had in no way prepared me for this.

Andrea wasn't just beautiful. She was stunning—fucking breathtaking.

Curves in all the right places. Soft where a man wanted his woman soft. Her breasts were full, swelling over the cups of her top, and her waist curved in and flared out sweetly at her hips. Her body reminded me of those old-school pinup models I'd been obsessed with in high school. She was a fucking goddess, and didn't even know. Lust pounded in me, like I was under a jackhammer. I was so still, my body so hard that taking a breath required effort I couldn't spare. Every muscle in my body was rigid with need, with the desire to cross the distance between us and sweep her into my arms, and to feel her softness against my body.

Fuck me, I had it bad for her.

Her hands fluttered to her sides and then to the water lapping at her thighs. "Why are you staring at me like that?"

The quiet question blasted through me. "I can't look away."

Andrea's cheeks pinked under the sun. "That's weird."

"Oh no, being *able* to look away would be weird. No. Not just weird," I decided. "It would be fucking sacrilegious."

Her lips parted and then she smiled, and fuck if it didn't feel like I'd just won something. As she glided past me, I ground my teeth until my jaw ached, denying the urge to reach out and just…fuck, just touch her.

I watched her slip under the water, my starving gaze following her as she swam to the other side. When she broke the surface of the clear water and glanced over her shoulder at me, my heart thundered in my chest.

Like she was some kind of siren, her look alone lured me across the pool. I ended up next to her, both our arms resting on the ledge of the pool, our feet not touching the bottom.

The sun dipped behind a dark cloud, and Andrea looked up, her forehead scrunched. "Do you think it's going to storm?"

"I don't know." I didn't look away, which told me I was bordering on being a creeper at that point. "I saw that they were calling for some storms this week. It's August. Expected."

Her legs floated, brushing mine. The mere touch, the slight glide of her skin against mine, packed a hell of a punch. "I just hope they're not caught out in the rain or something. I know they're talking about going hiking again on Thursday or Friday."

"You're not going to go with them again?"

She shook her head and laughed. A curl fell forward, sticking to her cheek. "No."

"Me neither." I reached over, scooping up the curl and tucking it back behind her ear.

Her eyes shot to mine, the brown hue warm. There was a multitude of questions in her gaze. Silence stretched out as we studied each other, and I'd have cut off a finger to know what she was thinking in that moment. I knew what I was thinking. A whole lot of *want*. I wanted to kiss her. I wanted to see if her eyes darkened when she felt pleasure. I wanted to know what her expression looked like when she came. And I wanted to know what my name sounded like when she screamed it. Then she looked away, ducking her chin. The connection was broken.

Man, I needed to get control of my head. And my cock. Especially my cock, because if she looked down between us, there'd be no hiding how aroused I was, and that put the *dic* in "fucking ri*dic*ulous."

Searching for something to take my mind off the hard-on of a lifetime, I cleared my throat. "So what makes you volunteer at a hotline like that?"

She tilted her head to the side. "I…I don't know. I guess…" Trailing off, she sighed. Several seconds passed while it seemed like she searched for the right thing to say. "Those people, you know, they're just like you and me. They've hit a rough patch in their lives and most of them just want someone to talk to—someone to listen to them. Actually hear them. I can do that."

Instinct told me there was more to it. "Still has to be hard."

"It can be," she said quietly, squinting as the sun peeked out. "I've had a couple of calls where the people wanted to talk, and you think it's going to be a normal call, but then you realize that they've already taken pills or something like that. Those…those are hard," she admitted. "We really don't know what happens to them. If the police got there soon enough—if they are even alive right now. If they tried again or if they found someone else to hear them. So, yeah, that part is hard, but their world? Those people calling? Their world is a lot harder than whatever I deal with when I answer those phones."

Working at the fire department meant I saw a lot of terrible shit. Car accidents. Burn victims. Floaters in the river. And sometimes we were called in when the police or EMTs couldn't get through a door. Found a lot of OD victims that way.

"So why aren't you going into psychology?" Curiosity consumed me. "Seems like you might have found your calling."

She smiled a little. "I don't know if I have the empathy to pull that off every day of the week for the next forty years. Syd does. I don't."

I wasn't so sure about that.

"What about you?" she asked. "Why do you want to be a cop? You seem to like doing the fireman thing."

My lips curled up on one side. "It's what I've always wanted to be."

"Because of your father?"

Surprise shuttled through me. I'd had no idea she knew that my father was a cop. Had to have been Kyler. "Yeah, but not the reasons you're probably thinking."

She twisted toward me, her thigh glancing off mine. "What do you mean?"

My father was the last person I wanted to talk about, but I found myself running my mouth anyway. "Walter—my father—was a shit husband and dad, but he was even more of a shit cop."

Andrea blinked, obviously taken aback.

I laughed under my breath and looked away, casting my gaze to the woods surrounding the pool. "He couldn't keep his dick in his pants and he couldn't keep his nose clean, you know what I mean? He'd let people slide if they could do things for him, like cut him deals on shit. Not drugs and that kind of shit, but you'd be surprised by what people will do to get out of tickets. When I was younger, I didn't get why my mom cried all the time or why my dad didn't always come home after his shifts. I didn't get that he was a bad cop, probably wouldn't have if it wasn't for his partner. She was the one who showed me what it was like to be a cop, to respect that uniform and your role in society. I have no idea how she dealt with my father as long as she did—or how my mom did—but because of her I knew I wanted to be a cop." I took a breath, feeling the tops of my ears burn. "Anyway, I guess I wanted to be one because I could somehow make up for how shitty my father was at it."

"Wow," she said, placing her sun-warmed hand on my shoulder. "I didn't know any of that."

My gaze fell to where her small hand rested. Such an elegant and graceful hand, one that could've wielded a scalpel artfully, just hopefully not to my heart.

Heart?

Why in the fuck was I thinking about my heart and her cutting into shit?

And I was still hard.

Her hand slid down to my forearm. When she reached my wrist, she squeezed gently. "You know, you don't have to make up for how lousy he was."

"I know." My voice was rougher, abrasive.

Her slight smile grew. "But you'll make an excellent cop. You're a good guy. Most of the time," she teased.

I wasn't having good-guy thoughts right then. Nope. Not at all. I couldn't help it. I had to touch her. I needed to, and my control thinned and then snapped. So I did.

### Andrea

I saw the change in him immediately. Those baby blues darkened to azure, and I stilled, barely breathing. Part of me wanted to dive underwater, but that was such a small part. The rest didn't want to move.

My heart skipped as Tanner moved, but it wasn't closer to me. He pushed away from the ledge. But before I could feel a second of disappointment, he shifted so that he was behind me, his forearms resting on either side of mine on the pool ledge.

I sucked in air as I tensed, keeping the front of my body against the slippery side of the pool. What in the world was he doing? My imagination fed me a ton of naughty images as the clouds darkened over us again.

His breath was warm on my shoulder as he spoke. "Can I tell you something?"

Closing my eyes, I nodded. "Sure."

"I'm glad you didn't want to go hiking. I like having you all to myself." He moved one hand off the ledge and it landed on the bare skin of my side, underwater. I jerked back and came into contact with his large body. I didn't move. Not even when his chest rose sharply against my back. "Are you?"

All thoughts scattered when his hand slid to my hip. The small stretch of material did nothing to block the feel of the rough calluses on his palm.

"Andy?"

My breath stuttered. "Yeah…yes."

"That makes me happy to hear." His hand drifted off my hip, over my belly, stopping just above my navel. I didn't even have a chance to think about sucking in my stomach. My mind was blown by the touch and my arms shook. "Are you okay with this?" he asked as he flattened his hand.

I could barely get the words out. "Okay with what?"

"With this." He leaned into me. His entire front pressed against my back as he used his hand against my stomach to hold me in place. Against my lower back, I could feel the hard length of him, and my blood trilled through my veins. "You feel me and you're okay with that?"

Lust blurred my thoughts, mingling with confusion. While my body was a hundred percent on board—hell, it was on a train that had already left the station—I didn't understand why he wanted this—wanted me now. But I wasn't sure if that mattered—if the past really had any place in the here and now. And when had I ever really stopped to think about anything? Obviously not often.

He skimmed his hand up my side, and the answering shivers radiated throughout my body. "Andy?"

Normally, I hated it when he called me that, but right then, he could pretty much have called me anything, and I'd have been okay with it, especially with his hand so close to my breast. "I feel you," I whispered. "I'm…okay with that."

He made a deep, raw sound, and I thought I felt his lips brush my shoulder. "Thank. God." His hand stopped just below the swell of my breast. "Because if you'd said no, I think I might have cried."

My lips twitched. "Seems a bit extreme."

"You have no idea how badly I've wanted to touch you. Actually, I don't even think *I* had any idea," he mused. Then his hand was over my breast. "No idea."

I arched my back as a moan escaped me. "Oh God…"

His hips pressed against me, and I thought for a moment I'd slip right under the water. A tempest of sensations rose swiftly, like the summer storm brewing over our heads. His hand closed over my breast, gently kneading. "What I'd give to see them," he said, his thumb swiping over the crest of my covered breast. "But that'll have to wait."

I didn't want to wait.

But I didn't have to.

With incredibly nimble fingers, he slipped them under the cup of my bikini top. Heat exploded as the tips of my breasts tightened to the point of pain and my body sparked alive. My nipples had never been that sensitive before. Normally, I could do without them being touched, but now?

My hips rocked back against his as a jolt of pleasure moved from my breast and then straight down my belly. "Tanner."

"Fuck. I like it when you say my name like that." His mouth touched a spot below my ear as he caught my nipple between his fingers.

I cried out, stunned at the fierceness of the sensation pounding through me. My chest ached, felt swollen with need. His lips moved over my neck, trailing hot and wet kisses to my shoulder as he continued to touch me.

My chin fell and I opened my eyes. In a pleasured haze, I stared at his hand. He'd tugged the cups of my top down and my breasts were exposed, above water but blocked by the side of the pool. In reality, Syd and Kyler could return at any moment, but I didn't want to tell him to stop.

"I couldn't wait. Fucking beautiful," he said, kissing my neck, and I knew the moment he'd lifted his head and stared over my shoulder. "Jesus. They *are* perfect."

Sometimes I was insecure about the size of my breasts. Syd hadn't understood why, and time and time again, she'd told me that she wished she had what I did, but with bigger breasts came bigger problems. They weren't perky like smaller ones. Bluish veins were visible on the sides. The skin puckered and did weird shit sometimes. But the way he touched me was reverent, and with the combination of his fingers and the water teasing the tips, my insecurities were quickly floating away.

Tanner murmured something against my neck and then his hand left my breast, gliding down my stomach. When the tips of his fingers reached the band on my bottoms, I held my breath, and those tiny kisses picked back up along my neck, scorching me.

He waited. "What do you want?"

*Oh God.* That was all I could think. Over and over. *Oh God.* Then I wasn't thinking as his hand moved over my bottoms, between my thighs. His fingers played over the material, causing me to jerk against the arm he used to hold himself afloat.

"What do you want, Andrea?" he asked again, voice husky.

"Please," I whispered, and I wasn't even sure what I was asking for, but my body moved, seeking relief from the torment he was creating.

He cursed again and then his hand was slipping under the thin material of the bikini bottom. As he kissed my jaw, he touched me—*really* touched me. He cupped me with his longer fingers. "You're so warm," he said. "So hot."

Oh my God, he was doing it…right here, in this pool, and in broad daylight. This was really happening. Hadn't I just told him yesterday he had no chance of getting laid? Boy, I really hadn't put up much of a fight, but I wanted him—had wanted him for so very long, and I didn't want to think about all the *nothing* that came after this.

I'd never been more turned on in my life.

I didn't have a chance to say any of that. His thumb pressed down on the bundle of nerves, and I cried out his name, trembling as startling pleasure rose violently. He didn't even get a finger in me, didn't even try. He worked with pressure as his other finger skimmed my center.

"Andrea." His voice was raw, primitive in my ear. My hips moved against his hand almost frantically, and I whimpered, so close to release. "That's it. Let go."

I did.

I let go. Every muscle in my body tightened and then the release whipped through me so quickly I was left breathless and dizzy, spinning me into the kind of freedom a bottle could never give me. My arms turned to mush, and I would've slipped right under the water if it hadn't been for Tanner pushing his body against mine, wedging me against the side of the pool.

My head fell back against his shoulder, my breathing rapid as his thumb slowed against me. I don't even know how much time passed before he slipped his hand out of my bikini bottom, but I could feel him against me, still so hard and practically burning. He fixed my top without saying anything, his hand lingering in the most delicious way.

"You," I said hoarsely, wetting my lips. "What about you?"

He pulled back just enough that he was able to turn me in his arms. Thrown off, I gripped his shoulders. My eyes met his and held. A heartbeat passed as he stared down at me. Our legs tangled and then he pressed in between mine. I felt him, right against my core. A strange sound rose from the depths of me, part moan and part yearning.

"Me?" He lowered his forehead to mine. His hips did this remarkable and downright sinful roll. "I can—"

Sharp bright light cut through the sky above us, wrangling a gasp out of me. Tanner's grip tightened, and a moment later thunder boomed so loudly it felt like it rattled my bones.

"Oh my God," I said, eyes wide.

Tanner was already turning me around, lifting me with one arm, which was freaking impressive. "We need to get out of the pool before we're fried."

I *so* was not going to dispute that.

We scrambled out of the pool, and I stopped to grab my dress just as the sky ripped open and cold rain pounded down, causing me to shriek. Tanner laughed as he grabbed my arm, dragging me over the deck as our feet slipped in the rapidly gathering puddles.

Neither of us said anything as we stared at each other in the chilled air of the house, soaking and dripping wet, but there was nothing that needed to be said. The truth lay in the open between us.

Everything had changed.

# Chapter 9

*Tanner*

We stared at each other as the thunderstorm raged outside, the thunder cracking so loud it rattled the windows. The storm mirrored what I felt inside. My fingers still tingled from where I'd touched her, and her cheeks were flushed, eyes still shining with bliss.

Dammit, I was harder than a rock.

I wanted to go to her, but she stumbled a step back and hastily drew the dress on over her head. Once she had it situated, she swallowed hard as she looked out the windows. Rain pounded the deck. "God," she said, voice scratchy. "Syd and Kyler are out there in this."

"They'll be okay. Kyler will make sure of that."

She cast me a quick look over her shoulder. The passion had faded from her gaze, replaced by a keen wariness. "So will Syd. She can take care of herself."

"I didn't say that she couldn't." I scrubbed my hands through my wet hair and then grabbed a towel that had been left on the back of a bar stool. I soaked up as much water as I could and then dropped the towel on the puddle I'd created. The dress Andrea wore was soaking up the wetness and clinging to her curves in a way that made my mouth water, but she had checked out of the fun and naughty stuff.

I didn't blame her. I hadn't planned on that happening. Okay. Maybe I'd planned on kissing her, but I hadn't expected it to go that far, especially when we hadn't even kissed. Now I had no idea what she was thinking as she turned around, her gaze bouncing off mine.

"I think I'm going to go nap," she said, not meeting my gaze.

My chest tightened. "Andrea, what happened—"

"It's okay. I mean, it was *great*." Her cheeks flushed as she edged around the island, steering clear of me. "We don't have to talk about it or anything."

I frowned as I tracked her across the kitchen. "But I *want* to talk about it."

She neared the living room and the stairwell. "No guy *wants* to talk about that…whatever that is. I don't have crazy expectations, so you don't need to set me straight or anything like that."

My mouth flopped open. "What?"

Her face matched her hair. "I know that what happened doesn't mean anything. I know it doesn't—"

"Excuse me?" My voice rose as irritation flooded me. "It didn't mean anything?"

Confusion pinched her pretty face as she stopped at the bottom of the stairs. "Did it?"

Did it? Holy fuck, I stared at her, and the only good thing I could think at that moment was the fact that I no longer had a raging, rock-hard boner. "Of course not," I snapped.

Andrea flinched—fucking *flinched* like I'd hurt her feelings or some shit. She nodded jerkily and then turned, racing up the steps in her bare feet. I stepped forward, partly worried she was going to fall and break her neck and also to run after her.

But I stopped myself, knowing I was too damn angry to have a normal conversation that wouldn't end in us screaming at each other. Whirling from the stairs, I stalked back into the kitchen, stopping at the glass doors with my hands on my hips.

What the fuck? That didn't mean anything? What did she think I did? Went around randomly getting chicks off for shits and giggles? Well, actually, she probably *did* think that.

"Shit," I groaned, dipping my chin.

Based on what she knew about me—what she'd seen from hanging out with me—I was an equal opportunity fucker. Hell, why would she think she was any different than the slew of girls that had come before? But she *was* different, and damn she had to know that. I wouldn't just fuck around with a friend of Sydney's. That was obvious, because if that was the case, I would've tried to get between those pretty thighs the first time she'd mouthed off at me.

I heard the front door open and I turned, spying Kyler and Sydney. They looked like they'd swum in a river to get there, but both were smiling.

"Holy shit," Kyler said, dropping his backpack by the glass door. Laughing, he shook the rain out of his hair. Droplets of water flew in every direction. "That storm is crazy."

"Yeah," I murmured, heading to the fridge. "It came out of nowhere."

Sydney moved to the sink, where she wrung her hair out. "We checked the weather. Wasn't calling for anything until this evening."

"We didn't even get far," Kyler complained. "As soon as we saw those clouds rolling in, we started to head back."

I pulled a bottle of water out of the fridge and tried to force myself to pay attention to the conversation, but honestly, I didn't give a fuck.

Sydney straightened and turned around, frowning. "Where is Andrea?"

"Taking a nap." My hand tightened on the water bottle until it crackled.

Her brows rose. "I think I'll go check on her."

I raised the bottle to my mouth, having no idea what Andrea was going to say to Sydney. God only knew. After her steps faded, Kyler eyed me from where he stood. "What's up?"

"The sky," I replied.

He rolled his eyes. "Did we miss anything interesting today?"

Like I was going to go there with Kyler. "We hung out in the pool for a while, before it stormed."

"Uh-huh." A knowing look crossed his face. "I guess Andrea was just worn out from the exertion of hanging out in the pool?"

"Guess so," I muttered, finishing off the water. "I've got to get out of these wet clothes."

Kyler said something, but I wasn't paying attention. I headed upstairs as the thunder continued to rumble outside. I almost started toward Andrea's bedroom, but figured Sydney was with her. Stripping off the swim trunks, I grabbed a pair of shorts and dragged them on. I sat on the edge of the bed, blowing out an aggravated breath.

Rubbing my temples, I closed my eyes. Maybe I was off when it came to Andrea. Yeah, she wanted me, and today proved that, but it didn't mean she wanted more. Wait a second. Did *I* want more? I already knew the answer to that.

"Fuck," I muttered.

That was pretty much the only word that summed it all up.

### Andrea

The storm subsided briefly and then came back with a vengeance. Rain pounded the roof and the pool was starting to overflow. Water lapped over the edges, seeping through the deck boards. Lightning cut through the black sky and thunder shook the cabin.

I stood by the window, watching the sky light up like someone was setting off fireworks from the cusp of Seneca Rocks. I blew a breath out and watched it fog the window.

*Of course not.*

Squeezing my eyes shut, I tried to shake those three little words off. At no point had I ever entertained the idea that Tanner's sudden interest in me had anything to do with long term. He was a...virile man, and I'd turned to putty in his hand—literally. I shouldn't feel any regrets, but I did.

I always did.

Because for once, I wanted to be…I wanted to be something more than just a hookup. I wanted to be…*worth* more. I wanted to not feel the need to sneak downstairs and get a drink. I wanted to not be feeling this way. Resting my head against the cool glass, I sighed.

Truth was, I wanted to be with Tanner. I wanted to lose myself in him, give away a little piece of myself and not to think past that moment.

Dinner hadn't been too awkward as Tanner pretty much seemed to forget that I was sitting in the same room as everyone else, and afterward, we'd all gone down into the media room. The boys had had an epic air-hockey death match, and about an hour ago, I'd left, claiming to be exhausted. I hadn't looked to see if Tanner had watched me leave, because I was pretty sure he hadn't.

I'd thought my little speech in the kitchen about it not being a big deal would've smoothed things out, but I had the distinct feeling I'd made it worse. And I had lied. It was a big deal. The way he'd handled me, how he touched me, had erased every incident I'd ever had with a guy before. He'd made me forget. Everything. One could not put a price on that. One could not pass up that kind of opportunity.

But I had a feeling that I had without realizing it.

Moving away from the window, I sat on the edge of the bed and stretched my legs out. I had that habit—a habit of making things worse without really even trying. Like when I'd changed my majors. I could've gone with a nursing degree, then at least it wouldn't have been like I was tossing away nearly four years of education. There were more examples I could give myself, but I really didn't want to travel down that depressing road tonight. I stood and headed for where I'd left my purse on the dresser. Opening it up, I poked around the red bottles until I found the one with the sleeping pills in it. I'd just started to pop the cap when there was a soft knock on the bedroom door.

I guessed it was Syd, so I dropped the bottle back in my purse and padded over to the door, opening it. My eyes widened.

*So* not Syd.

Tanner stood in the doorway, his hands planted on the frame, head bowed. A moment passed before he lifted his chin. His eyes were a cobalt blue, intense as they immediately latched onto mine. My breath caught in my chest.

"I lied," he said.

"What?"

His hands slipped off the frame as he straightened. "I lied earlier. While we were in the kitchen. What happened between us in the pool? It did mean something to me."

# Chapter 10

**Tanner**

The moment those words came out of my mouth, I knew how true they were and there was no taking them back.

When I'd come upstairs, I hadn't planned on stopping at her bedroom, but it was like my brain had shut the hell down and I found myself standing in front of her door. There was no way I could go to sleep with her thinking I didn't give two shits.

And now I was here and Andrea was staring at me like she'd never seen me before. I had no idea what to make of that, but a tense second passed, and then she took a step back, and then another.

I took that as an invitation.

Stepping into her room, I held her gaze. "Tell me it meant nothing to you, and I'll pretend like nothing happened. Just say the word, Andy. We can forget it ever happened, but if it did—if it meant anything—then there is no way in this fucking world I'm going to act like nothing happened."

Her chest rose sharply as she lifted her hands, tucking the wild curls back behind her ears. "Tanner, I…it…" Her eyes closed briefly. "It did mean something to me, but—"

"There doesn't need to be a 'but' right now," I cut in, feeling like I'd just won the damn lottery. How desperate was that? "Okay? We don't have to—"

"Think past now?" she whispered so quietly I almost didn't hear her. Her lashes lifted. "I can't think past now."

I honestly didn't know what she meant by that, but then she reached down, wrapping her fingers under the hem of her loose T-shirt. My fucking heart stopped as she lifted the shirt over her head. The material dangled from her fingers and then slipped to the floor.

Andrea wore a white bra, with delicate lace that framed the cups and a tiny bow in the middle. I'd seen her in a bathing suit before, so it should've been no big surprise to see her like this now, but it *was* different. More intimate. Meant more.

I closed the door behind me, breathing heavily, as if I'd just run two miles. Unable to pull my gaze from her, I thought I'd probably see nothing more beautiful than right here, right now—seeing her standing there like she was. As much as it killed me, I had to tell that coming to her tonight wasn't about getting between her legs. "Andrea, I didn't—"

"Don't." Her chest rose with another deep breath, straining the cups. "I don't think we need to talk."

"I think we do." My voice had deepened, turned rougher.

Shaking her head, she walked up to me, each step slow and purposeful. I was rooted where I stood. She stopped when her feet brushed mine. "I don't remember kissing you before." Her eyes met mine as she tilted her head back. "And you didn't kiss me earlier."

"I didn't." I barely recognized my own voice.

Andrea placed her hands on my chest and I felt the fine tremor coursing through them. "I want to remember kissing you."

Damn. "I want you to remember that too."

She leaned in, her breasts pressing against my chest. The centers of her cheeks flushed pink. "Will you kiss me now?"

Oh man, I'd really had no intentions of any of this when I'd come up here. I had just wanted to talk to her. To clear the air and put it out there—where I stood when it came to us. But I wasn't a saint. On a good day I didn't have much willpower, and right now, my restraint snapped like a rubber band pulled too tight.

One hand landed on her hip, and I curled the other around the nape of her neck, tilting her head back further. I lowered my mouth to hers, and this time—yeah, this was a *real* kiss.

Her mouth was soft under mine, and when her lips parted there was no lingering taste of liquor on that mouth. Hell no, it was a hundred percent all Andrea and she still tasted sweet. She slipped one hand up to my shoulder, her fingers curling into my shirt as I ran my tongue along the seam of her mouth.

She parted her lips, and I delved in. Fuck. Her hot mouth was consuming me. The way she flattened her body against mine was driving me to the edge. And the feel of her warm, bare skin under my hand as I trailed my fingers up the side of her waist was undoing me.

Stretching up on the tips of her toes, she lined up our hips and when she rolled hers against mine, I groaned into the kiss. Like a haze had clouded my thoughts, I was brimming with the need to bring her to pleasure again, to hear those soft cries in my ears and to feel her body break in such a beautiful way once more.

I walked her backward, right up to the bed, and then I guided her down. Cheeks flushed, she stared up at me, her chest rising and falling heavily as she watched me. Reaching around the neck of my shirt, I tugged it over my head and then tossed it behind me.

Andrea's gaze dipped, and I stood, letting her look her fill. I liked it—fuck, I *loved* the way she looked at me like she could possibly get off just by staring at me. That was one hell of a boost to the ego right there.

I came to her, planting my knees on either side of her hips and then I slipped my hands along her waist. Lifting her up, I moved her so her legs didn't dangle off the edge. And then I swallowed her surprised gasp with a kiss as I settled onto my side next to her.

Cupping her cheek with my hand, I turned her face toward me, dragging out the kiss until we both needed to come up for air. "Damn, Andrea, I could live on the taste of your mouth."

"You're so full of it," she whispered, lifting her mouth to mine.

Tightening my grip on her chin, I pulled her mouth from mine. "I'm *not* full of it." I smoothed my thumb along her bottom lip. "I'm going to prove it."

She swallowed. "Then do it."

One side of my lips kicked up. "Listen to you. All bossy and shit."

"You're not proving anything when you're talking."

A chuckle rumbled out from me. "Oh, you are so fucking in for it."

Before she could respond, I claimed her mouth once more, harder and rougher than before, and there was no mistaking that I *was* claiming her. Our lips mashed together, teeth clinked. I would've worried if it weren't for the way her hand curved around my neck, pulling me down harder.

My pulse pounded throughout me as I slid my hand away from her chin, down the delicate arch of her throat and between her breasts. My hand kept going until I reached the waistband of her jeans. I flicked the button free. Then I reached up, dragging the strap of her bra down on one arm and then the other. As my tongue swirled along hers, I grabbed the center of her bra and yanked it down. She made this lovely little sound that I fucking ate right up.

I was on fire as I lifted my head, breaking the kiss. My gaze dropped. Fuck. Every possible time I'd imagined what her breasts looked like bare did not even compare to the real thing. Her breasts were heavy and perfect, the swells rosy and the tips hard. I ran my thumb over her nipple, wanting to shout when her back arched and a soft whimper parted her lips.

"You're beautiful, so fucking beautiful," I told her as I flicked that tight little nub, my body tightening as she made that sound again. I lowered my mouth, circling the peak with my tongue, wanting to pummel my chest with my fists when she cried out and clenched the back of my neck, holding me to her breasts.

I suckled her deep and hard, reveling in all the delighted moans and gasps coming from her. I was in heaven as I moved my mouth to her other breast and felt the weight of the other in my hand, but I wanted to use my fingers for so much more.

Reaching up, I wrapped my hand around her wrist and brought her hand down, to her breast. I watched her eyes darken as I closed her fingers over it.

"Tanner," she whispered, her cheeks heightened with color.

I wet my lips. "Look at you." I closed my hand over hers, using her hand to knead her own breast. "I will never forget the way you look right now."

She was breathing heavily as I moved her fingers, using them to toy with the tip. "What…what are you doing?" she asked.

"Living out a fantasy." I watched the tip of her breast harden further and then I bent my head, flicking my tongue over it. "Don't stop doing this. Promise."

"I…"

My gaze flipped to hers. "Promise me."

Her body trembled. "Promise."

I brought my mouth back to hers, rumbling with approval when she kept her hand on her breast. Her touch was hesitant at first, but she didn't stop as I slid my hand down her soft belly and then under the band of her jeans. It was nothing to slip under her panties, and when I felt the first brush of wetness gathering between her thighs, I almost fucking lost it.

"Don't stop touching yourself," I ordered a second before I slipped a finger through her softness. "God damn, don't stop."

Her breathing hitched. "I won't if…if you don't."

"Nothing in this world could make me stop."

And that was the damn truth. Nothing. Not a damn thing. I shifted my hand so my palm pressed down on that area that I knew drove her crazy. I feasted on her lips and tongue like a man starved, and I fucked her with my fingers. She was so tight and wet and perfect, there was a good chance I was going to spill without even getting my pants off.

I don't even think I'd care if I did.

When I eased another finger into her, the movements at her breast picked up, and I lifted up, looking down. "Holy fuck," I grunted. This was a dream. Had to be.

My fingers pumped in and out of her, and I felt her start to shake, and I wanted to taste her cry when she came. I moved my mouth over hers as her hips rose, matching the thrust of my fingers. The rise and fall became frenzied as she tightened around my fingers. The first spasm I felt around my fingers had me grinding against her thigh. Her hips were coming clear off the bed and her body began to shake. I shoved a leg between hers, my hips riding her, mimicking her movements.

I was lost in her.

Andrea's back arched and her hips stilled when she came, her inner muscles clenching my fingers. I caught her cries with my tongue, but I felt them in every cell. I nursed her down, slowing my fingers as she fell back to the bed, her hand falling away from her breast, lying limply on the bed beside her thigh.

Easing my fingers out of her, I kissed her gently. Fuck— tenderly. Yeah, this was a tender kiss. A slow sweep of my lips against hers despite the fact my blood was boiling and I was so hard it actually hurt. But as I rose and stared down at her flushed face, I soaked in her parted lips and those thick lashes that fanned her cheeks. I knew in that moment that I could never get enough of her. I knew, that no matter how crazy it sounded, there was no girl like her.

And as barbaric as it sounded, it was still true. Andrea was *mine*.

## Andrea

I came back to my senses slowly, my muscles weak and my skin buzzing. The peace, the calmness that invaded every cell was better than any drink or pharmaceutical could ever provide.

Tanner kissed the corner of my mouth and then he trailed a stream of tiny, hot kisses down my throat, across my shoulder. If I wasn't careful, I could get addicted to this.

Blinking my eyes open, I looked down at me—at us— and lost whatever air was in my lungs. Beyond him, I could see the tip of one of my breasts, the slope of my belly, and my eyes then tracked his arm—his hand. He was now just sliding it out from between my legs. I swallowed hard. Good Lord, the image of us was branded forever in my mind.

Caressing my stomach and waist, he shifted, and I could see quite plainly that he was aroused—*very* aroused. I'd felt it earlier, in the pool, and when he was pressed against me just now. He was thick and hard, and this was the second time he'd brought me to the greatest heights of pleasure without really seeking his own.

I hadn't been able to think past the fact he'd been in my room and he'd been saying those things. When he looked at me like that, when he touched me like that, I didn't feel like I was barely holding onto everything by the tips of my fingers. I felt confident, sophisticated, worldly and beautiful. I felt happy and in control, and most of all, I felt normal.

But part of me knew this was so dumb and dangerous. Just because he'd said what happened between us meant something to him didn't mean that once he discovered more about me that he'd hang around. I knew he wouldn't.

I didn't expect him to, not after he'd peeled back a few more layers. My head was messed up sometimes, and the last thing anyone needed was to get tangled up in that crap.

However, all that common sense was absent as I placed my hands on his shoulders and pushed him onto his back beside me.

"What are you doing?" he asked in that deep, sexy voice.

"Returning the favor." I sat up and swung one leg over his.

His hands settled lightly on my hips. "You don't need to."

Glancing down at the hard line clearly visible through his nylon pants, I lifted a brow. "I think I do." I bit down on my lip as I straddled his legs. "Unless you don't want me to."

"Babe, I want to do whatever the fuck you want to do," he said, eyes heavily hooded. "And trust me, I want you to do whatever it is you're planning, but I just want you to understand you don't *have* to."

Oh dear, I felt the back of my throat burn as I ducked my chin.

"I don't *expect* that from you," he said.

I kept my gaze lowered as I swallowed around the sudden lump in my throat. I couldn't think of the last time it wasn't expected from me after a couple of drinks and a few nice words. Hell, I couldn't remember the last time someone had gotten me off before today, especially as easily as he had.

"I want to do it." My voice was light.

He made a deep sound that made my blood hum. "Then you have me."

*If only.*

I started to fix my bra, but he caught my hand. "I like you like this," he said, his eyes like blue fire. "I'll never forget you looking like this."

I sucked in a shaky breath. "Who knew you could say all the right words?"

"I know, right?" He chuckled. "Usually I'm saying all the wrong ones."

That could be said for the both of us, but I was beyond talking. We were a disaster in the making, but as I slid down his body, I couldn't stop myself. Neither of us could stop. I'd deal with it later. I was good, if not great, at pushing things away to deal with later.

His pecs were hard and smooth under my mouth. I tasted his skin, reveling in the salty mixture as I kissed my way down his tight abs, closing my eyes as I forged a wet path down to the loose fit of his pants. His body was a work of art—hard and like silk stretched over steel. I could worship him all day long.

I tugged gently on his pants and he lifted his hips. "Look at me," he said. "Being all helpful."

"So surprised," I murmured, giggling.

The laugh died off though when I got my first real glimpse of him. His pants were down to his thighs and he was exposed in all his glory, and boy, was it *a lot* of glory. Every part of him matched up in size, and he was huge.

I trailed my finger down the center of him, grinning when his entire body jerked at the touch. "You like that?"

"That would be a 'hell yeah.'"

Smiling, I wrapped my hand around the base. He throbbed against my palm. I knew what to do. I'd done this before, many times when I didn't want to go…well, those times didn't matter, because I wanted this. I wanted to *do* this.

I moved my hand in a slow pace, watching him through my lashes. His eyes were almost completely shut, his jaw locked down tight, and his hips followed my rhythm. It was so natural, and I wasn't really thinking about anything when I scooted down further and lowered my head. The tips of my breasts brushed his thighs as I circled my tongue over the head.

Tanner all but growled out, "Yes."

*Yes. Yes.* That word cycled in my head over and over. I closed my mouth over him and took him in, running my tongue as I went as far as I could go.

"Fuck. Your mouth," he groaned. "God. Damn. I'm not going to last."

I would've laughed, but I was so caught in the act of pleasing him. Normally this…this seemed like such a chore. With Tanner, it felt sensual and promising. Mutual. Give and take. Sexy and beautiful.

His hand tangled in my hair, but he didn't hold me to him, and that was a…a nice change up right there. He moved, thrusting his hips, but he held back, and he was right, he didn't last long.

"I'm about to come." He tried to pull away, but I wouldn't let him. Closing my eyes, I took him deeper. "Andrea," he moaned, his hips rising off the comforter.

The feel of him coming apart was something that I would never forget. The musky, salty taste, the way he pulsed and how he held my neck so gently—all of it was as shattering as the pleasure he had brought me.

As I slowed down and lifted my head, I saw that he was staring at me with wide eyes and in a way I couldn't decipher. I didn't move as he sat up and gripped the sides of my face, and I sure as heck didn't breathe when he hauled me against his chest and kissed me. And it was no small kiss either. It was deep and scorching, lighting me up.

When we broke apart, he rested his forehead against mine and let out a short breath. "Well, Andy, this, by far, has to be the best trip to a cabin *ever.*"

A slow grin pulled at my lips and then spread into a full smile—a real smile, and before I knew it, I was laughing, and it felt like the first real laugh in a very long time.

# Chapter 11

*Andrea*

We lay side by side, our heads propped up on the abundance of pillows stacked at the head of the bed. I'd finally fixed my bra and had pulled my shirt back on, but Tanner was still rocking his bare chest hotness and I was okay with that.

He'd gone downstairs at some point and had grabbed us two sodas. Normally I drank diet, but I slurped up the good old-fashioned kind without complaint. He'd also brought up a block of cheese that he'd pulled apart in chunks, and I think I might've fallen in love with him a little at that moment.

Because cheese equaled happiness.

I had no idea where Syd and Kyler were or if they had any suspicions about the kinkery that had just gone down in this room, but I was trying not to do a lot of thinking, because thinking led to stressing and stressing led to stupidity for me.

Tanner talked about some of the calls he'd responded to while working at the fire hall. The funny ones—like when someone had locked themselves out on the balcony of their apartment...naked as the day they were born. Or when the department was called by an overeager child who'd just learned in school what to do in case of an emergency and was more of a show than tell when it came to explaining to their parents what they'd learned.

He laughed a lot, and I liked it when he did. It was a good sound, one I had tried not to pay attention to before, but now I couldn't help but smile when I heard it. I was slow to realize that he was always laughing. I just had to pull my head out of my ass and pay attention.

"So how did your parents react when you changed your major?"

My eyes widened. "Oh, my God, they flipped out. They think I'm throwing away all of my education and that I'm ruining my life by wanting to become a teacher."

"I don't think becoming a teacher is ruining your life," he said. "Plus, it's just as important as becoming a doctor."

I raised one hand and rubbed my thumb and pointer together. "Money. A teacher makes way less money."

"And that's all they care about?"

Was it? "That's a hard question to answer, to be honest. Money is important to them. I don't think it's the only thing." I frowned slightly. "I think they just want to make sure I have a…a good life, you know? That I don't struggle."

"That's understandable, but being a teacher doesn't mean you'll be dirt poor."

I laughed softly as I bent one leg. "Yeah, and they also wanted me to become a plastic surgeon like them—like Brody was going to do. Unless I decided to specialize in emergency procedures, I'd spend my life augmenting boobs and noses."

"Did Brody change what he's doing? He's in med school, right?"

Surprise flitted through me. I had no idea that he remembered anything about my brother. He'd met him once, though it had been brief. "He's not doing plastic surgery. He's going for trauma. I think he likes the adrenaline."

I also think he liked the whole God complex that came with the job. Good fit for him.

"My parents have accepted it," I added as I wiggled my toes. "Begrudgingly, but hey, at least Brody hasn't disappointed them, so they have that."

He cocked his head to the side. "You haven't disappointed them."

The way he said it was almost like he completely believed that, but I knew better. They *were* disappointed. One day they'd fully get over it, and I was sure it wasn't the only decision I'd made or would make in my life that would upset them. I really didn't want to think about that.

It was so…different hanging with Tanner like this. Not like we hadn't had moments, lots of them, when we weren't trying to kill one another, but this was kind of like we were *together*, really together. Of course, I knew we weren't, but…

I cradled the can against my chest, staring down at it, smiling as Tanner's laughter faded. "You've gotten quiet," he said, knocking his knee off mine. "You okay?"

Shaking my head, I glanced over at him. "I'm okay. Really good. It's just…this is nice," I said lamely. "I mean, I haven't just sat like this with a…"

"With a dude?" he supplied.

I nodded. "Not for a long time."

"How long?"

I coughed out a dry laugh. "A really, embarrassingly long time. Not since I dated this really dumb quarterback in high school." My cheeks heated. "So, yeah, that long."

Tanner didn't respond.

Ugh. I peeked at him again, expecting to see him looking at me like I was some kind of sad specimen of a person, but he was just…he was just looking at me, his eyes soft. "What?" I whispered.

"I'm glad you picked me to do this with, then," he said after a moment.

My heart fluttered like a little bird. "I think you kind of picked yourself."

"Whatever," he chuckled, and then leaned over me, placing what was left of the cheese and his soda on the nightstand.

"You know, there's a stand on your side," I pointed out.

He leaned back against the cushions and gave a lopsided shrug. "Yours is better," he said, and I laughed at the absurdity that was all him. "But it's hard to believe that you don't do this."

"I don't." I lifted a shoulder and something really stupid blurted out of me. "I liked doing what I did to you."

A slow grin curled his lips. "I did too. I really, *really* liked it. Basically, whenever you feel the need to do it, you just let me know. I don't care where we are or what we're doing. I'll make sure you can do it."

Laughing, I shook my head. "I'll keep that in mind."

"You do that." He paused as he crossed his legs at the ankles. "Seriously, though, I didn't expect that. Made it all the more sweet."

There he went again, saying possibly the most correct thing in the world. I looked away, staring at my soda. "It never felt like that. I mean, anytime I did *that* before, I kind of felt like I had to, you know?"

A moment passed. "No. I don't know. Explain?"

"Guys just kind of expect it," I said, toying with the tab on the can. "No one goes home from bars expecting to chat."

There was another stretch of silence. "Maybe people shouldn't go home with others if they think they'll owe someone something." His words were clipped, stern.

My head jerked up and our gazes met. "I'm not sure if that was an insult or not."

He frowned. "It's not an insult. You should never feel like you owe a guy that. No matter what. I don't care if they ate you out or gave you a million dollars."

I raised my brows. "Ate me out or a million dollars? Nice use of examples there. I don't know, Tanner. I think if someone gave me a million dollars, I'd be down for just about anything."

His frown turned into a scowl.

"I was joking," I added softly.

Tanner's stare was unnerving. "Have you ever been… forced into doing that, Andrea?"

His question caused me to flinch back. "What? No! That's not what I meant. It's just sometimes…" I trailed off as what I was saying really sank in. The soda curdled in my stomach, and I wished I hadn't shoved the huge chunks of cheese into my mouth. My head raced back through the nights that I'd gone home knowing the guy expected to get laid, but not wanting to. I'd done that, because at that time, I'd thought there were no other options. Stupid. There were always options. Like "no," for example.

Then there were those nights I really couldn't remember.

Jesus. I felt sick. I didn't like where my head was going with this. Sweat dotted my palms. It wasn't like I'd been… I couldn't even finish that thought. I didn't know what that meant—doing things because I felt like I had to, or not remembering what I did sometimes. Or maybe I did, and I just didn't want to grab hold of those thoughts.

I needed a drink.

Okay. That was probably not the best response to the situation.

Tanner reached over, tapping his fingers along my arm. "I'm thinking some pretty bad things right now."

I couldn't look at him.

"I hope it's just my head jumping to conclusions unjustly," he added.

The next breath I took hurt for some reason. "It's jumping to conclusions."

His hand stilled and he wrapped his fingers around my wrist and squeezed softly. "Hey," he said gently. "Look at me."

Drawing in a shallow breath, I lifted my gaze and our eyes met. Held. A heartbeat passed, and I felt stripped bare, more exposed than I had been earlier.

"I just want you to know that if you ever need to talk to someone, I'm here. No matter the time of the day. You got that?"

And then I saw it plain as day in his gaze. There was no mistaking it. Not just sympathy. Part of me could've dealt with that, but there was more lurking in those blue eyes.

Pity.

He stared at me, full of *pity*. Every muscle in my body tightened. Skin prickled with uncomfortable heat. The urge to get away rushed through me. I couldn't do this.

**Tanner**

I saw the exact moment Andrea shut down on me. As soon as I told her that she could talk to me about anything, shutters closed over her eyes. The girl who'd sat next to me and laughed was gone. The girl who opened up about her parents had left the room. And the girl who had cried out, surrendered herself, was nowhere to be seen.

Shit.

"Andy—"

"I'm really tired." She swung her legs off the bed and stood before I could respond. "I think it's time for me to get some sleep." She started toward the door, seemed to remember that we were in her room, stopped, and placed her soda on a dresser. Her back was to me.

Heart dropping, I scooted off the bed and held myself back. I had a feeling that going to her would somehow make this worse. "Andrea, I didn't mean to—"

"You didn't do anything." Slowly, she faced me and plastered a smile across her pretty face. Fake. Plastic. "I'm just really tired all of a sudden. You wore me out." Her laugh was brittle-sounding. "I need my beauty rest."

I opened my mouth, but clamped my jaw shut as her smile spread—the kind of smile doctors wore when giving patients bad news.

She gathered up a bundle of clothing from the chair, cradling the items close to her chest as she stopped in front of the bed. "I'll see you in the morning?"

A huge part of me wanted to demand to know what the hell was going on, but there was no mistaking that her walls were up. I watched her hurry into the bathroom and quietly close the door.

I briefly considered plopping my ass down and waiting for her, but I'd accidentally hit a raw nerve, and frankly, I was too pissed to really have this conversation. Not angry at her, but if she really had done things with guys because she felt like she had to instead of wanting to, it was likely I'd punch a wall.

Thank God I did not have a sister.

If I couldn't deal with the thought of assholes treating Andrea like that, what the hell would I do if I had a sister? Fuck. I'd end up in jail.

Angry and beyond frustrated, I gathered up our drinks and what was left of the cheese and left the room, taking them downstairs. The first level was dark and quiet, and after grabbing a bottle of water, I ended up back upstairs, in my room.

Shit.

Dropping down on the bed, I ran my hands over my face. Things were all over the place with Andrea and me, but I felt like we'd moved forward. It wasn't just because what she and I had done in that bed, but because of everything before, during and after that. But now? I couldn't shake the feeling that we'd taken one huge step backward.

# Chapter 12

**Andrea**

My brows rose as I watched Syd place a backpack by the kitchen island. It looked like it weighed more than she did.

"You're going to carry that while hiking?" I asked.

"Yep." She tugged her hair up and secured it with a hair tie. "It's really not that bad and it's smart to be prepared in case something happens."

"Like when a rabid bear tries to eat you?"

She grinned. "I don't think we're going to run into any rabid bears. And we're not just going to hike. We're going to camp out for the night."

I gaped at her. "Seriously?"

Walking over to the counter, she grabbed the pot of coffee and began pouring the steaming liquid into her Thermos. "Yeah." She looked over her shoulder at me and laughed. "You should see your expression. It's like I just told you that we're going to go camping on Mount Everest or something."

I hopped up on the barstool. "When did you guys decide this?"

"Last night. After you went to bed." She screwed the lid on the Thermos and faced me. "You know, after Tanner *also* went upstairs."

Schooling my expression blank, I picked up my mug. "Okay."

"Yep. Kyler and I thought it would be kind of cool to do. We used to camp out all the time when we were kids, so it'll be fun." Syd skipped over to me, placing the Thermos on the counter. "We were going to invite you and Tanner."

"Oh really?" I murmured.

She nodded. "Actually, Kyler went upstairs last night to ask Tanner if he wanted to camp with us."

My hand tightened around the warm mug.

"Strangely, Tanner wasn't in his room." Syd paused, lowering her voice. "And the funny thing was, he heard these noises coming from your—"

"Stop it," I said, cheeks flaming. "I know where you're going with this."

Her eyes narrowed as she climbed onto the stool next to mine. "You need to spill, right now, and make it quick before Kyler gets his butt down here."

Any other time I would've given her all the juicy details, but I shifted uncomfortably. Tanner could walk in on us at any moment. I took a deep breath and said in a quiet voice, "We didn't have sex."

She gave me her best serious look. "Don't you dare lie to me, Andrea."

I rolled my eyes. "I didn't say we didn't do other things, but we didn't do that."

"What other things?" A wide smile broke out across her face as she smacked my arm. "Tell me. Tell me now."

"Stuff. Things. Use your imagination."

She folded her arms and waited. "My imagination sucks. I need help."

I glanced at the stairwell. "It involved his hands and my mouth. How about that?"

"Oh!" she chirped. "You dirty girl. He's a dirty boy. You all are getting dirty together."

"Oh my God," I moaned, tucking a stray curl back. "You shouldn't be talking. I know the dirty things you and Kyler do."

"Hells yeah," she replied, giggling. "The things we did last night were pretty freaky. Loved every second of it."

I simply stared at her.

She tilted her head back and laughed, and I shook my head. "We spent most of the time just hanging out, to be honest," I admitted after a moment. "It was really nice."

"I'm sure it was." Sincerity filled her words. "Tanner is a really good guy and you're awesome. So it had to be nice."

I wanted to deny that last part. Tanner was an awesome guy, and I was...well, I wasn't sure what I was on most days.

"You two have always been circling one another," she continued, drawing my focus. "It's about time that you let go of what happened freshman year and he recognizes what's been in front of his face a lot longer than he even realized."

My heart stuttered and then sped up. I thought about the way he'd looked at me last night. "I don't know, Syd. I'm..." I was afraid to open myself up, to expose myself to all that hope.

She touched my arm. "Just don't stress out about it, okay? And if you feel up to it, give it a chance. Give it one shot. Use your time alone with him and see what happens. Kyler and I aren't planning to come back until tomorrow evening. You two will have all day today and tomorrow."

Understanding seeped in. "You guys are going camping because of us—"

"We're going camping because we want to." Her sly grin said otherwise. Footsteps sounded from above, nearing the stairs. She hopped off the stool and then leaned in, kissing my cheek. "Have fun."

I said nothing as she danced off toward the stairway. Sitting there, I stared into my mug as my pulse began to race. Sweat dotted my palms, but I regulated my breathing, taking deep breaths before the overwhelmed feeling could take hold and spread like a virus.

When I heard Kyler's deep voice, I looked up and closed my eyes. In a lot of ways, I was a coward. And I didn't like that about myself. Not at all, but it was scary—the idea of giving us a chance when I wasn't even sure Tanner would be on board.

But there'd been last night, and there'd been the time in the pool. He had said it meant something to him, and maybe...I wasn't seeing what I thought I saw in the way he looked at me. Maybe I was reading too much into that and not enough into what he was actually saying. I opened my eyes, I decided that I could at least try.

I would try.

### Tanner

I normally wasn't a suspicious man, but I had this distinct feeling that Kyler and Sydney's impromptu camping trip reeked of a hidden agenda. With them gone, Andrea and I had the whole place to ourselves.

And I totally wasn't complaining.

When we got back to Maryland, I was going to buy Kyler a drink, or maybe one for Sydney—for whichever was the mind behind their deviously brilliant plan.

The two of them had left about three hours ago, and I was still giving Andrea some space. She was downstairs for the most part, at least not hiding, and neither was I. I'd plopped myself in the living room and had been flipping channels for a while when she reappeared in the room.

My thumb paused over the remote as I glanced over at her. Her red hair was pulled up in some kind of twist so there was no hiding the pretty flush creeping across her cheeks.

Fingers clasped together in front of her, she shifted her weight from one foot to the next. The skirt of her lavender dress swung just above her knees. She was barefoot, and I noticed that the paint on her nails was a different color than before. They were now a pale blue.

I had never, in my entire life, noticed a chick's toenail polish until now.

"I was going to go outside." Her gaze met mine and then flickered away. "I wanted to see if you wanted to, um, to join me?"

What I wanted to do was jump to my feet and thrust my fist into the air, but I managed to calmly turn off the TV, place the remote on the couch, and stand. "Yeah. I can do that."

Her smile was quick, but beautiful nonetheless. As she turned around and walked toward the glass doors, I trailed after her, wanting to start spewing poetry and shit. Rubbing a hand along my jaw, I shook my head as we stepped outside. She went to the side of the pool, sitting down and dipping her feet into the water. The rain last night had raised the levels, and the water nearly reached the edge.

Following her, I rolled up the legs of my jeans and did the same. Since the storm yesterday, the temps had dropped. While it was still warm, it was bearable—we could sit outside and not have sweat pooling in uncomfortable places.

Andrea stared at the slowly rippling water. "So…when you leave for the police academy, how long will you be gone?"

The question caught me off-guard, because I was surprised and glad that she wanted to know, but I recovered quickly. "It's about six months."

She glanced at me quickly, eyes wide. "That long?"

I nodded. "But we do get time off. We can leave after a little while, and people can visit us on assigned days. It's not like no contact for six months." At first I wasn't sure why I was telling her all of that, but then I realized I wanted her to know that I'd be around, available. For her. "So, I'll still be around."

Andrea seemed to mull that over. "Are you excited?"

"Yeah," I admitted, splashing my feet. "It feels like I've been working toward it since forever."

"You don't have to go to college to enter the academy, right?"

I shook my head. "No, but it gave me a foot up on those who didn't. Plus, having a degree in criminal justice and having experience on a police force will allow me to move more easily into federal positions."

"That's what you want to do? Federal law enforcement?"

"Eventually," I nudged her with my arm and grinned. "Because while I know I'll look damn good in a police uniform, just imagine what I'd look like in a suit."

Andrea tipped her head back and laughed. "I can second that."

"Damn straight."

Smiling, she paddled her feet in the water. "When you end up pulling girls over, they're going to willingly accept whatever ticket you're giving them."

I chuckled, admittedly basking in the compliments she was paying me. Fuck. I was ready to roll on my back and let her rub my stomach.

"It's so dangerous, though. The job." She started to toy with the hem of her skirt. "Does that scare you?"

I thought about that for a moment. "I think I'd be stupid or reckless to say that it's not scary. I think there's a healthy level of fear. It keeps you on your toes."

She nodded slowly. "That's an interesting way to think of it."

"What about you?" I asked. "You have to be terrified, too."

Her lips turned down at the corners. "How so?"

"You're going to be working with kids," I explained. "Nothing more terrifying than that."

Andrea giggled. "But you know what? I don't have to take those kids home with me."

"And I won't take the job home with me," I admitted, meeting her gaze and holding it. "It'll be hard, but I refuse to do that shit."

She didn't look away. "Did...did your dad do that?"

I raised a shoulder. "I don't think he knew how to separate the two, but that was the least of his fuck-ups."

"Do you have any contact with him?" she asked.

"Not really. I'm cool with that, though. I still see my mom." I leaned back, resting on my elbows. "What about you? Are you close to your parents? You've never really said before."

"I am. We get together every other Sunday for dinner. All of us. Mom likes to cook, so it's a grand affair for her." A loose curl blew across her cheek. "I kind of look forward to it."

My gaze traveled across her face. "That's good." Sitting up, I reached over and caught the curl with my fingers. She stilled as I tucked it back behind her ear. Her wide eyes latched onto mine. "Your brother, if I remember correctly, isn't a redhead. How about your parents?"

"My mom is," she answered, swallowing. "My dad has brown hair and blue eyes. Brody takes after him."

The tips of my fingers had minds of their own. They trailed down the smooth curve of her cheekbone. "So you take after your mom?"

Her lips parted. "Yes."

"Then she must be beautiful."

The hue of Andrea's eyes deepened. "You know what?"

"What?" I grinned as my finger reached the corner of her lips.

"You can be a real charmer when you want to be."

"And I want to be." Leaning toward her, I replaced my finger with my lips, kissing the corner of hers. "With you."

Andrea pulled back slightly, ducking her chin as she peered up at me through thick lashes. "I don't know what to do…with you."

I didn't let her get very far. Curling my hand around the nape of her neck, I brought our foreheads together. "Yeah, you do, Andy. Just do whatever you want."

Her eyes squeezed shut. "What I mean is, I don't know how to do *this* with you."

My heart thumped heavily. "You're doing just fine." I paused. "Most of the time."

The corners of her lips quirked up. "Yeah, maybe about fifty percent of the time."

Placing my other hand on her cheek, I smoothed my thumb along her jaw. With Andrea, I never really knew where I stood with her. One minute, she was sweet as sugar to me. The next, she had a bite more venomous than a copperhead. But I had great instincts. Always have. I knew she liked me, and I had a feeling that like ran deeper than friendship or lust. I was going to have to be the one to take the first step, to really put it out there so there was no mistaking what I wanted or expected from this.

I pulled back just a little, cupping both sides of her face. "When we leave this cabin at the end of the week, I want to see you."

Her lashes fluttered up. "We'll see each other."

I grinned. "I know, but that's not what I mean. I want to *see* you, Andrea. You get what I'm saying?"

Andrea's gaze searched mine, and I was seriously hoping I wasn't going to have to write it down. Like those notes back in grade school—*Do you like me? Circle yes or no.* But then she drew in a deep breath and said, "I get what you're saying."

Thank God. "So, what's your answer?"

"Yes," she whispered. "I want to *see* you, Tanner."

# Chapter 13

**Andrea**

"You're not paying attention at all."

Fighting a grin, I denied the truth. "I am totally paying attention."

"Liar."

I was a total liar, and I barely smothered a giggle as I refocused my attention on the movie Tanner had found after dinner in the stash inside the cabinet. All I knew was it was a *Transformers* movie, but I had yet to see a Dinobot.

Today had been one of the most…chill days I'd had in a long time. After our talk by the pool, when I thought I could float right up to the sun, we'd hung out there for a few hours, talking about nothing in particular until we were both starving. Yeah, we'd picked at each other, but it was teasing instead of fighting or being mean. It was almost like we were together, like *really* together. And it had been years since I'd felt that way.

At some point, around five minutes after the movie had started, Tanner had gotten hold of my legs and placed them in his lap. And that was pretty much at the point where I'd gotten distracted. It wasn't my fault.

Totally all Tanner's fault.

He started off with his arms folded across his chest, not touching my legs while I rested against a pillow I'd shoved between my back and the arm of the couch. But then his hands had dropped to my ankles and I'd jumped a little at the contact. All he'd done was cast a sly grin in my direction, and my tummy had tumbled a bit. His fingers had curled loosely around my ankles at first, and as I pretended to pay attention to the movie, he pretended not to be doing anything.

I bit down on my lip when his thumbs started to move in slow circles around my ankles, and I almost tasted blood when one of his hands traveled up my calf. Those fingers worked deftly, easing the tension out of my muscles, but creating a whole different kind of tautness throughout the rest of me. When he reached the sensitive spot behind my knee, I swallowed a moan that would've embarrassed me.

Each pass of his fingers, each touch sent waves of heat licking up my leg. Blood simmered in my veins as I desperately tried to curb my body's reaction. There was really no point, though. By the time his hand had reached the inside of my knee, I was having trouble sitting still and not squirming.

Tanner's gaze was fastened on the many explosions occurring on the TV, and it almost seemed like he had no idea what he was doing to me, but I doubted his innocence and I also doubted how I'd be able to successfully pretend I wasn't affected.

But the most amazing thing that was happening had nothing to do with the pleasure he was slowly creating inside me, but everything to do with the fact I was even sitting there. I was trying, like I'd said I would, and I wasn't letting my head get in the way or allowing all the self-doubt to pile up on me. I was just there—right there and no place else, and I wasn't letting myself go anywhere else. And there were no outside influences. Well, other than the rather major influence Tanner was turning out to be.

His hand reached the spot where my legs were pressed together, and I swore my heart skipped a beat as I stared at where his hand rested. Slowly, I lifted my gaze. He was no longer paying attention to the movie. Our eyes locked, and even in the low light of the living room, those bedroom eyes of his were full of heat.

I caught my lower lip between my teeth as I opened my legs to his wandering hand. One side of his lips tipped up in response. He didn't look away as he slid his hand further up, the tips of his fingers nearly reaching the sensitive crevice near the apex of my thighs.

My heart was pounding as his hand moved underneath the skirt of my dress. I could barely catch my breath as he turned his attention back to the movie. I was completely lost, though. No pretending. My eyes drifted closed and then my head fell back against the thick cushion. His touch was featherlight against the inside of my thigh, but it was still driving me crazy. With each pass of his fingers, he came dangerously close to my center. He never quite reached there, and it was the sweetest kind of torture. A tingling warmth invaded me, quickening my breaths. He touched, he explored and caressed all without touching me *there*, but my desire was ramped up. A fine tremor danced over my skin. I wanted him, *needed* him to touch me where I ached.

Unsure of how much time had passed, I opened my eyes and found him watching me. For a moment, I couldn't move, couldn't even drag in a deep enough breath. Then I was moving without thinking, and there was something beautiful in that, the freedom.

I shifted onto my knees, and Tanner must've been thinking along the same lines, because he gripped my hips and hauled me into his lap. A heartbeat passed before our mouths came together, and there was no slow seduction in that moment.

We devoured each other, and when I pressed down, I felt how affected he was. He might've looked like he'd been paying attention to the TV, but he'd been focused on what he was doing.

His hands slid down my hips, under my skirt. The rasp of his calloused palms over my skin was probably one of the most sensual things I'd ever felt. "I was wondering how long it would take you," he said, his lips brushing mine. "I was starting to get disappointed over here."

I laughed softly, but it ended in a moan when he raised his hips against mine. I clasped his cheeks, loving the way the bristle along his jaw tickled my palms. "You were driving me crazy."

"Were?"

I kissed him. "Are."

"That sounds better." His hands smoothed over my bottom and squeezed, causing knots to form low in my belly.

My body rocked against his as he broke free from the kiss and blazed a path down my throat. His hands moved deftly, sliding back down my legs, and then they were at the top of my dress. Before I could take my next breath, he'd tugged the top part down, exposing me.

The dress had one of those built-in bras, so now there was nothing between me and his hungry gaze. I cried out, my head falling back as his mouth found the way to the tip of my breast. He licked and nipped as he teased and taunted me.

There was another explosion on the TV, and I was close to exploding myself. He sucked greedily once his mouth clasped down, and a riot of sensations floored me. I moved on him, riding him in a way that made me wish there were no clothes separating us.

One of his hands—I couldn't keep track of which one—made its way under my dress again, and I really loved where it was heading. His fingers slipped under the band of my panties, toyed there for a few moments, and then slipped out. I didn't have a chance to be disappointed, because the next thing I knew, I was on my back on the couch and his hands were on my knees.

"I want to taste you," he said, voice rough, and I shivered.

My mouth dried, and there was no mistaking what he meant when he said that. I didn't protest when he eased my knees apart. This was so intimate, almost *too* intimate. Air lodged in my throat, and I fought against the urge to close my legs.

Thick lashes lifted as his eyes met mine. "You want this?"

Nervous and excited, I could barely get the word out. "Yes."

"Thank fucking God, because I've been dying to know what it's like to have you come on my tongue."

Goodness, the words alone almost sent me over the edge. He rucked the skirt of my dress up above my hips, and then his hands slid up the side of my leg. He reached my panties and tugged them aside.

Cool air washed over me as his lips parted. "Fuck. I want to get in there."

I wanted him in there, wanted him everywhere. As he lowered his mouth to mine and kissed me softly, my heart seemed to swell in my chest. It was such a simple kiss, a beautiful one.

Then his hand was moving again, finding me with unerringly precision. He skimmed his finger along the center, causing my hips to jerk. He made another pass as he lowered himself down my body, stopping to linger at my breasts, and then his head was between my thighs.

"Oh God," I whispered. The image alone, of seeing him down there, was almost too much.

Then he pressed a kiss against my thigh.

The swelling in my chest increased and there was a good chance I'd float straight to the ceiling, maybe even beyond that, but he tugged me back down when his mouth brushed over me.

"Tanner," I gasped, my hands fluttering to his head.

The intimate kiss spun my senses, and he *so* knew what he was doing. It was wet and hot and shattering. He kissed and he licked and he did things with his tongue I didn't think were possible. The way he worked me told me that he enjoyed doing it. No chore for him—oh no, he couldn't be happier.

Neither could I.

My head was kicked back and my hips arched against the steady delving of his tongue. I met his strokes, repeating his name over and over. Raw and primal sensations pounded through me. Tiny noises I didn't recognize were making their way out of me, and then I felt his finger slipping through my wetness. My entire body clenched. He went deeper, harder.

My eyes flew open as I coiled tightly, and all I saw was him.

The release took me off-guard, pounding through me, and I was swept up in the intense pleasure. Liquid heat poured through me. Tanner pulled back, kissing my inner thigh before he rose above me, planting one hand on the arm of the couch.

He breathed heavily as he stared down. "I've never heard anything more beautiful than the sound of you calling out my name like that."

Every few seconds, an aftershock traveled through me, and I was still shaken and breathless. "I never felt anything more beautiful than that," I admitted.

The blue of his eyes seemed to have deepened. "Then I guess it was a first for both of us."

That swelling in my chest was turning into an epidemic. "Yeah."

He drew his hand down to my thigh and squeezed gently. There was something in the way he stared down at me that made me feel like one of the most beautiful women in the world, and there was something priceless about that. Just a look, but it was possibly more powerful than any words that could've been spoken.

And that's about when the craziest words known to man tiptoed to the tip of my tongue. *I love you.* Oh God, those words were legitimately resting on my tongue, ready to be spoken. My heart stuttered. I *loved* him? Was that really what I was feeling? The swelling in my chest? Or was it just lust? No. I'd been in lust before. I knew the difference. This…this tingling feeling in my fingers and the warmth in my chest was not lust. It was hope and yearning and anticipation. It was tenderness and acceptance and a thousand other endless wants and needs. When in the world did this happen? I had no idea. Did it start all the way back during my freshman year? Or was it over the course of a handful of days?

*I love you.*

For three little words, they were really terrifying. It was the power the words symbolized, the ability to change everything.

I couldn't say them, because no matter how wonderful he was being to me, he couldn't feel the same way as me. There was no way. My heart wanted to go there, but my brain was like *hell to the no*, but I could show him.

That was the best that I had.

I could show him just how much I cared for him without truly putting that out there between us, and most likely ruining everything.

My hand shook under the weight of what I was feeling as I cupped his cheek. I took a deep breath. "Can we go upstairs? To bed?"

Tanner stilled above me as understanding crept into his handsome face. When he spoke, his voice held an edge that sent a shiver across my skin. "Babe, if we go upstairs and we end up in a bed, I'm gonna…well, I'm going to have one hell of a time stopping myself from getting between those pretty legs."

My cheeks flushed. "I wouldn't want you to stop."

His eyes flared and a long moment stretched out between us. "You sure?"

*I love you.* "Yes," I whispered. "Yes."

# Chapter 14

**Tanner**

I was literally at a loss for words as Andrea took my hand in her smaller one and led me up the steps. It was like I was fifteen again and minutes away from losing my virginity. No shit. That was how it felt. Nervousness. Anxiety. Anticipation. All of those feelings were rolled together.

Never in my life did I think I'd feel that way again.

Wasn't sure if that was even a good thing.

As we rounded the top of the stairs and Andrea looked over her shoulder at me, smiling shyly, I realized that yep, that was a *damn* good thing.

She started to turn into her room, but I stopped her. I wanted her in my room, in my bed. I pushed open my door and then closed it behind me. She stopped a few feet from the bed as I walked over to my duffel bag and rooted around until I found what I was looking for.

"You brought condoms with you?" she asked as I tossed a few on the nightstand.

I grinned, somewhat sheepishly. "I try to keep them on me. You never know when they'll come in handy."

She arched a brow. "I'm not sure if that's a good thing or not."

"It's a good thing." I turned to her. "At least, it's turning out to be a good thing, but seriously, I didn't think I'd be using them this week."

"Really?" Doubt crossed her face as she walked toward me, wrapping her hands around the edge of my shirt. "I remember that bet you made with me."

"Actually, there was no bet. You wouldn't play along." I lifted my arms, letting her tug the shirt off.

Her gaze flicked up to my face and then down to my chest, and I saw the appreciation in her gaze. "I do remember telling you that was never going to happen." She slid her hands down my chest, to the button on my jeans. "And yet here I am."

"Here *we* are."

She leaned forward and kissed the center of my chest as she reached down, cupping my erection through my jeans. My body jerked at the bold, hot-as-fucking-hell touch. "Does that make me easy?"

"Fuck no. Do you really think that?" If so, this shit was going to stop right now. I caught her wrist, pulling her hand away. "Do you?"

She lifted her chin, inclining her head. "Not with you. No," she answered after a moment. She pulled her hand away and then pushed me down so that I sat on the edge of the bed. "It's strange."

"What is?"

Her gaze traveled over me, hungry. "I never thought that I'd be this comfortable around you."

I wanted to gather her in my arms and lose myself in her warmth. "I'm glad you do."

Andrea stepped back. She had fixed her dress downstairs, which had been a real visual disappointment, but now I was thrilled. As I sat on my ass and she stood in front of me, lifting her fingers to the tiny-ass straps of her dress, I was going to get to see her undress, and shit if that wasn't a beautiful thing.

She slipped the straps down her arms, letting them dangle as she reached behind her. The tinny sound of a zipper going down had me aching.

I spread my legs out, but it didn't help. "You're killing me."

Her lips curved up. "You killed me earlier."

"I did?"

The loose curls around her face bounced as she nodded. "What you did down there, on the couch?" The dress loosened around her and she caught the material before it slipped down her breasts. "I thought I'd died for a moment."

I leaned forward, my eyes never leaving her. Hell, a flesh-eating zombie could stroll into the room and I wouldn't look away. "I'll take that as a compliment."

"It was," she said softly, and then let the dress slip down her body, pooling at her feet with a soft *whoosh*.

Holy damn, my heart rate doubled. It was like seeing a goddess in the flesh, and I suddenly didn't feel worthy of laying my eyes on her. The delicate skin of her throat flushed pink and that blush spread down to her full breasts. My mouth watered at the sight of those hardened tips and my fingers tingled just imagining sliding down her ribs, over the sweet curve of her waist and to those damn silky panties that covered her rounded hips.

"Is there a bow on your panties?" I asked.

"Yes. Because I'm sweet and demure."

I chuckled hoarsely, but then straightened as she stepped toward me. My gaze was fastened on that purple bow right up until the moment her fingers slipped under the sides of her panties.

Never in my life had I been so fucking turned on.

Andrea bent slightly, and I sucked in a sharp breath as her breasts swayed and that scrap of purple lace slipped down her thighs, joining the dress, and then she was completely nude.

"Holy fuck," I groaned, shaking my head slightly as I looked my fill.

She curled one arm across her waist, over her navel. "Is... is that a bad thing?"

"No. Hell, no." I stood on oddly weak legs. "Andrea, you're beautiful."

The pink in her cheeks brightened as her lashes lowered. "I feel beautiful when you…you look at me this way."

"I'm always going to look at you this way, so you better get used to it." My gaze drifted over her body, lingering on some areas more than others, but I found myself staring at her feet. One foot was turned toward the other and her toes were curled. It was such a shy and sweet position that it tugged at my chest.

I wanted to do right by her.

Slowing this down was one of the hardest things I'd ever had to do, because I was so hard, so ready to be inside her that it was almost painful, but I didn't want this to be fast. I wanted her to remember this always and I wanted this to erase every fucker that'd come before me.

As I approached her, she lifted her gaze and her lips parted. Gently, I touched the sides of her face with the tips of my fingers and tilted her head back. Lowering my mouth to hers, I kissed her softly, taking my time to explore the depths of her warm mouth and her sweet taste.

I moved closer, welcoming the feel of her body brushing mine as the kiss went deeper and became more erotic. Our tongues tangled, and when her hands dropped to my pants, finishing with the zipper, I moaned as she barely touched me.

Stepping back, I finished with the jeans and the boxer briefs, shedding them quickly. I straightened, grinning when I saw what she was staring at. "You like?"

Her tongue darted over her plump lower lip. "Yeah. Yeah, I do."

Another husky laugh radiated out from me and then I took her hand, drawing her to the bed. As she lay down, I grabbed the condom off the nightstand and tossed it beside her.

Andrea arched a brow, and I grinned as I reached down, wrapping my hand around the base of my cock. "Keep an eye on that condom. Make sure it doesn't run off."

Her gaze dropped. "I don't think it's going anywhere."

"You never know." I put a knee on the bed beside her as I slowly moved my hand along myself. She seemed to like that by the way her chest rose sharply. "You like that, don't you?"

"Like what?" Her voice turned richer, thicker.

I moved my hand faster. "This. You like watching me do this."

Dammit, I loved the way her cheeks could turn pink at a drop of a hat. I expected her to lie, but after a moment, she nodded. "I do."

My jaw was beginning to ache from how hard I was grinding my teeth. "I'm going to have to file that little piece of knowledge away for later."

"Later?"

I smiled. "Oh, there's going to be a later. Lots of laters."

Andrea seemed to relax in that moment, and I hadn't noticed how much tension filled her until then. "I like the sound of that."

Staring at her, I felt my heart do something funny in my chest. Like it had jumped. Damn, she was going to break me in the best possible way.

I forced myself to lie down, stretching out on my side beside her. Drawing my hand down the length of her body, I idly brushed my thumb over the rosy peak of her breast. Fuck, I really liked the way she felt. I really liked the tiny feminine sound she made when I caught her nipple between my fingers. I liked the way she tilted her head back, lifting her chest in a silent invitation for more. Man, I just really liked her. My heart was pounding in my chest like a steel drum as I leaned over, placing a kiss on the little dip at the base of her throat.

"I like that," she said, running her hand up my arm. "I like everything you do."

I smiled against her skin, more than pleased to hear that. I rolled the tight nub as I kissed my way down her lovely breasts. She shuddered, and there was nothing sweeter than that. I could eat her up, one lick and nibble at a time, but there was no way I'd last if I went for round two of that.

Trailing a path along the underside of her breast, my hand drifted down her soft belly. I lifted my head, watching my own progress as my hand disappeared between those sweet thighs. I slipped a finger through the wetness there. She was tight and hot and wet. She was ready.

The foil package was already in her hand, and I had to laugh as I grabbed it from her, carefully ripping it open. My damn hands shook as I rolled it on and then I rose above her, forcing myself to breathe slowly as I shifted my weight onto one arm and kneed her thighs apart.

Her warm brown eyes held mine as she spread her fingers across my cheek. "I want you."

I closed my eyes briefly, shaken by the need I felt. "I will never grow tired of hearing that." I reached between us, guiding myself to her entrance, and then I grasped her hip, tilting her up. "I've wanted this since the first time I laid eyes on you."

A strange look crossed her face, gone so quickly I wasn't sure if I even saw it. She smiled. "Let's not wait any longer."

Magic words spoken right there.

I eased into her, groaning as her tightness enveloped me inch by fucking torturous inch. She was so tight and hot, a tremor rolled down me. I stilled, gasping. "You're okay?"

Andrea's hands slid down my sides to my hips. "Yes," she whispered.

Her gaze was dark and warm, and the restraint evaporated like smoke. I thrust my hips forward, filling her completely. Her head kicked back as she gasped, my name falling like a musical note between us.

I moved over her and in her, slow and steady at first, and she drew her legs up. Her feet slid along my calves until her thighs pressed against my hips, holding me there as she rose to meet each thrust. I had never felt such intensity, never such rightness. I hadn't even known it was possible to feel that way.

My back bowed as I drove into her, fisting one of my hands in her hair, yanking her head back. Our mouths met. The kiss was fierce, my tongue plunging into her, just like my hips were. Sweat dotted my brow and my back. The bed shook under the force. I devoured her with a hunger I didn't even know I was possible of experiencing.

I was losing control.

Maybe I'd never had control. My hips pistoned in and my hand dug into the flesh at her hip. I tried to pull back, mentality and emotionally, but I couldn't. In the back of my mind I was afraid of hurting her somehow, but she tightened around me, clamping down.

"Oh God," she gasped, her eyes going wide and smoky with pleasure. "Tanner, I…"

"Let go," I grunted out. "God, just let go, because I'm gonna—"

Andrea let go. Throwing her head back, she cried out. Her body spasmed around me as her fingers dug into my skin. There was no rhythm or grace in how I moved. I drove into her, the pounding motion moving both of us across the bed. Her lashes swept up and our gazes collided for an instant. What I saw in her stare proved that she hadn't broken me before, because I broke right then, splitting wide open. An intense, all-consuming release powered down my spine. My senses were fucking obliterated. It was all too much.

I came, my hips jerking wildly as I buried my head against her neck. The sounds of her pleasure were lost in my pounding heart and my own harsh groans. Fuck. I came for what felt like forever, the spasms never ending. My hand tightened around the back of her head as I shook and trembled.

I had no idea how much time passed before my body slowed its roll, but I slowly became aware of her hand gliding up and down my spine. Dragging in a ragged breath, I lifted my head.

Her half-hooded gaze met mine. "Hey," she whispered.

My lips twitched. "You okay?"

"Perfect."

Another rough breath parted my lips. "I'm probably crushing you."

She shook her head slowly. "I don't mind."

Neither did I, but seriously, I wasn't a small guy. I shifted onto my arm and carefully eased out of her. My legs felt strangely weak as my gaze dropped to hers. Again, I was at a loss for words as I leaned down and kissed her softly.

When we parted, I was unwilling to leave the bed, but I had to. "I'll be right back."

She nodded as I rose. Padding across the floor, I got rid of the condom and then made good on what I'd said, getting right back to where I was.

But Andrea was sitting up, drawing her knees up to her chest. "I can leave now if you—"

"What?" I shot her a look as I dragged the covers back on one side. "Leave?"

She glanced at me and then her gaze darted away. "I mean, I can hang out with you in here if you want or I can go back to my room."

I stared at her for a moment. "Get your ass under this blanket."

Her brows shot up. "Excuse me?"

"You're not going anywhere," I told her. "I want you in here, with me. So get that pretty ass under these blankets. I want to snuggle."

"Snuggle?" She didn't move for a moment and then she did, shaking her head and then scrambling under the blanket, on the far side of the bed.

I climbed in before I fell in, and as soon as my ass hit those cool sheets, I reached out and circled an arm around her waist, drawing her back against my front. "Snuggling," I explained, "requires two people to be close together."

"Understood," she said, and then wiggled her bottom a little, as if she was getting comfortable. "Tanner?"

"Yeah?"

I felt her draw in a deep breath. "Thank you."

I frowned. "For what?"

"For…for all of that."

Lifting my head, I looked down at her, and I froze for a moment. Thick lashes fanned her cheeks, and her slightly swollen lips were parted. The height of her cheeks was flushed, and even though we'd just fucked like two wild animals, there was still an odd air of…*peace* around her. It didn't make sense, but that's what I saw and felt. It had to be one of the rarest moments to see her like that.

I settled back down. There were a lot of words I wanted to say as I kissed her shoulder. There were a lot of things I was feeling as I closed my eyes, resting my forehead against her shoulder, but at that moment, words didn't seem adequate compared to what I was feeling, so I held her tighter to my chest and did something I couldn't recall doing before, with anyone.

I fell asleep with Andrea in my arms.

# Chapter 15

**Andrea**

For the first time in forever, I woke up with my body tangled with a man's. As my senses slowly kicked back on, the first thing I thought was that I'd never stayed a night with a guy before. Not even my boyfriend back in high school, for obvious reasons.

This…this was a huge first.

I was still lying on my side and Tanner was still pressed against my back. For several minutes, I dared not to make any sudden moves to disturb him, because I liked the way I was cocooned in his embrace. No. Not just liked. I *loved* it, and as I stared at the wall across from his large bed, I knew I could easily get used to this. Maybe I should, because he had said there'd be a later for us, lots of *laters,* if I remembered correctly.

Last night had been one of the most amazing nights of my life, and no matter what happened between Tanner and me, I wasn't going to let myself regret one single moment of it. No way.

So I lay there, soaking up every second like a sponge, and I don't know how much time passed, but I felt him harden against my bottom. I sucked in a sharp breath, unsure if he was awake or not. Well, *part* of him was definitely awake.

The arm resting over my waist moved slightly and my eyes popped open when his large hand closed over my breast. Yep. He was awake.

Lips brushed my shoulder. "Morning," Tanner spoke in a rough voice.

"Good morning," I said, my gaze dropping to his hand. He ran his thumb over the tip of my breast and squeezed gently.

"You sleep okay?" Tanner shifted, wiggling his leg between mine.

My heart skipped a beat. "I slept like a baby."

"Hmm. Wonder why?" His lips skated over the slope of my shoulder. "Guess what?"

I hesitated and then lifted my hand, folding it over his. "You're horny?"

His deep laugh stirred the hair at the base of my neck. "I'm hungry."

"Oh. Well then, this is awkward."

He nipped at the sensitive spot below my ear as he slid his hand down from my breast, to the space between my legs. "I'm hungry for you."

"Isn't that the same thing?" Arching my back, I pressed my bottom against him.

His groan turned me on even more.

"You're right." His hand slipped further between my legs. Sensation trilled through my veins. "You're totally right."

His hand disappeared from between my thighs, and I felt him move behind me. Then I heard a wrapper being torn, I started to roll to face him, but the hand on my hip stopped me. I stilled, biting down on my lip as that hand trailed up my side and then smoothed down the center of my back. Since I couldn't see what he was up to, the anticipation had a razor-sharp edge to it, almost desperate.

"Tanner," I whispered, wanting.

"Damn." His body was flush against mine again, and I could feel him hot and hard against my lower back. "You're already ready, aren't you?"

Before I had a chance to respond, he moved again. Both hands landed on my hips as he rose behind me. I was on my belly, my legs spread and he was between them, one hand remaining on my hip. My pulse sped up as I slid my hands up the sheet, bracing my weight on my forearms. I turned my head, peering back at Tanner over my shoulder.

Goodness, he looked incredible behind me. Sleep still clung to his features, but his eyes were a vibrant blue, full of potent heat and arousal. He started kissing me again, starting at my shoulder and working his way down my back, blazing a trail that ended just above the cleft along my bottom.

He used the hand on my hip to lift me. His warm breath danced along the back of my neck. "This is the kind of morning I'd love to repeat over and over. Actually, this moment, right here," he said, and I felt him poised behind me a moment before he thrust deep into me.

My back bowed as I cried out. The feeling of him—it was more intense, fuller and tighter, stretching every nerve ending to the edge. But it was more than him just being inside me. There wasn't so much as an inch between our bodies. His much larger body was curled around me, sealed to mine.

"You okay?" His voice was dark, gruff.

"I am," I managed to breathe. "God, Tanner…"

He kissed my cheek and then his lips moved to my ear. "I'm going to need you to hold on, because I'm going to give it to you hard."

I shuddered.

And then he did just what he said he was going to do.

Tanner moved fast and he hit deep, only slowing down to grind against me before picking his pace up. In this position, there was nothing I could do other than meet each of his thrusts and I did so happily, willingly. He was in control at this moment, and as I clenched the sheet, a riot of sensations lit me up.

"Oh God, Tanner," I gasped, rocking back against him. "Yes, yes, yes."

He made this sound, like a rumble of approval, and I felt it wash over me, through me. I was panting and he was making harsh noises. He got a hand under me, and then he started to touch me between my thighs as he slammed into me. The pleasure was so quick, it was sharp and near violent.

"Fuck," he grunted against my neck.

Suddenly I was on my knees and my hands were pressed against the headboard. One of his arms was around my hips, holding me in place as he thrust forward, the other was beside my arm, his hand closed over mine on the headboard. In a daze, I opened my eyes and stared at our joined hands.

My breath caught and I lost a little of myself at the sight, and then I lost a larger part in the way he moved behind me. And I was completely gone as the room filled with sounds of our bodies meeting together, our moans and soft curses. There was no rhythm between us. What became of us was a wild dance. The tension spiraled tight, and I was tossed right over the edge. I threw my head back against his shoulder as my body clamped down. The most exquisite rush of pleasure poured into my body, stunning me with its intensity. It whipped through me, heightened by every powerful thrust. My arms came out, but he caught me, sealing me tight against his body as he came, only his hips jerking.

There wasn't a single muscle in my body that worked in those precious moments of pure bliss. I was limp as a noodle, trembling as he guided me down and then left the bed to deal with the condom. I was where he'd left me when he came back to the bed and somehow we ended up face-to-face, his arm around me, his hand smoothing over my flushed cheek. I was completely sated. I hadn't known it could be like this. I wanted to tell him that, but my tongue was too heavy.

Tanner tucked me against him. "I think...I think I now need a nap."

A tired but light laugh escaped me. "Same here."

"Then we have a plan."

"We do?" I murmured.

"Yeah." He kissed my forehead. "Since we don't have shit to do and we can do whatever we want, we're going to nap now."

I smiled as I snuggled into him. "Sounds like the best kind of plan."

Late in the afternoon, I stood in front of Tanner, a package of raw chicken in my hands. "I know I'm right."

He arched a brow as he leaned against the counter. "I have never heard of such a thing."

"I'm sure there are a lot of things you've never heard of."

"No way," he drawled lazily.

I rolled my eyes. "If you boil the chicken first, then it doesn't take as long to grill it and then you always make sure it's not undercooked."

"I get what you're saying, but it just seems repetitive."

"But it's not the same thing. You're not cooking it completely," I tried to explain for what felt like the hundredth time. "Forget it. Just let me do this."

He grinned as he waved a hand, as if granting me permission. Choosing to ignore that, I set the package on the counter and then cranked the heat up on the pot of boiling water.

"At least it's stopped raining," he said, and when I turned around, he was staring out the glass doors. "I bet Kyler and Sydney are wishing they'd stayed here."

"They're probably all cuddled up in a tent, making little Syd babies."

He smiled and then winked. *My* heart toppled over itself. "Kind of like what we've been doing all day?"

Heat flashed across my face.

"Except we fall into the category of doing practice runs," he continued, his grin sly. "Though I'd love to see a little red-headed Andrea."

Oh my word, my eyes widened. Did he really mean that? My tummy dropped in a pleasant way and my heart started to dance, but I turned around, catching the end of the package. There was no way he was being serious, and I was not going to allow myself to read into that comment. Nope. I was not going to let my brain do anything stupid.

Earlier, while Tanner was in the shower, and I'd gone into my head—those quiet moments…they hadn't been so great. And while I'd showered, my thoughts went to familiar places filled with doubt, areas where overthinking ran rampant.

Sometimes…sometimes it felt like there were too many thoughts running around in my head, and that was one of those moments. I started to panic as I stood under the showerhead. Would Tanner regret last night and this morning? Did it mean anything to him? What would happen if I told him that I thought…that there was a good chance that I was in love with him? Did he really even know me?

The answer to that question was what scared me the most. I didn't think that he did know me. At least not the "me" that existed when there were quiet moments, and that was a "me" I didn't know how to deal with.

But it wasn't just about Tanner. Those feelings of panic and uncertainty. Those feelings were never about just one thing. If they were, they'd probably be easier to deal with.

"Was that too honest?" he asked, and his voice was closer—real close.

I shivered as I continued to rip open the package of chicken and then picked up the tongs. "I just don't think you…you really mean that."

"Are you inside of my head?" His hands settled on my hips and I gave a little jump. "Do you know what I think?"

That question hit too close to home. So I took a moment and picked up the chicken with the tongs, plopping it down in the boiling water. "I don't think I want to know what's inside your head."

"Uh-huh." Tanner circled an arm around my waist and pressed into me. He kissed the side of my neck. "I think you'd like the things that go on inside my head."

Despite my earlier thoughts, I smiled as I picked up the last piece of chicken. "Okay. Maybe."

"Definitely," he murmured, dropping a kiss against the sensitive space below my ear.

"Possibly."

Tanner stepped back as I took the tongs over to the sink and washed them. When I turned around, he was staring into the pot with a look of disgust on his face. "This...this is gross-looking. All that white stuff floating to the top?"

I laughed as he shot me a look. "Don't be a baby."

"Will it get me spanked if I act like one?"

"Oh God." I laughed again, shaking my head.

Grilling the chicken and then eating dinner pretty much consisted of us bickering and then Tanner making some kind of random, perverted statement that either made me giggle, blush, or both. There were no quiet moments, not for a while, not even when Syd and Kyler returned from their camping trip.

But those quiet moments surged back with a vengeance as we all sat in the basement's media room.

Rain had started up again, shortly after Syd and Kyler had shown back up, and we were currently watching the boys engage in an impromptu air hockey death match once more. Kyler had a beer. Tanner had a beer. Even Sydney, who rarely drank, had one of those fruity beers.

I wanted a drink. Bad.

So much so that I sort of felt like banging my head against a wall, but I didn't want Tanner to look at me like—actually, I *wanted* Tanner to look at me. That was the thing. Once our friends had shown back up, he hadn't really looked at me or...or paid attention to me.

At first, I thought it was just me being stupid. No big surprise there. Sounded legit, because my history of being stupid was well-known. When Kyler and Syd returned, there was a lot of commotion, and they were hungry and wanted to talk about their trip while they ate our leftovers. I'd been nervous, unsure of how I should act, if I should just walk up to Tanner and grab his junk or something or wait to see what he did, so I didn't do anything really. And when Syd had gone upstairs to shower, Kyler had monopolized Tanner's time, and then when Syd had returned, my mother had called, and I ended up having to listen to how epically proud they were of Brody and how worried they were for me. By the time I got off the phone, I really, badly, needed a drink, but I resisted.

So Tanner and I obviously hadn't had a lot of time to make googly eyes at one another or to expose our sudden, undying passion for each other, but as the evening eased into night, the indifference he'd started showing when Syd and Kyler returned continued.

Maybe that wasn't a bad thing. I wasn't sure. But I'd thought that he would at least pay attention to me. Honestly, I think we'd exchanged a handful of words. There were no long looks of lust or stolen touches. When I'd gone upstairs to get a freaking soda, he hadn't followed or anything.

So maybe he *was* treating me differently, because usually we did talk…or argue…or whatever, but now it seemed like he didn't want….

I cut myself off before I could finish that thought.

I didn't know what to make of any of it.

But my heart was pounding in a way that was so not pleasant and my stomach was twisted in knots as I watched Tanner strut around the side of the table, grinning as Kyler smack-talked him.

God, I really wanted a drink.

However I wasn't sure if I could have just one drink. I mean, I thought I could, but the last thing I wanted was for anyone, especially Tanner, to comment on my drinking. Not that at the moment they truly had any room to talk since they all had drinks in their hands. It wasn't fair. They could drink, but I couldn't?

It was close to midnight when I finally called it a night. The air hockey game had ended and everyone was still chatting, but I was ready for the night to be over. Tomorrow held a lot more promise than what I was seeing now.

After saying goodnight, I headed for the stairs. Tanner did look up then, and my heart got all floppy when he grinned and said, "Goodnight, Andy."

"'Night," I repeated, and then all but dashed up the flight of stairs and then to the top floor like a dork.

*Goodnight, Andy.*

Was that code for you'll be seeing me later…or just telling me goodnight? Probably code. Definitely code. Should I have used a code that signaled I was okay with that? It didn't matter. I took a ridiculously long time getting ready for bed. I brushed my teeth and then got the knots out of my curls. Then I washed my face and then engaged in some major wishful make-up—applied mascara and blush. For bed. Whatever. Then I slathered on the lotion that smelled of peaches. Searching for something sexy but didn't look like I was trying too hard was more difficult than I imagined. I ended up settling on a pair of super cute sleep shorts and a cami.

I didn't lock the bedroom door before I climbed into bed. Tanner would come—especially after yesterday and today, he would come. And we would talk, because we needed to be on the same page with what things truly meant. He said there were *laters* and that he wanted to see me once we left here, but that could mean anything—secret friends-with-benefits or an actual, real relationship.

My heart dropped with the thought of him wanting to be closet fuck buddies, and I wasn't even going to pretend that I'd be okay with that. In all honesty, I wasn't okay with the random hookups that only happened after I'd had a few drinks under my belt and wasn't thinking right. In the darkness of the room, I could acknowledge that, even as hard as that was. And if Tanner wanted to be in a relationship, I needed to be honest with him and up front about some of the things he didn't know about me. I guessed, in a way, he needed to make an informed decision.

*Informed decision?* I rolled my eyes. Wasn't like he was voting for president or something.

I rolled onto my back and glanced at the clock. Tiny balls of ice filled my stomach when I realized an hour had passed since I'd walked into my bedroom. My gaze flicked to the bedroom door. Wasn't he coming? Better yet, should I be okay with him sneaking into my bedroom even though he really didn't pay much attention to me once our friends showed back up?

Then again, had I paid attention to him?

I bit down on my lower lip as I stared up at the ceiling, only able to make out the shape of the quietly moving fan. In all honesty, it wasn't like I'd gone out of my way, either. I mean, I hadn't been sure what to do or how we should act.

Squeezing my eyes shut, I told myself that all I needed to do was wait. Tanner would show. He would. So I waited.

And I waited—waited while the seconds turned into minutes, minutes into hours, and my door didn't open and Tanner…he never came.

# Chapter 16

**Andrea**

Two. No. Three. Maybe it was four? Hell. I tipped the bottle of beer to the side, frowning as I stared at the label. Maybe I should ask Syd. She'd know. She always knew.

"It's five," Syd said with a troubled-sounding sigh.

Straightening the bottle, I looked at her. She sat in the chair across from where I was stretched out on the still-damp chaise lounge on the deck. It had rained most of the day and the sun had only peeked out behind the thick clouds a couple of hours ago. "Huh?"

"That's your fifth beer," she explained, reaching up and pulling her thick hair—God, I wanted her hair—into a ponytail. "You have that look on your face. I recognize it. You're trying to remember how much you've drank."

My lips turned down at the corners. "I have a look?"

She nodded. "Yeah, you do. The look usually comes before you ask me how many you've had."

"Ha," I laughed. "I *was* just about to ask you. Huh." Tipping the bottle back, I took a huge gulp. Immediately, I felt the need to burp that baby out, but as I glanced to where Kyler and Tanner stood, I decided that wasn't very ladylike.

Tanner.

Ugh.

I took another drink and then rested my head back against the cushion. I couldn't even look at him without reliving everything that we'd done in, like, real-time, and that was just awkward. Really awkward, because as soon as I thought about what we'd done, I thought about the fact he'd virtually ignored me all last night and had never showed up. And then I had to acknowledge that I'd probably gotten played. I'd gotten played *hard*. What in the world had I been thinking earlier? I hadn't been thinking. That was the problem.

"But if you're counting the shot of vodka you did between beer number two and beer number three, I'd say you're probably at six or seven," Syd added.

My eyes narrowed on her. "I do not follow your logic."

She glanced over to where the guys were. Since the storm had cleared out, we'd ended up grilling steaks. Ribeyes—the good, fatty kind. Like my thighs. Except I doubted my thighs tasted good when chargrilled.

God, I think I might be a little tipsy.

Opening my eyes, I turned my head to the side and my gaze collided with Tanner's. I sucked in an unsteady breath. Kyler was talking to him, but it didn't look like he was paying attention at all. So now he wanted to eyeball me like—like he had every right to do so. What the fuck ever. I looked away and I finished off what was left in my bottle.

I did not want to think about him. I did not want to think about how wonderful it had been the few fucking hours that I'd had him. And I sure as hell did not want to think about how…how nice it had been to just talk with him, to have that bond that I thought went beyond sex. And I really, super-duper did not want to think about how pathetic he must believe I was, because here I was, in love with him, and there he was, probably counting down the days until we would leave. Not that I'd told him that I loved him. Thank God. Anyway, I didn't want to think about any of that.

"So what are you guys doin' tomorrow?" I asked, and then grinned, because I was positive I didn't slur my words.

Syd shrugged dainty shoulders. "I don't know. What's on the schedule, Kyler?"

"Spending all day in bed," he replied.

I laughed—loudly.

She pursed her lips. "Yeah. No."

He pouted, and I admitted to myself that Kyler looked good with a pout. A man pout. Ha. "Whatever you want to do, Syd. I'm at your service," he added.

A grin crossed her face. "I like the way that sounds." Looking at me, she shrugged again. "I really don't know. I think we're going to try to go hiking again tomorrow. Oh! Or go fishing. There was this lake we came across. It would be perfect. You're more than welcome to join us."

I laughed again and just as loudly as the first time. "No."

"Then I guess Tanner's going to skip, too," Kyler replied blithely.

Tanner shot him a look that should've knocked him flat on his ass, but Kyler chuckled as he tossed his bottle in the trashcan on the deck.

I could feel Syd's gaze on me, and whatever relaxation I'd gained faded as the muscles along the back of my neck tightened. She had been trying to get me to talk about what had gone down between Tanner and me while they'd been camping, but my mouth was shut. No way was I talking about any of that while I was still stuck in this stupid cabin and I was likely to lose my shit. "He can do whatever he wants," I announced.

Tanner's arms folded across his chest and his biceps stretched the sleeves of his shirt in a way that should've been indecent. "Thanks, Andy, for reminding everyone that I can do what I want."

I snorted. "You're welcome. That's what I'm here for."

"To point out the obvious?" he replied.

"Oh dear," Syd murmured under her breath.

A wide smile tugged at my lips as I fastened my gaze on Tanner's handsome face. Now *this* I could deal with. The smartass Tanner. That was who I was familiar with. Not the sweet and charming Tanner who made me think that I was different—that *we* were different—before painfully reminding me that in fact nothing was any different. "Well, if I don't do it, who will?"

Tanner arched a brow. "No one else?"

I shrugged a shoulder. "Whatever. I'm getting another drink." I glanced at Kyler. "Want one while I'm up?"

He opened his mouth, but I saw his eyes shoot to where Syd sat. "No. Thank you."

There was most definitely something up with that, but I didn't care. Swinging my legs off the lounge, I stood. And then I wobbled.

"You sure you should have another?" Tanner asked, stepping forward.

I shot him a nasty look. "Did I ask you for your opinion?"

"No. But I'm going to give it to you."

A very unattractive snicker came out of my mouth. "I bet you're going to try."

"Um," Kyler said.

Tanner's jaw flexed, but before he could reply, I volleyed back at him. "But again, not something I'm interested in."

Understanding flared in his eyes, and he barked out a short, dry laugh as he turned his head to the side. "Yeah, you know, that's the funny thing about my opinions. You usually just ignore them because you know they're right."

"I don't understand what is happening," Syd said under her breath.

"You know what else is funny?" I asked sweetly as I dropped the bottle in the trash.

"What?" He looked bored.

Meeting his gaze, I raised my right hand…and my middle finger. "This."

"Oh. Wow," he said. "Keeping it classy, I see."

My eye-roll was so powerful, I thought my eyeballs would roll back in my head, never to be seen again. "Oh, whatever. My middle finger offends you when every other word out of your mouth is 'fuck?'"

"She has a point," Kyler commented.

I bestowed him with an awesome smile. "Thank you."

"Don't encourage her," muttered Tanner.

Choosing to ignore him, I turned and headed for the door. I walked inside, and not once did I stumble, so Tanner could kiss it.

My cheeks flushed with that thought. Okay. No kissing of anything, even though I liked the kissing. He was so damn good at it.

The bottles jangled so prettily when I opened the fridge door that I wanted to do a little dance in tandem with the tune. I grabbed a beer and made a mental note to head to town tomorrow for more. I had a feeling I was going to need a twelve-pack to get through the rest of this trip. Maybe a forty-pack. Did they make forty-packs? God, I so hoped so.

Shit, I just needed a keg.

Screwing off the cap, I flipped it onto the counter with a sigh and watched it spin dizzily across the granite. As I stood there, the bottle cool in my hand, I struggled to put a name to the cause of the restlessness crawling across my skin. It wasn't just Tanner. God, it was never just one thing. It was always a bag of stupid crap that had me feeling this way.

All day I'd been stressing over a lot of things—the phone call with my mom, going back home, being stuck in life when everyone else was moving on, and of course, what was going on with Tanner. And for some reason, I started thinking about what I'd said the first night with Tanner, about how I felt when I'd been going down on Tanner. Had I been forced before? None of the guys had pressured me. I'd gone home willingly with all of them, but had gone under the impression they were expecting something from me. After all, why else would they be taking me home? That pressure... God, it was *inside* me. Nothing they had done that I could recall. But it was *me*. I'd felt that pressure to do it, to avoid the actual sex, because why else would they be with me?

Why else had Tanner been so nice to me? He'd obviously wanted some and he'd gotten some. He hadn't even really had to work for it. I'd just handed it right over.

I wanted to bang my head off a wall, because it sounded so pathetic, like the way Tanner had looked at me when we'd talked about my past experience with guys.

This was stupid.

Everything was stupid.

I sighed again. Great. I was moving from happy, I-don't-care-about-anything buzz, to go-stick-my-head-in-the-oven buzz. I winced the moment that thought completed itself. That wasn't cool. Not cool at all.

"Andrea."

I jumped, and sticky beer sloshed over my hand. "Jesus." I turned around, finding Tanner standing on the other side of the island. "What are you doing? Stalking me?"

"Yeah," he replied blandly. "That's why I called your name, because that's what stalkers do when they are trying to be stealth."

"Really stupid stalkers would do that." My heart slowed in my chest. "Get what I'm saying?" As soon as I asked that, I felt like the ass, but anger...anger had always been so easy to grasp onto.

His shoulders rose with a deep breath. "You've been avoiding me all day."

"Have not."

He cocked his head to the side and raised both brows. "You practically hid in your room or attached yourself to Syd all day."

"I was...I was spending girl-time with her," I said. "And napping."

"Andrea..."

He'd been right. I *had* avoided him. Apparently, I wasn't doing that great of a job at it.

"The same with last night. You barely talked to me."

"What?" Dumbfounded, I felt like screaming that word. "*I* barely talked to *you*? *You* ignored *me*."

He stared at me. "Andy, I—"

"This is stupid. This whole thing is stupid." I lifted the bottle.

A moment passed and he asked, "Do you really think you need another beer?"

Annoyed, I slowly brought the bottle to my mouth and took a long drink. "Does that answer your question?"

The hue of his blue eyes deepened. "Look, I'm not trying to be a dick—"

"You might want to try harder. Just sayin'. Might just be my opinion, but thought I'd share."

He opened his mouth and then snapped it shut. Several seconds passed. "You know, I didn't say that shit to you to piss you off."

I wanted to point out everything he'd done to piss me off, but...but shit on a brick. Anything that I told him would betray how I felt about him, and well, I was already embarrassing myself enough without going there. "You breathed," I decided, nodding, and totally proud of myself. "How about that?"

Shaking his head, he rested his elbows on the island. "You can usually do better than that."

"It's not worth my time to do better." I flounced past him. Well, I might have staggered past him, but in my head, I flounced like a Grade A Uppity Chick, and it was awesome.

"I wish you wouldn't drink so much."

My feet stopped. Dammit. My feet had a mind of their own, and they had stopped because he'd said that so quietly, not with an ounce of derision or scorn. Actually, it sounded like a plea. The alcohol churned in my stomach. All I could see was his look of pity.

"Why do you drink like this?" he asked.

*To relax. To not act like a freak. To forget. To remember. To be funny. To have people like me. To not care if they do or don't. To have fun. To just not care.* A burning sensation rolled down my back as my head continued to shout out the answers. I just didn't want to *care.*

I didn't say any of that. "*You* drink."

"I do. And sometimes I drink and I get drunk, but not every time."

Slowly, I faced him. He wasn't looking at me. His eyes were on the island. "I don't get drunk every time."

He shook his head again. "Andrea, you either get plastered or damn near close. Every time."

"That's not…" I trailed off, and yeah, even I could see where he was right. I could probably count on one hand how many times I'd only had two beers or two shots and then stopped. Come to think of it, I wasn't sure if I *ever* had.

"My dad got shitfaced all the time," he continued. "Never thought that I'd be interested in a girl who was the same way."

My brain registered two things at once. He was interested in me, which wasn't a big duh. I mean, he'd had his hands in my pants more than once, so yeah, I should've known that. But he compared me to his dad, a man I'd recently discovered he pretty much loathed, which pretty much canceled out the first part. Hurt invaded every cell and festered under the skin. The back of my throat burned and I wanted to rush away.

But I didn't. "That kind of makes you twisted."

Another weak laugh came out of him. "I guess it kind of does."

My hand shook as I lifted the bottle, but I didn't take the drink. I just stared down at it, hurt and angry and a thousand other emotions I couldn't even begin to sort out. "Then maybe you should spend some time reflecting on that instead of on my drinking habits."

"Did you ever think it's because I care?" Pushing off the island, he angled his body toward mine. "Has that ever crossed your mind just once?"

"When?" I laughed, and then I did take a drink. "Was it between fucking random chicks? Or when you ignored me as soon as our friends showed up?"

"Ignored you?" His eyes narrowed. "I didn't want you to be uncomfortable—"

"Why are we even having this conversation?" I interrupted, and anger—that ugly, red-hot feeling—sank its claws in me. "It's stupid, and I'd appreciate it if you'd mind your own fucking business for once."

"You think I'm going to mind my own business after what happened between us?"

My laugh came out like a snort. "Why wouldn't you? Doesn't seem like what happened between us changed a damn thing. It doesn't matter anyway." The words hurt to speak. "It was just a good time. It didn't mean anything."

Tanner stared at me as his lips thinned and frustration flashed across his face. "No wonder you've been single the entire time I've known you," he said, turning away.

An icy hand trailed down my chest and fisted in my stomach. "What?"

"This." He faced me again, throwing his hand up in a wide circle. "You're always fucking drunk, and when you're not, you're actually a decent person to be around. But that shit doesn't last long enough to put up with this mess."

# Chapter 17

**Andrea**

I couldn't move as Tanner's harsh words settled over me, seeping through my skin and digging in deep, below the muscles and bone. I stared at him as this God-awful burn started in the pit of my stomach and crawled up to my chest, getting lodged there.

I wanted to fire back with something clever. I wanted to act like his words didn't bother me and what he thought didn't matter. I wanted to tell him that I didn't care about being a mess and being single, but I couldn't get my tongue to work. It was glued to the roof of my mouth and his face had started to blur.

A tense moment passed and then Tanner cursed under his breath. He lifted a hand and ran it over his head as he looked away, a muscle flexing along the strong cut of his jaw. "Andrea, I—"

"Don't," I cut in, my voice shaking. I wasn't sure what I was telling him not to do, but the last thing I wanted to hear was an apology. Even though my thoughts were a little fuzzy, I knew you couldn't own those words and then take them back. But under that hurt, the truth was just as painful, if not more. It wasn't like I was a victim in all of this. Tanner's words were harsh, but they were dipped in fact, and even being half-drunk, I could recognize that.

And that's what made all of this so much harder to swallow.

"You can't take that back," I whispered. "You can't take that back."

He flinched.

I drew in air, but it seemed to get stuck in my throat. A series of fine shivers rolled down my back. "Fuck you, Tanner."

Setting the bottle on the counter, I turned and started walking toward the steps. My hands shook.

Tanner wheeled around, blocking my path. His eyes were wide. "I'm sorry. I shouldn't have said what I said, not like that."

His words hit and bounced off. "Get out of my way."

"Andrea—"

"Get out of my way!" I screamed so loudly that a streak of pain shot down my throat. I stumbled back as the tips of my fingers started to tingle. "I get it. Okay? You regret being with me—"

"Wait. What? I never said that, Andrea. I don't regret a moment of being with you," he said, shaking his head. "If you don't believe me, I'll walk right out there and tell both of them exactly what we did and what it meant to me."

I laughed, but the sound also got caught around the knot in my throat. For the tiniest moment, it felt like I couldn't breathe. Even though I knew I could, knew I was breathing right then, my lungs seized up. It was like vise clamps had been secured around my chest and tightened. The tingling spread up my arms as the corners of my vision started to dim. Blood pounded through me as my heart rate kicked into overdrive.

Tanner was talking, but I wasn't hearing him. There was a roaring in my ears, drowning him out. I tried to side-step him, but stumbled and lost my balance. I bumped into the wall. He reached for me, but I needed to get out of there. I needed to go upstairs. I needed my medication.

The sliding glass door opened, and it sounded like a high-pitched whine to my suddenly sensitive ears. Air wheezed in and out.

"What's going on in here?" Kyler asked from somewhere in the kitchen, and it sounded like he yelled it, as if his voice boomed like thunder.

"He won't...let me go...upstairs," I mumbled, leaning against the wall. "I need...to go...upstairs."

The room spun as I pushed off the wall, my legs shaking as I reached the step. I thought I heard Syd's voice, but they now sounded far away, somewhere back in a tunnel. I needed to get upstairs, so I could breathe. I needed to breathe.

A hand landed on my arm, but I kept going. Pure determination drove me up the stairs and toward the bedroom. My purse...it was somewhere in the room with my meds.

"Andrea, what the hell is going on with you?" Tanner was right behind me, his voice coming back in, loud and clear.

*Please. Just go away. Please. Just go away.* I wasn't sure if I spoke those words out loud or not. I thought I did. I needed to, because the room, the world, needed to go quiet so that I could make *this* stop.

I stumbled across the room, toward the dresser, but I didn't see my purse. Where was it? God, I needed to find it. I was frantic. Had I not brought it with me? Did I leave it somewhere? Panic exploded in my gut like buckshot. It was going to happen. I could feel it building at the base of my neck.

"Leave me alone," I said, and as I spun around, I saw Tanner standing just inside the room, but I didn't really *see* him. "Leave me alone!"

### Tanner

I froze, hands at my sides as I stared at Andrea. I had no idea what was happening. I didn't even know if she knew what was going on. Was she that drunk? Fuck. I wanted to help her, but I didn't know how.

I stepped toward her and then immediately stopped as she shrieked, "Leave me alone!"

I halted once more. Something was very wrong with Andrea. Her face was flushed, too red. Her eyes were glazed over, maybe from the drinks, but they were darting too fast. Even from where I stood, I could tell her pupils were dilated. My stomach dropped and a horrible, insidious thought crept in. Was she on something?

"What can I do?" I asked. "Tell me what I can do to help you."

Andrea shook her head and then she doubled over, folding her arms across her waist. Concern overrode any other thought. I moved forward, but a smaller form shot past me, heading straight for her.

It was Sydney.

She rushed to Andrea's side, wrapping an arm around her shoulders. "Come on, Andrea, take a deep breath. You need to stop and take a deep breath."

Andrea was trembling so badly that Sydney was shaking. "I need…"

Either Andrea's legs gave out or Sydney had gotten her to the floor, because they were both huddled there. "What's happening?" I asked.

Sydney didn't answer. She was focused on Andrea.

One of her small hands was on the center of Andrea's back, the other above her chest. "Take a deep, slow breath. That's all you've got to do. Take a breath…"

Never in my life had I ever felt so damn helpless as I stood there, watching them. I was trained to help save people, to rush into burning buildings and use instruments to pry open the mangled wreckage of vehicles. I'd given CPR and stopped gushing wounds, but I never felt more useless than I did then.

"I need…" Andrea gasped out between a broken-sounding sob. "…my meds…"

Her meds?

"I can't give them to you," Sydney said, running her hand down Andrea's back.

Andrea's cries grew stronger, and I couldn't stop myself. I moved closer, kneeling down.

"I'm sorry, Andrea. I can't," Sydney continued, holding Andrea tight. "You've been drinking. I can't give you those pills. Not when you've been drinking."

"I can't breathe," shrieked Andrea.

"I'm going to get you to breathe again, okay? Just listen to me. I'm going to get you to breathe again." Sydney paused, looking over at me. "You need to leave."

Fuck that. "Is she okay?"

"She will be," she replied softly. "But please leave. She's not going to get better with you in here."

I didn't understand that, but as I glanced at Andrea, my heart fucking shattered a bit. She was practically curled into a ball.

"I'll make sure she's okay." Sydney met my gaze. "But please leave. Let me take care of her."

But I wanted to be the one to take care of her. After all, I had a feeling that I'd caused this—or at least added to whatever the hell was going on. Never did I suspect my ignorant words would have driven her to this, and maybe it was partly due to the alcohol, but I was a part of this.

"She has panic attacks," Sydney said when I hadn't moved. "That's all this is, okay? It's a panic attack."

Panic attack? My internal thoughts were a parrot. I had no idea. Never once had Andrea mentioned anything like that or even appeared like she suffered from them. Obviously it was something relatively common if Sydney knew about them and Andrea had meds—meds she couldn't take because she'd been drinking.

Oh man, I knew what alcohol could do if mixed with certain meds. I didn't know what kind of meds she was supposed to take in this situation, but what if she had gotten up here and taken them? Good God, it could've ended in a tragic disaster.

I found myself nodding as I slowly rose and I wasn't even aware that I was out in the hall until I spotted Kyler waiting by the steps. I walked past him. "I didn't know," I said. "I didn't know she went through that."

Kyler said nothing as he followed me downstairs. I didn't know where I was going, but I needed to keep moving. I hit the kitchen and stopped, running both hands over my head. "Did you know?" I asked when I heard Kyler behind me.

There was a pause. "Syd mentioned it before."

"Shit." I dropped my hands. Tension crept across my neck. "And no one thought it would be a good idea to tell me?"

"Why would we? I mean, that's some personal shit right there."

I faced him. "Sydney told you."

"I'm her boyfriend, and it wasn't like I was going to tell people. And you—not to be ignorant—but you're just some guy who hangs out with Andrea every once in a while."

My hands closed into fists. "I'm not some random fucking dude."

He arched a brow. "You're not?"

"Fuck no."

"You're her friend then?"

"I'd say we fall in the 'more than just friends' category," I responded and turned away. Spying the beer bottle on the counter, I snatched it up and walked over to the sink, emptying the fucker out. "What? You're not going to ask for details on that statement?"

"I really don't think this is the time for me to get info out of you," he replied calmly. "All things considered."

"Hell." I threw the empty bottle in the trash and then gripped the edge of the counter. My head dipped. "I'm a dick. A total fucking dick."

I shouldn't have said what I did. There was something to be said about being too honest and those words had been too honest. They were also hurtful as fuck. Anger and frustration had gotten the better of me, and that really made me no different than my father.

Knowing that burned like a mother.

How many times had my father lost his cool and said ignorant shit to my mom? To me? More times than I could count. Sometimes it was the truth. Mom wasn't perfect either, and neither had I been growing up, but just because something was true didn't make it right to throw it in someone's face. And just because what I'd said to Andrea was true didn't make it okay.

Well, what I'd said was partially true.

I had no idea why she'd been mostly single since I'd known her. Most guys would overlook the drinking. Hell, I could overlook it if I…if I didn't care about her. And that was the whole thing. I *cared* about her. A lot.

And I had hurt her.

What I'd said needed to be said, but that hadn't been the right way to go about it. Clenching the counter, I watched what was left of the foam from the beer bubble its way down the drain. I wasn't sure an apology was going to be enough.

"It can't be that bad."

I'd forgotten that Kyler was even in the room. "Oh, it was."

"She was drunk and she…she has some issues, Tanner."

"With anxiety?" I pushed off the counter, ready to defend the whole "issues" statement. "A lot of people have problems with that. It's not that uncommon."

He raised his hands. "I'm not saying it's bad that she does or anything like that, but you've got to understand, that probably had some kind of influence on her reaction. You probably weren't the only cause of what just happened."

"Maybe," I muttered. "But man, just trust me on this. I shouldn't have said what I did. Not the way I said it."

Kyler stared at me a moment. "Okay. So now I'm going to get all up in your business at the most inopportune time possible."

I raised my brows.

"It's obvious that you really care about her. Something went down between you two while we were camping." He grinned in a way that kind of creeped me out. "This is great."

I frowned. "I don't think this is a good thing right at this moment."

"No. It is. Well, after you apologize for being a general shithead and Andrea...well, when she feels better." He tilted his head to the side, studying me. "It doesn't bother you that she has anxiety issues?"

My frowned deepened. "No. Why would it?"

"Some people...well, I'm gonna be real. There are people out there who are assholes and don't understand something like that. They judge."

I folded my arms across my chest. "I'm not one of them."

Kyler nodded and then asked, "What about the drinking?"

And that was the million-dollar question. I wanted to be able to overlook the drinking, because underneath it all, there was a damn-fine woman there. Andrea was smart and she was funny. She was kind and she was beautiful. And she was a damn firecracker in and out of bed, but the drinking...

The girl had a problem, even if she didn't want to acknowledge it.

I shook my head, unable to answer that...and damn, that was probably answer enough. Maybe for a while I could ignore the drinking, but long-term? Yeah, I couldn't deal with that. Disappointment rushed me. I felt like something cherished had just been snatched away from me.

"What got her so pissed off at you?"

Part of me didn't want to talk about it, but guilt was a noxious acid in my stomach. "You were right. Things did change between Andrea and me while you guys were gone— hell, *before* you guys left. It got heated—in a good way. But when you guys came back, she was so nervous and I...I didn't want to make her uncomfortable. I wanted to see how she played things out, but..."

But she hadn't really acted any different toward me, and so neither had I. Last night, I'd planned on sneaking into her room, but I figured we probably should talk first and I knew talking would've been the last thing I would've done. So I'd decided to wait until today to talk to her. And then she'd played keep-away all day. If I could go back and change things, I would.

I never ended up elaborating on what I was saying to Kyler. I was done talking about shit and I spent the next couple of hours roaming the house until I finally got tired of waiting for Sydney to reappear. I headed upstairs, past my room. The door to Andrea's was cracked open, and taking a deep breath, I eased it open.

I was relieved to see that neither of them was still on the floor. Andrea was asleep on her side, facing the door. Curled inward, her face was no longer flushed but her hair appeared damp. Her pale lips were parted.

Sydney sat on the other side of her, leaning against the headboard and legs crossed at the ankles. She glanced up from her phone as I stepped into the room.

"Is she okay?" I whispered, not wanting to disturb Andrea.

Lowering her phone to her lap, Sydney nodded. "She's out cold." Her voice was low. "A truck could drive through this house and she'd sleep through it. It's like that after… after these instances."

My chest spasmed. "This…this happens a lot?"

She studied me for a moment as uncertainty flickered across her face. "As far as I know, not when she's been drinking, but it's happened a couple of times since I've known her."

"She normally uses the meds then?"

Sydney nodded again. "It's not her fault. Her brain… Well, it's like a faulty house alarm, you know? Your brain is wired to alert you to danger. Gets the adrenaline going, all of that, but with people who have anxiety attacks, the brain isn't working correctly. It's like a house alarm going off when no one is breaking into the house. Sometimes something triggers it—something big. Other times, it can be an issue that would be minor for the rest of us."

"I didn't think it was her fault," I whispered. "I just didn't know. I had no idea. Andrea seems so…"

"You know, usually the people who smile the most and laugh the loudest are the ones who…suffer the most," she said quietly as she glanced down at Andrea and sighed wearily. "I knew…I knew the drinking was bad, especially with the anxiety. I've talked to her about it, you know? But I never really pushed her on it, and I…I should've. I *know* better. It's just hard to see everything clearly when it's someone you care about."

Damn, that was… All of this was painful to hear. For a moment, I couldn't move. All I could do was stare at Andrea. The bright red curls were spread out behind her like flames. Her hands were folded under her chin, against her chest. I had no idea how she'd gotten herself in that tiny ball, but she looked much smaller, much younger.

"I messed up," I said out loud, to no one in particular.

A heartbeat passed and Sydney said, "So did she. So did all of us."

# Chapter 18

*Andrea*

It was the butt-crack of dawn Saturday morning when I found myself wide awake with a pounding headache and a really vile taste in the back of my throat. Throwing off a quilt I didn't remember grabbing, I sat up and the room did this really weird funhouse thing. I made it to the bathroom with just seconds to spare, enough time to turn on the shower to drown out the sounds I made when I dropped to my knees in front of the toilet.

Pain shuttled up and down my ribs by the time I finished, and I sat there for a minute, clean water in the basin of the toilet and steam filling the bathroom, replaying messy images from the night before, over and over like I was stuck in some kind of twisted instant replay of random, blurry flashes that didn't make a lot of sense.

Last night...I'd gotten plastered and not only made a complete idiot out of myself, I'd had an anxiety attack. My cheeks burned as I vaguely remembered Tanner standing in the room, me screaming at him...not being able to breathe.

How in the world would I ever face Tanner again?

I dragged myself to my feet and, after stripping down, I stepped under the warm spray. It was a nice shower— multiple body jets and an overhead rain showerhead. I liked to think the drenching and pounding washed away all the lingering alcohol seeping out of my pores.

Brushing my teeth twice, I practically made love to the mouthwash before I pulled on a lightweight maxi dress and quietly sneaked downstairs. It was too early for anyone else to be up and even though I wanted—*needed*—coffee and its wonderful caffeine, I didn't want the aroma to turn the house into a Folgers coffee commercial. So I settled for iced tea that I took outside.

Tired and my head thumping dully, I set the tea aside and padded over to the side of the pool. My toes curled as I stared at the water. I felt...detached from last night. Like it hadn't been me who'd gotten so drunk or had freaked out. Just a movie I watched or something I was a bystander to. But that was how it always felt after an attack, and it *had* been me.

Lifting my head, I closed my eyes and I tried not to think, but it was a quiet moment. My body tensed, and I wasn't sure what I was preparing myself for, but every muscle trembled.

When I opened my eyes, nothing had changed.

I walked over to the lounge chair and sat down, tucking my feet under the hem of my dress. Since it was so early, the sticky humidity and the overbearing heat hadn't rolled in yet. The sky was cloudless, a beautiful blue that...that reminded me of Tanner's eyes.

Tanner.

My shoulders rose with a deep sigh. Last night had been such a disaster. I hadn't planned on drinking as much as I had, and I'd be lying if I said I didn't know why I'd done it. After what happened between Tanner and me, I'd been a nervous wreck, especially after Kyler and Syd had returned. Besides being thoroughly confused, everything had changed between us. I could no longer be around him and see him just as a friend. Now I was conscious of every little thing I did or said in front of him, and looking back, I knew I had let my head make more of a deal out of his behavior Thursday night than it should have and I had started drinking yesterday so I could relax. That had been the plan, but like Tanner had said, I hadn't stopped.

I never stopped at one or two drinks, because I didn't know how.

Closing my eyes, I let myself sink into the cushion as I sipped the tea. A huge part of me wanted to shout at the top of my lungs that I didn't have a problem. I wasn't the dreaded A-word. I knew what an alcoholic looked like.

An image of my father formed in my thoughts.

For many, many years, he'd hidden the truth from his colleagues, but not from us. Every moment he was home, he drank. Didn't matter if it was my birthday or Brody's. Or Thanksgiving or Christmas. So many special moments he'd missed, passed out on the deck or in his bedroom. Ten years ago, when Mom had threatened to leave him, he'd sobered up, started going to AA meetings and all that jazz. It had been a rough start and he'd had to take a sabbatical from his practice, but he'd made it through.

I wasn't like my dad.

I didn't drink every day, but…as I drew in another shaky breath, I opened my eyes. I wasn't stupid. Alcoholism didn't mean someone drank all the time, but I didn't have that problem. No way. I would not slip down that rabbit hole, especially after seeing what it had done to my family. I wasn't that weak.

Maybe I did drink too much on occasion. Okay. I totally did that. And maybe very few people who knew me in real life actually took me seriously because of it. And maybe… God, I was a mess with or without a drink sometimes.

A lot of times.

Sipping the tea, I let my gaze wander over the tall pines surrounding the backyard. What in the world was I going to do about Tanner? Just the thought of him caused my chest to clench. He thought I was *a mess*.

That…that had hurt. Still tore through me, because I *was* a mess. I'd proved that last night, hadn't I?

Blinking back the sudden rush of tears, I gave a little shake of my head. I felt like I'd disappointed him somehow. Like I had let down my parents when I'd told them I no longer wanted to go to med school. Like I'd disappointed

Sydney when she had kindly suggested that I talk to someone when she discovered I had anxiety attacks and I'd told her that I didn't need to talk to anyone.

But worse yet, I was disappointed in myself, and I couldn't go back and change anything.

The last couple of times that I'd had *that* feeling of being overwhelmed and out of control, I'd been able to stop it before I'd needed meds. It had been well over a year and then some since I'd actually had one. If I hadn't been so drunk, I knew I would've been able to stop it. I just knew it.

The sliding glass door opened and I looked over, my heart lodging in my throat when I saw that it was Tanner. Sleep clung to his eyes. The shadow of growth along his jaw gave him a rough, sexy appearance. Normally, he was so clean-shaven. He only had on a pair of flannel bottoms as he stopped in the middle of the deck, raising a hand and idly rubbing his palm against the center of his chest.

I was struck mute, partly embarrassed about last night, and his disheveled look was really just too damn attractive for this early in the morning. When I rolled out of bed, I looked like a redheaded Chewbacca.

"Hey," he said, his voice gruff as he lowered his arm. "You're up early."

I nodded, clutching my tea to my chest. "I…I got a lot of sleep last night."

He nodded slowly, and when he didn't respond, the silence stretched out between us until it became so awkward that my cheeks started to burn. I was about to get up and flee, which probably also included shoving my head under a blanket, when Tanner cleared his throat.

"Mind if I sit?" He jerked his chin at the space at the end of the lounge chair I sat on.

Pressing my lips together, I shook my head. Quiet, I watched him sit down, resting his arms on his bent knees. I knew we were going to have *a talk* after last night, but I'd really hoped it wouldn't be this soon, because I had no idea what to really think about everything and I felt like I needed a hard drink to fortify myself for this conversation.

Well, *that* wasn't the right thought to have, all things considered.

He angled his head toward me and his troubled gaze met mine. My stomach dipped as his shoulders tensed. "About last night," he started, voice low. "I want you to know that… what you went through? The anxiety attack? I wish I'd known you had those."

And I wished he'd never found out.

"I would've liked to have been able to help you through it, but I want you to know that I don't think anything… weird about it. That I don't think any differently about you because of it."

Only a very little part of me believed that to be true.

"I want to get back to all of that. I want to learn more about it," he continued. "But, first, I need to tell you this. I shouldn't have said what I did, the way I said it."

A moment passed. "No. You shouldn't have," I agreed, lowering my gaze to my half-drunk tea. "But…you were right about it. I'm a—"

"You're not a mess," he cut in.

If only he really knew how messy my head was sometimes. That attack last night? Just the tip of a Titanic-sized fucked-up iceberg.

"Seriously," he continued. "That was a dickhead move. I shouldn't have said that. So I'm sorry. Really, I am." He paused. "I've been saying 'I'm sorry' a lot lately."

"You have," I murmured, setting the tea on the small, round table beside the lounge. "Tanner, I don't…I don't know what to say."

He stretched out his legs, wiggling his toes. "I worry about you," he said after a moment, surprising me. I'd vaguely recalled him saying something like that last night. "I didn't mean to lose my cool with you. It's just that you—"

"I drink," I finished for him, flushing. "That doesn't make me an alcoholic."

Tanner didn't respond for a long moment and then he raised his shoulders in a helpless shrug, and I knew my statement had fallen like a pile of bricks between us. A few may have landed on my head. I folded my arms around my waist, wishing I had something other than my word to back up what I'd just said, but I really didn't.

What I did say, I hadn't planned on. "I'm single because I haven't dated anyone that made me want to put the effort into a relationship."

His features tensed. "Andrea—"

"The guys I date aren't really relationship-worthy," I said, and I couldn't shut up. Once I opened my mouth, the words kept coming. "There are guys that are. Like you and Kyler. The ones you want to latch onto and never let go. And there are guys who are good for going out with to the bar and maybe spending a couple of hours with. Hooking up. Nothing more. You bring them home, hoping they don't puke all over the place." I laughed hoarsely as he watched me. "That is, *if* you bring them home. So, none of them I've ever wanted to be in a relationship with. Hell, half of them I wouldn't look twice at while sober."

His brows knitted.

"Well, let me just clarify, that it's not like an entire football team worth of guys I've been with. Nothing like that, but that's not the point." I shrugged. "I'm just the female version of them."

"What?" Shock colored his tone.

"You know. I'm not really relationship-worthy. I'm the girl who drinks too much, does stupid shit, and is either really funny when drunk or really annoying." My lips trembled even though my tone was light. "I *am* a mess. I know that."

"No." Tanner shook his head. "You are not that. You're not a mess. You *are* relationship-worthy, Andrea." He twisted toward me, expression taut. "Fuck. What I said last night—I'm sorry. I'm really sorry if it makes you think that."

I waved my hand. It was dismissive, but that was the last thing I felt. Nothing about this was something I could throw away. "I know what I am, Tanner. I know what guys think when they see me at a bar. It's the same thing I think when I see one of them. Good for a few things, nothing long-term."

"Don't say that."

Meeting his gaze, I smiled weakly. "I'm not trying to wallow in self-pity or make you feel bad for me. I just know what you all—"

He moved incredibly fast. Standing, he reached down and cupped my cheeks, tilting my head back. I had a second to take a breath as shock held me immobile. He lowered his head to mine.

Tanner kissed me.

# Chapter 19

**Andrea**

His mouth on mine was the last thing I expected. Shocked straight to the core, I didn't move. Every muscle in my body locked up, and I wasn't even sure if I breathed or not. He was kissing me again.

And dammit, he *really* knew how to kiss.

Tanner swept his lips over mine, once and then twice, the touch slight and soft as a whisper. In the back of my mind, I couldn't remember being kissed so…so gently. Like he was asking permission for more with the touch of his mouth. All of the kisses I could ever recall were hard and wet and oftentimes messy, but this was soft and warm and so incredibly tender. A lot like the ones before, but this…this felt different.

He tilted his head to the side and the pressure of his mouth increased sweetly as he curved his hand around the nape of my neck. My brain clicked off, and the entire conversation faded away like smoke caught in a fierce wind, as did everything I'd been feeling up to that moment. All I could feel was his kiss.

And then he took it beyond the questioning tenderness.

He made this sound in the back of his throat when my lips parted to his, and that questioning kiss became something else, something deeper and more sensual. His tongue glided over mine, and he tasted of mint. I decided in that moment that was the best flavor in the world.

My heart pounded and my pulse skipped fast-forward, and his hand tightened along the back of my neck, his long fingers tangling in my still-damp curls. His mouth moved over mine in determination and when his tongue flicked over the roof of my mouth, there was no stopping the breathy moan.

Tanner shifted, stretching his long and lean body over mine as he guided me down against the lounge, pressing my back into the thick cushion with his weight. Oh dear. My hands fluttered to his shoulders. My heart moved into cardiac-episode territory. His chest was warm, seeping through the thin material of my dress. His other hand drifted over my hip and then squeezed, wringing a gasp from me.

My hands tightened on his shoulders, the blunt tips of my nails digging in. What he was doing was like taking a cannonball to my senses. Every part of me was scattered by the pure pleasure of a kiss, and I'd...I'd never been kissed like *this* before. Like I was something to cherish and worship. Like Tanner was doing everything to hold himself back from going for more, and I could feel the restraint in the taut lines of his body, in the way his body trembled and his hand clenched my hip.

When he lifted his mouth from mine, a sound I barely recognized came out of me. His answering chuckle was deep, husky, and when he rested his forehead against mine, I blinked my eyes open. I was in a daze.

And I said the first thing that came to mind. "What was that for?"

Tanner laughed again, and I could feel it rumbling through my body. "Only you would ask what a kiss is for." He slid his hand up to my waist, leaving a wake of shivers in his path. "You're worth a million times more than what you give yourself credit for."

All I could do was stare.

His eyes were a brilliant blue, the shade of the sky above us. "And I want to punch myself in the fucking nuts for putting that kind of thought in your head." He paused.

"Well, not right now. I think I'd do permanent damage if I did that at this second."

I blinked slowly as my hand slipped down to his chest. Under my palm, I could feel his heart beating nearly as fast as mine. "You didn't…" I swallowed hard. "You didn't put that thought in my head."

He cocked his head to the side. A moment passed between us. "Was it there before?"

The truth of what I'd just admitted was like being doused in ice water. Pressing against his chest, relief flooded me as he lifted up and returned to where he'd been sitting before our mouths had decided to get super-friendly with one another. I needed that space in that moment. My thoughts and feelings were all over the place, swirling together and forming a cyclone of messy emotions that whipped away the warmth of the kiss.

I shook my head, wishing I'd kept my mouth shut. I was sure "emotionally unstable" was already added to the list of traits Tanner probably strung together whenever he thought of me, but I really didn't need to add to it. Actually, he seemed to think highly of me. My heart did a little flip, but my stomach dipped when I realized his good opinion of me wouldn't last long. It hadn't before, so why would now be any different?

My lips still tingled from the kiss, but there was a sudden, sharp stabbing pain in my chest that felt so very real. It stole my breath and twisted up my insides. Tanner wasn't the person who made me feel like…like I wasn't *worth it.* Yeah, he'd said some crap that kind of reinforced it, but that thought—that mentality—had always been there, under my skin and dipping every thought in acidic bitterness. To be honest, that…that had always been in my head, ever since I was a young girl. There was no real reason other than *me* being the reason. I hadn't been bullied as a child. My heart had never really been broken. Sure, it had been wounded but never shattered. My father had been a drunk, but I'd grown up in a loving family with all the means in the world. I had access to more things than most, but my head…

My head just didn't work right.

The moment someone like Tanner truly realized that, he wasn't going to want anything to do with me. And I needed to be so very careful with that, because despite what'd happened when I'd been a freshman and he'd gotten with my roommate, he was the kind of guy who was worth it, and losing someone like him would surely smash my heart to smithereens.

"Andy," Tanner said as he placed his hand on my arm. "Talk to me."

Drawing in a shallow breath, I looked at him and I wanted him to kiss me again. I really did. And I wanted him to pull me into his arms. I really wanted that, but that's not what I did. I sorted through all the emotions churning inside me and I mentally recoiled from the spark of hope and anticipation that blossomed in my chest. I settled on the one tangible thing I always latched onto, the one emotion that protected me no matter what.

Anger.

It was the wrong thing. I knew that and I also knew the kind of sadness I felt, the restlessness that seemed to invade my very core, it was more destructive than any risk I could take, but I couldn't…couldn't do this. "I don't want to talk to you." As his eyes widened with surprise, I swung my legs off the lounge and stood. "And I prefer to pretend that nothing happened between us."

Tanner drew back like I'd kicked him in the face, and I didn't feel a moment of satisfaction. There was only a riptide of frustration and bitter self-loathing that chewed through me like a cancer.

Our gazes met, and the stark disbelief in his stare was hard to acknowledge, but even harder to look upon was the twinge of hurt I saw lurking in there. Guilt flooded my system, and I turned away.

I'd made it to the door, my fingers brushing over the handle when his voice stopped me.

"Don't walk away from me," he said. "Please."

**Tanner**

Coming to my feet, I was prepared to chase her ass down if she ignored me and opened that door. There was no way I was letting her walk away after what'd just happened. No fucking way.

My heart pounded like a steel drum and my pulse was still thrumming. All from a kiss—a simple kiss. Never had a kiss made me feel like that, and I'd be damned if she stomped all over it with absolutely no explanation.

Andrea faced me, her face pale enough that the freckles stood out. She opened her mouth, but didn't speak.

I took a step toward her, stopping when I saw her hands close into fists. Knowing her, I wouldn't be surprised if she threw a punch. "I didn't intend on doing that. Kissing you," I admitted. "But I sure as hell do not regret doing it or anything we've shared, and you're going to stand there and tell me you do?"

Her throat worked on a swallow. "I didn't say that."

"You didn't?" My brows flew up. "You want to pretend I didn't just kiss you? That you didn't kiss me back?"

Color poured across her cheeks. "I didn't kiss you back."

"Oh, bullshit, Andy, you kissed me back. We both know that," I said. "Your tongue was dancing just as much as mine was. Both of us are damn old enough to admit we liked something. I more than liked that. You can't tell me you didn't."

She looked away, shaking her head as she folded her arms under her chest. "You...you don't remember."

"What?" I ran my hand over my head, clasping the back of my neck. "Are you talking about the classes you said we shared?" I still couldn't believe that. There was no way I wouldn't remember her.

"See? You don't even remember seeing me, not once, but I noticed you." The words came out in a rush, almost too hard to follow. "I had the biggest crush on you and every time we had class, I tried to work up the nerve to talk to you." She laughed hoarsely. "Yeah. I was…I was practically horrified by the notion of going up to you and doing something stupid, but I never did work up the courage. Or maybe my roommate Clara just got to you first."

There was that name again. *Clara.* I lowered my hand as a weird sensation filled me. Her roommate got to me first. I felt my stomach dip as an old, worn-out memory wiggled free—of me and this girl I'd met one night, at a UMD game….

Oh shit.

She stared at the deck. "I came back to the dorm late one night, and normally Clara hung a sock around the doorknob if she had someone with her, but she didn't. I opened the door and—"

"You saw me with her," I finished as the spotty memory formed. "Shit, Andy. I barely remember her."

She snorted. "Nice."

I winced. "Yeah, okay, that sounds bad, but it's true. I remember the door to the room opening, but when I looked—"

"When you stopped screwing my roommate long enough to look," she corrected.

Wow. Okay. "You're right. Shit. I don't know what to say, but I didn't know you back then. I wish I had." The truth of that statement surprised even me. "But I didn't, and it's probably a good thing. Obviously, I was a man-whore back then."

"You're not now?"

She was baiting me. I knew that, and, boy did it take everything for me not to fall for it. I felt like shit knowing that she had walked in on something like that. "I know this is no excuse, but we didn't know each other. Not really. I'm sorry if I hurt you—"

"Just forget about it," she snapped quickly, lifting a hand and thrusting her fingers through her hair. Curls shot in every direction. "It doesn't matter now."

"Obviously it fucking matters, because you're still holding it against me," I shot back. Striving to stay cool, I took a deep breath. "I am sorry, Andrea. Really. You walking in on something like that isn't cool. The fact I don't remember you isn't either. Especially when you liked me. Did you really have a crush on me?" I said, hoping to lighten the conversation.

Frowning, she still didn't look at me. "I did."

My stomach dipped a little. "You *still* do."

Her shoulders rose with a sigh, and it seemed like she was about to say something, but the door behind her opened and Kyler stuck his head out. He looked like he'd literally just woken up as he gave us a sleepy look.

"We're hitting the road soon," he announced. "But I'm going to make omelets."

I started to tell Kyler he could shove the omelets in a place that would probably upset Syd, but what he said sank in. "Hitting the road?"

"Yeah." He stepped out, shutting the door behind him. "Syd and I talked it over, and we think it's best if we go ahead and cut this short and head home."

"What?" Andrea said. "Why? We have two more days left."

Kyler scrubbed his fingers through his messy hair. "We know, but both of us are ready to just get back to our place."

I was calling bullshit on this.

So was Andrea. "It's because of last night, isn't it?' Her voice cracked, and I took a step toward her, wanting to somehow comfort her. "That's why you all want to leave?"

Kyler dropped his arm and opened his mouth, but Andrea rushed on, clasping her hands across her waist. "I'm not going to drink anymore and I won't fight with Tanner. Please."

Damn, it was like having a hot poker shoved in my chest and feeling it twist as she continued. "I promise. I don't want to be the reason you guys have to leave. I know how much you two were looking forward to this."

"That's not the reason," Kyler said softly, too quietly. "We're just ready to head home."

"But what about fishing? I remember Syd mentioning something about fishing." Andrea's gaze swung to mine, her eyes wide and pleading for me to somehow change this. "There's still stuff to do."

"She's right," I jumped in. "Man, you guys don't have to do this."

Kyler drew in a deep breath and he smiled, but it didn't quite reach his eyes. "We're leaving in about two hours." His tone said the decision had been made. He reached for the door, sliding it open. "But I'm going to make some omelets. With green peppers and mushrooms. Yum."

Andrea didn't move as she stared at the closed glass door, but then she turned to me, her lower lip trembling. "I've ruined everything."

# Chapter 20

*Andrea*

Although the omelets smelled amazing, after one bite the fluffy eggs and veggies turned to sawdust in my mouth. I couldn't eat or force myself to pretend that I could. Between blurting out how I'd first met Tanner and then Kyler's announcement, I was ready to go cry somewhere. I dumped my food and quickly washed the plate, leaving the kitchen to find Syd. I didn't look at Tanner as I left the kitchen.

Syd was in their room, packing. I hesitated at the door, feeling like absolute crap. Guilt churned restlessly as she glanced over her shoulder at me. "Thank you for last night," I said, watching her fold a shirt. "For helping me. I appreciate it."

"It's no big deal. It's a practice run for me, right?" she teased. "You're feeling better?"

I nodded. My headache was partly due to the anxiety attack and mostly because I'd gotten plastered. "Syd, we don't have to leave."

Syd dropped a ball of socks into the suitcase and turned toward me. Her expression was pinched, somber. "Yeah, we do."

"But—"

"Both of us are ready to go home, and it's actually calling for rain again, later tonight and all day tomorrow. So if we stayed, we'd be stuck inside," she continued. "And honestly, none of us need cabin fever."

I shifted my weight from one foot to the next. "It's because of last night, isn't it? I promise—"

"Andrea, you know I love you. You're my best friend. Seriously." She sighed as she walked over to me, and I tensed. "I just don't think this is good for you right now. Honestly, I probably shouldn't have pushed you toward Tanner. That wasn't a smart move."

My mouth dried as my stomach tightened.

She looked up at me with all seriousness. "I know you haven't told me that anything happened between you two, but I'm not stupid. Something did, and maybe it shouldn't have, not right now."

"Not right now?" I heard myself repeat.

Sydney drew in a deep breath and let it out slowly. She squared her shoulders, and I prepared for a blow. "Like I said, I love you. I do. And it…it kills me to see the way you were last night. You never would've gotten to that point if you hadn't drunk so much. And you know, deep down, that is true."

I did. I *so* did.

"What you need right now isn't a guy," she said quietly. "What you need is help."

*You need help.*

Those words recycled over and over in my head. She hadn't stopped there. She'd talked about meetings and therapy and getting to the root of *my problem*. I was like a chunk of ice by the time I left her room and started gathering up my stuff.

*You need help.*

My brain couldn't shake those three words, couldn't let them go. I felt like I was going to be sick. Like at any given minute, I could just hurl all over the shorts I was stacking in my suitcase.

*You need help.*

Was it that bad? Was I that bad? I'd just made a stupid decision last night. Well, a stupid decision fueled by other dumb decisions that were rooted in a whole bunch of idiocy. If I could just stop making dumb decisions, I'd be fine.

I'd just shoved my undies into the suitcase when I felt a presence behind me. I didn't even need to turn to see who it was. I just knew. It was the guy that I apparently didn't need.

"I really don't want to talk," I said when he didn't speak.

There was a pause. "I think that's the problem. You never *want* to talk when you really *need* to talk."

I laughed hoarsely. "Jesus." I slammed my makeup caddy into the suitcase and whirled around. He'd changed from earlier, wearing jeans and a worn shirt that clung to his broad shoulders. "Is today the day when everyone tells me all about all my problems? Because if so, can we fast forward to the part where I say none of this is fucking news to me?"

Tanner blinked, taken aback. "Okay. Look—"

"No. There is no 'okay' or 'looking.'" My voice shook. "We ruined this for them. Or I ruined it for them. It doesn't matter. This trip was ruined. Okay? So there's really nothing I want to talk about right now."

He opened his mouth and then closed it. A long moment stretched out between us, and in that time, I wanted so much—so damn much. I wanted to redo this whole trip, our whole freaking relationship. I wanted to cross the little distance between us and throw my arms around him, because it wasn't that I *needed* Tanner. I *wanted* him. I wanted to tell him that I was sorry, but I wasn't sure what I was even sorry for or what I *wasn't* sorry for.

And all I did was stand there and stare at him.

"Okay. You don't want to talk. You don't want to figure out what's going on between us. I respect that." He exhaled loudly. "That's why I'm not going to force this. I'm not going to chase you down once we leave here. You come to me when you're ready, and if you don't? Well, that's a damn shame, because I think that no matter what is going on in your head, we could have something real between us."

My tongue wouldn't move. My jaw was locked down, because whatever Tanner thought we had between us would swan-dive out the window when he really got to know me.

Tanner's shoulders rose with another deep breath as he rubbed the palm of his hand over his chest, above his heart. His voice was flat when he spoke, and his gaze distant, almost cold. "Later, then."

He left the room without so much as a glance back. I closed my eyes, holding my breath until my lungs started to burn, and I went beyond that moment, right up until when I had to drag in air.

"Later" didn't sound like a promise. "Later" sounded almost like a goodbye. "Later" was totally expected.

As expected, the ride home was a sad and awkward affair. There were no long or teasing looks between Tanner and me. Kyler wasn't grinning at us in the rearview mirror. Syd had her nose buried in her eReader, and that was about the only thing that was similar to the trip up.

The sky was overcast and cruddy, and as we drew closer to Maryland, it started to drizzle. Tanner was the first one to be dropped off.

He climbed out, hesitating as our eyes met, and then he closed the door. I pressed my lips together and told myself not to look when he walked out from behind the car with his duffel bag, but I did.

I looked up, peering out the window. He stopped by my side, tapped the window, and then moved on to Kyler's window. "I'll text you later," he told him, and then he was off.

Tanner didn't speak to me, not that I was expecting that, but my chest still ached. When Kyler pulled up in front of my apartment, Syd followed me upstairs.

I stepped inside, suddenly weary to my very bones. Dropping my suitcase just inside the door, I faced my very closest friend. Neither of us said anything, and I almost said the things I'd never said to her before.

"I'm sorry," was all that came out of my mouth.

Sydney's smile was somewhat sad as she said, "I know."

The next few days flat-out sucked.

I spent them in my apartment, ignoring the calls from my mom and dad. I knew nothing had happened, because if so, Brody would've showed up. I just wasn't in the mood to deal with them. They'd mean well, of course, but I never felt like I…like they were proud of me when I got off the phone with them. Their disappointment always lingered like a festering wound.

I'd slept most of Sunday and Monday away, holed up in my bed. At some point during that time, I decided I needed a dog or a cat. Weird and random, but I thought then maybe my place wouldn't seem so cold and empty.

By Tuesday afternoon, I'd ventured out of my bedroom and ended up spending the majority of the day roaming around my apartment aimlessly. So much was floating around in my head, and I wanted to talk to Syd, but I didn't want to bother her. Although she hadn't said she was upset, I knew she had to be. I didn't blame her. I was pissed at myself.

I needed a change.

Standing in my living room, I took a drink of the beer I had left in my fridge while I turned in a slow circle. I ran my fingers through my hair. I didn't like where the TV was, and that was an easy fix. Over the next hour, I moved the television to the other side of the room, dragged the couch across the floor, and rearranged the leaning bookshelves. My arms ached as I studied the walls. Maybe I needed to paint. It wouldn't be the first time. I'd gone through at least three different colors since I'd moved in, and now I was regretting going back to the sandy beige color.

Maybe that's what I'd do tomorrow.

I still had a couple of weeks before classes started, and I wasn't volunteering that week, so obviously I had time. Plenty of time.

*You need help.*

Sleep last night was elusive, even with the help of the sleep aid and the three beers I'd drunk. I hadn't meant to drink that much, and I wondered if it was somehow counter-effective to the sleeping pill. I shouldn't have taken it, but I kind of forgot that I'd been drinking when I'd popped it in my mouth. Or maybe I just didn't care.

I lay in bed, unable to shut my head down. I kept picking up my phone, but who would I call? Syd would be asleep, and I couldn't call Tanner, but damn, I wanted to. I had no idea what to say to him.

He'd told me there might be something real between us, but he…gosh, he deserved better than *this*.

So I played a game. Then I checked Facebook. Then played another game. Finally, around four in the morning, I drifted off to sleep, not really even looking forward to tomorrow, because I figured it would be like today. Today sucked, much like yesterday and the day before.

I slept most of Wednesday away, but it wasn't a useful type of sleep. I never seemed to hit a deep enough level and when I did, I dreamt of being in a house, and I couldn't find my way out. In the dream, I wasn't alone, but I could never find the person who was there with me. They seemed one step ahead, and I was simply lost, never finding the correct door, the one that would let me out.

The quiet moments were getting to me.

Around six, I drank the last apple-cider-flavored beer, but that didn't relax me. Nothing was on TV, and I dismissed the idea of rearranging my bedroom. The only thing left to do was to get the paint. At least I could do that. Maybe I'd invite Syd over, and we could have a painting party. I could get one of those cheese and meat platters. And I could also get a slew of hot guy movies—movies with Theo James and Jude Law and Tom Hardy and other hot British dudes. Were all of them British? I didn't know. Their voices were hot and that was all that mattered.

Grabbing my purse and keys, I headed out to where my Lexus was parked and made my way to Lowe's. Before I headed in, I texted Syd a quick rundown of my plans and then found myself standing in front of a million and one paint choices.

Well, crap.

Probably should've decided on a color. It took a God-awful amount of time before I settled on a charcoal gray and even longer to find someone to mix the damn paint. Two hours had passed by the time I'd made it back to my car and into the grocery store down the street.

It wasn't until after I picked up the yummy summer sausage dish that I realized I hadn't heard my phone ding. Sitting in the parking lot, I dug my phone out of my bag and saw that Syd had texted me back.

*Not 2night. Maybe this weekend.*

Disappointment rose so swiftly, it was like being caught in a summer storm. I stared for so long at the text, the words blurred. I tossed the phone back in my purse and I sat there, staring at the empty car across from me.

Now what in the hell was I supposed to do with the summer sausage? Probably should've checked my texts before I'd bought the stuff. I rolled my eyes. God, that was stupid.

Anger flashed through me like a strike of heat lightning. It was irrational. I had no reason to be mad at Syd. Wasn't like this was planned. Wasn't like she had a need to hang out with me after this weekend. Wasn't like—

I cut those thoughts off, dug my phone out of my bag, and then sent her a quick *okay*. My attention wandered back to the vacant truck. I couldn't go home. I'd go crazy if I went back to my apartment.

I didn't even remember driving to the bar that we usually hung out at together. With college not back in yet and being the middle of the week, the place was pretty dull. As I crossed the floor I'd danced on more times than I could remember, I grabbed one of the many empty stools at the bar.

"Hey there," the bartender moseyed on up, smiling. He was cute. Older. I think he recognized me. "What can I get you?"

As I played with my phone, I considered a beer. "How about a Long Island?"

"Coming up." He wiped his hands on the towel. "Tab or pay as you go?"

"Pay," I mumbled as I dug out my wallet. Seemed ridiculous to run a tab on a Wednesday night.

My eyes watered when I took the first drink of the Long Island Iced Tea. Goodness, it was strong, but I slurped it up, welcoming the burn as it blazed down my throat and chest.

I finished off the drink and then ordered a beer as I glanced around the bar. A few guys were by one of the two pool tables. One of them looked vaguely familiar. My gaze moved on as I drank. At the other end of the bar were two middle-aged men. They looked…tired.

"Another?"

Surprised, I glanced up at the bartender. "Excuse me?"

"Drink." He gestured at the bottle with his hand. "Do you want another? You're out."

My brows furrowed as I glanced down. Holy crap, I was. When in the world did that happen? "Sure," I said. "Just one more."

The words seemed to laugh at me, because when he showed up with the drink, he also placed a glass of water in front of me.

Wednesday night and I was at a bar. Alone. At least my tummy was warm.

I glanced down at my phone as I thumbed through my contacts. I stopped when I got to Tanner. Was he working?

I bit down on my lip. He'd told me to call him when I was ready to talk, but that was a big question. Was I ready? Because talking….

The sounds of the bar increased around me as I stared at his name. Talking went beyond him and me, didn't it? Talking meant being honest about more than just us. I mean, after all, I was sitting—

"Hello."

I jolted at the sound of a male voice and looked up. A guy around my age stood beside me. He was kind of cute, I thought as I stared up at him, and he'd been one of the guys over by the pool table. I glanced around. He was talking to me. "Hi."

He leaned against the bar, grinning. "It's been a while."

Um.

Reaching out with one arm, he tapped mine. "I haven't seen you around."

Oh crap. Did I know this guy? I *knew* knew this guy, didn't I?

He cocked his head to the side and then laughed under his breath. "You don't remember me, do you?" He laughed again, and I felt my cheeks start to heat. "Man, wow."

I winced. "I'm sorry…"

"Ah, it's okay. It was a wild night. Lots of tequila." He winked, and my stomach dropped so fast, I thought it fell out of me. "You drinking tonight? I can get you a drink."

Oh my God.

Understanding smacked me in the face with the force of a baseball bat. Vague and wispy memories surfaced of him… and his truck—his truck that smelled like fast food, and I had—

I averted my gaze, suddenly sick to my stomach. An ugly tide of embarrassment washed over me, suffocating with its severity. I should've stayed home, stuffed my face with summer sausage and cheese, and painted the damn walls myself.

Except the walls…the walls weren't the problem.

I didn't need *a* change, I realized. Rearranging my living room wasn't going to change anything. Painting my apartment wasn't going to do it. Getting a pet wasn't going to make me any happier. *I* needed to change.

"Babe," he cooed, reaching out and brushing the back of his hand across my cheek. "You still here?"

Jerking back from his touch, I grabbed my phone and shoved it into my bag. I slipped off the barstool. "Sorry. I have to go."

I didn't look back as I rushed outside and all but darted into my car. Breathing heavy, I climbed in and hit the button for the engine. "Holy fuck. Shit. Damn."

My heart was pounding as I pulled out of the parking lot, heading for the interstate. I kept repeating those words, over and over. Holy fuck. Shit. Damn. I clenched the steering wheel to stop my hands from shaking as I merged onto the highway. It was virtually empty, so fucking empty. I started to shift over to the other lane. Headlights suddenly appeared in the rearview mirror. My poor heart lurched as I jerked the steering wheel to the right.

Everything happened so fast.

My car veered sharply to the right, too sharp. I tried to overcorrect, and panicked, slamming my foot down. The car lurched and the back started to spin. Lights spun. I dragged in a breath to—

A thundering force stopped the car and lifted it up. Metal crunched and gave way. I was tossed forward and to the side, suspended for a moment. Something white exploded. Powder flew everywhere. The crunching kept coming, like giant jaws eating away. Lights burst behind my eyes and then there was nothing.

# Chapter 21

**Tanner**

I stared at my phone, not paying attention to the hum of conversation buzzing around me. There was a game on the TV, and one of the guys was talking about some girl he'd met over the weekend.

I hadn't heard from Andrea since we'd gotten back, and damn, it was taking every ounce of my willpower not to call her. The fact I had to fight it so hard sort of ticked me off, but I'd done a lot of thinking over the last three days, and that I had to resist calling her spoke volumes.

I cared about her—*really* cared about her.

What I felt for her went beyond what I'd felt for other girls that had been in my life. Even before the trip to the cabin, I looked forward to seeing her, to getting on each other's nerves. To watch her cheeks flush with amusement and to hear her husky laugh. And now I wanted to feel her lips graze mine and to hear the soft sounds she made when I pleased her. To just be around her and have a thousand tomorrows with her.

These kinds of feelings had a name. I knew that. I didn't know how long I'd felt this way or what woke me up to realize it, but none of that really mattered. Nothing was going to change that. It was just how I was wired internally. Once I felt something or made a decision, I stuck to it. The end.

And I'd made the decision to let Andrea come to me. As much as it killed me, I was sticking to it. There was something going on with her and I had a feeling it didn't have anything to do with the anxiety attack she'd had. I wanted to be there for her, but she had to *let* me be there. I couldn't force it. Shit never turned out well when you did it that way.

But the shit she'd said, about her not being worth it? It made it so damn hard to stay away, because how in the hell would I prove to her that she was very much worth it by staying away from her?

"Yo. Hammond?"

My head snapped up. Daniels was standing a few feet from me, arms crossed over the gray company shirt. "What?"

"Just making sure you're alive over there." He grinned. "You've been staring at your phone like it's the hottest chick in this city."

I rolled my eyes as I slipped my phone into my pocket and then sat back, stretching out my legs. "The phone's more interesting than anything *you've* got to say."

Daniels laughed. "You wound me, man. Freaking wound—"

Static crackled across the speakers a second before dispatch's voice echoed through the fire hall. "Single motor vehicle accident with possible entrapment. EMT en route. Company 10 responding. Company 70 on standby." The voice rattled off the location of the MVA. I stiffened.

The TV muted and conversation lulled. Our company had moved to standby. If they were going to call out more than one company, the accident had left a mess behind. Company 10 was obviously going to handle the entrapment. We'd cover traffic if necessary.

"Shit," muttered Daniels as he dropped into the seat beside mine. "I hate accidents with entrapment."

Very rarely did an accident involving entrapment end with the person walking out on their own two legs.

I nodded as another guy roamed into the room, pulling up his turnouts. I already had mine on. All on duty moved out to the truck and waited for further instructions. We were ready to roll out if dispatch moved us out of standby.

The room was relatively silent as we waited to hear more. A handful of minutes passed.

"Entrapment confirmed. Company 10 is beginning extraction methods," Dispatch announced, the voice monotone. "EMS on scene. Patient is unresponsive. Medevac 1 on standby. Company 70 remain on standby."

Shit. I scrubbed my hand across my jaw. Calling on an air ambulance to move to standby wasn't uncommon if there was entrapment, if the patient was unresponsive, and if they couldn't get to the patient to assess the full extent of the injuries.

I exchanged a look with Daniels, and figured he was remembering the last extraction we'd done. It had been a kid and that call…yeah, that call hadn't ended well. No one had walked away from it.

"Patient is out of vehicle…Priority 1."

"Fuck," I said, closing my eyes. Priority 1 meant there was basically a heartbeat, one code above Priority 0, which in other words, was a DRT—Dead Right There.

Another voice crackled out and then dispatch confirmed, "Patient is Priority 1. EMT on scene have stabilized for transport. Medevac 1 off standby."

"That's good," murmured Daniels.

I nodded again and waited. If they were able to stabilize the person enough to transport via an ambulance, it was a good sign. Then again, it could also mean calling in the heli wasn't going to do shit in the long run.

Eventually we were called off standby and the accident scene ended up being cleared by the other company. We got a call for a fire alarm at an apartment building that turned out to be a false alarm, and then we headed out to grab a bite. Once we returned back to the fire hall, one of the EMTs from another company swung by to drop off something to one of the other guys.

I was barely paying attention when I heard Daniels ask, "You were on that MVA call earlier, weren't you?"

The EMT inclined his head. "Which one? I swear to God that's all I've responded to tonight."

"The Priority 1 call," Daniels explained. "How'd that turn out?"

"Oh. The one out on 495? Man, they had a hell of a time getting the side off to get her out of that damn car," the medic said. "We took her to Holy Cross. She had head injuries. Most likely internal ones. When we dropped her off, her pupils were still non-responsive."

I pulled out my phone, thumbing through my contacts.

"Strangest damn thing." the medic continued. "There was paint and summer sausage in the car. Weird combination."

Daniels snorted. "That is weird. Was the patient young or old?"

"Early twenties, I think. State Police were handling the notification. Pretty girl. Face a little busted up from the airbag. Damn shame." He rolled his shoulders, working out a kink. "There was no missing the smell of alcohol on her."

Icy fingers trailed down my spine. There was no other way to explain it. It's the same feeling when people say it feels like someone's walking over their grave. My thumb stilled over my phone. "What kind of car was it?"

The medic glanced in my direction. "A Lexus. A dark gray or black one."

No. No way.

Those icy fingers fisted in my gut. For a moment, I couldn't move, and then I was standing, my finger hitting Andrea's contact. I walked away from the group, ignoring Daniels calling out my name. Andrea's phone rang until voicemail picked up. Could be a coincidence. It was late. I called again. No answer. I called once more, this time leaving a message, telling her to call me.

My heart started racing as I turned around. The guys were staring at me. "What…what did she look like?"

"I don't know," the medic said, frowning. "She was cute and—"

"What was the color of her hair?" I shouted.

Daniels rose. "Hammond, you okay?"

I stalked to the medic, my hand tightening around my phone. "What was the color of her hair?"

The medic's eyes widened. "It was dark and there was blood, but I think it was red."

The floor shifted under my feet. My heart stopped in my chest. I said something to them. I don't even remember what I said, but I turned and walked outside. I called an older lady I knew, who was working that night in dispatch.

"Jodi?" I said, my voice hoarse. "It's Tanner."

"Hey, sweetie, what's going on?" she asked.

"I...I need you to do me a favor, okay? I know it's asking a lot, but please. There was a call tonight. A single MVA out on 495. A Priority 1 patient," I said. "Have they identified the passenger yet?"

"I believe so."

"What was her name?"

Jodi didn't answer immediately. "Sweetie, you know I can't give out that kind of info."

I screwed my eyes shut and forced myself to take a deep, slow breath as I paced in front of the open bay doors. Daniels was nearby, but I couldn't pay attention to him. "I know. I hate having to ask you this, but I think it's someone I know— someone I care about."

"Shit," muttered Daniels.

Jodi made a soft sound. "Oh gosh, let me...let me see what I can find out. Okay? Can you wait for a moment?"

That moment was the longest fucking stretch of time in my life, and I prayed—fuck, I prayed—during those moments. *Please not be Andrea. Please.* That's all I could think.

"You still there, Tanner?" Jodi returned. "I just talked to the trooper. Next of kin has been notified, so I feel...I feel okay with telling you who it was. Her name is Andrea Walters. She's—"

"God. It's her." I bent over at the waist. "It's her."

"Oh no, sweetie, I'm sorry…"

Jodi's voice faded out. I didn't remember hanging up the phone, but suddenly Daniels was there, placing his hand on my shoulder. I straightened.

"Go," Daniels said before I could say a word. "Get out of here and let me know when you can, okay?"

I was already halfway across the parking lot.

It was way past visiting hours when I showed up at Holy Cross, and it took a couple of minutes to find a nurse who knew me, who told me where to go, but warned I wouldn't be allowed to see her. Intensive care unit, recently moved out of surgery.

Fucking *surgery*.

As I rode the elevator up, I kept telling myself that it could still be a mistake. It had to be one. It couldn't be her. There was no way. Fuck. It couldn't be her. She would never get behind the wheel of a car after drinking. It couldn't be her.

The doors opened and I stepped out into the quiet hall. The nurses at the end didn't pay much attention to me as I wheeled a right. Maybe it was because of my uniform. I didn't care as I hurried down the chilled hall, looking above the windowless doors. I came to the end and turned left.

My feet stopped as if I'd stepped in cement.

Halfway down the hall, there was an older couple talking to a middle-aged doctor. The man was tall with brown hair and the woman was shorter with the deepest…the deepest red hair.

Both were pale as the doc reached out, clamping his hand on the man's shoulder. I couldn't hear what was being said, but the doctor spoke again, and the woman's face crumpled as she placed her hand over her mouth.

The hall spun as I stumbled against the wall. My gaze traveled to the room beyond them. The door opened and a nurse stepped out. All I could see was a curtain and a hand—a pale, small hand. It wasn't moving.

Fuck. I pressed the palm of my hand against my chest as the door drifted shut. Footsteps pounded up the hall, and I looked, recognizing the man who was only a year older than Andrea—her brother, Brody. He didn't even see me as he rushed past, his flip-flops smacking like cracks of thunder.

I leaned against the wall as it hit me, really fucking slammed into me. She was in that room. It *was* Andrea. No fucking coincidences. No point to hope there was some kind of mistake. It was her. Pain lit up my chest like someone had planted a fist in it.

My knees gave out and I slid down the wall, my ass hitting the floor. I dropped my arms over my knees and just stared ahead. It was her.

It was Andrea.

# Chapter 22

**Andrea**

The first breath I took burned and sent pain splintering throughout my chest and ribs. It hurt in a way that immediately forced my grimy-feeling eyes open. I winced at the harsh overhead lights in the drop ceiling. I tried to lift my hand to shield my eyes, but my arm felt like it was weighed down with lead.

*Sit up.* I needed to sit up, but as soon as I started that process, a sharp stabbing sensation shot across my abdomen, causing me to exhale harshly. Okay. I would not move.

A shadow moved closer to the bed, and as I blinked, a form took shape. Dad. My father was leaning over me. Deep shadows were grooved into the skin under his eyes. Taut lines formed around his mouth. His brown hair was a mess, as if he'd shoved his fingers through it many times. He hadn't shaved. When was the last time I'd seen him unshaven? Goodness, it had to be back when he still…he still drank.

Oh my God.

I had been drinking and—

"Honey, you awake?" Dad sat on the edge of the bed, and I realized his shirt was wrinkled. So were his khakis. Actually, *he* was wrinkled. "Andrea?"

I forced my tongue off the roof of my mouth. "Yeah."

He closed his eyes briefly, letting out a long and low breath. "You've been asleep for over a day. I know it's normal after these kinds of injuries, but I didn't want to leave this room until you opened your eyes. Your mother is going to be so upset to know she decided to pick up food for us at this exact moment. Are you in pain?"

Pain? *Everything* hurt—my stomach and my head, even my hand. My gaze drifted to my right hand and I suspected the giant, freaking I.V. hooked up to it was the culprit.

"Injuries?" I rasped out.

Dad reached out, picking up my left hand in his cool one. He squeezed gently. "You hit your head pretty hard. It's a concussion. And you're pretty banged up, but the…" He squeezed my hand again. "Your spleen ruptured. There was no saving it. It had to be removed, and you needed a blood transfusion. Without a spleen, there are going to be some complications. Issues with fighting off infections and…"

He continued on, but I wasn't really hearing him any longer. My spleen had burst and I no longer had one. Blood transfusion? A concussion? My mind raced back to the car, to the seconds before I heard the metal crunching and giving way.

"Did I hit someone?" I blurted out, ignoring the raw pain in my throat. "Did I hurt someone?"

Dad stopped and he stared at me so long that panic built in my chest. "Oh my God," I croaked. "Did I hit someone? Did I? Oh God, I can't—"

"You didn't hit anyone, Andrea." His throat worked as he stared down at me. "You hit a barrier wall on 495."

Only a smidgen of relief filtered through my system. I didn't hit someone. That was good, but I *could've* hit someone. Oh God, I could've *killed* someone.

"They ran a blood test. You were over the legal limit," he continued, his voice rough at the edges, brittle. "You were drinking and driving."

Pressure increased as those words settled in, seeped through the confusion and took root. I'd drunk and drove. Had I done that before? Never. I'd always waited at least an hour or more before I drove. I *always* made sure.

Oh my God.

Dad let go of my hand and his gaze moved to the blinds over the window. "I've failed you."

His words jarred me. "Dad—you didn't fail me. This... this was all me. I...did this." Truer words had never been spoken. Tears rolled down my face. "I did this."

He shook his head. "Your mother and I, even your brother, knew you drank. We kept telling ourselves that it wasn't that bad. That you weren't like me. That you wouldn't *become* like me. We were wrong." His gaze shifted to mine, and I saw that his stare was glassy. "I was wrong, but I will not let you become me."

The pressure was increasing, and it was becoming hard to breathe. In the background, I could hear the beeps from the heart monitor increasing. *It wasn't just the drinking*, I wanted to scream at him, but there were no words.

"And that's why we're stepping in right now," he continued doggedly. "As soon as you're well enough to leave the hospital, you're going into treatment. That's not up for discussion. If you say no or you fight me on this—" His voice cracked, and my shoulders shook. "I will completely cut you off."

I could barely breathe. Not because my family was forcing me into treatment. Not because all choice had been stripped away from me. No. I could barely get enough air into my lungs because I had made such a reckless, irresponsible decision. Not just one, but years' worth of them, and they all had been building and piling up on one another. I could've hurt someone—killed them. This was no longer just about me. This...this was out of control.

"Do you understand?" he asked.

I completely understood.

Before I'd left the bar, I had realized that I needed to change, and now more than ever I knew this. I wasn't going to fight this. Not now. I met my father's blue eyes and then his face blurred.

"Dad…" The tears rushed me, heedless of the sting they caused when they hit the incredibly raw splotches on my face. "There's something really wrong with me."

"I'm really proud of you."

My gaze shifted away from where Syd was perched on the edge of my bed. It was a day after I'd woken up in the hospital. I still hurt something fierce. "You shouldn't…be proud of me."

"Why not?"

I stared at the ceiling. "I drank and then I drove. I could've…" Absolutely disgusted with myself, I pressed my lips together and shook my head.

"I'm not proud that you did that," she said. "But I'm proud that you're getting help."

Closing my eyes, I sort of wished I was asleep. "It was my dad's idea."

"You could've fought it."

"He threatened to cut me off if I did," I told her, also wishing I had another blanket. It was chilly in there. "You know me. I like all my perks. Can't have that—"

"Knock it off," Syd snapped, drawing my attention. Her cheeks flushed with anger. "I talked to your dad. You didn't even *try* to fight it. Not one second. You know you need help. I'm proud that you're making that decision, so why are you acting this way?"

Why? Because I didn't deserve her kind words, and I sure as hell didn't deserve anyone to be proud of me. "I drank and I drove. I totaled my car. I don't…have a spleen anymore. I'm a loser. I'm going to have to go to court and I'm pretty sure I've lost my license. I'm not complaining. I deserve that."

My ass actually deserved to be in jail, and who knew, I might just end up there.

"Andrea…" She sighed as she tilted her head. A long length of dark hair fell over her shoulder. "You're not a loser. You—"

"I need help. I know." The wall I'd erected since my father left crumbled a smidgen. "I know."

Her lower lip trembled as she patted my hand. "When Tanner called and told us what'd happened, I thought my heart had stopped."

*Tanner.*

Now *my* heart stopped. This morning when my brother stopped by, he'd told me he'd seen Tanner the night I was brought in. At first, I'd thought that Tanner had responded to the accident, but Brody had ended up talking to him. Tanner had heard the call go out, but didn't realize until later that it had been me. When he had, he'd come straight to the hospital.

"I thought I'd lost you," she whispered, her voice wavering.

I squeezed my eyes shut again.

Several moments passed. "Kyler would've come with me, but I figured you probably didn't want a whole party in here." She paused. "Tanner wants to see you."

"I don't want to see him," I said immediately.

"He is so—"

"I can't." I looked at her then. "Please. I can't see him right now. I don't want to see him right now. I can't…I can't deal with that."

It was bad enough that Tanner had already been there. According to Brody, he'd actually been *in* this room while I'd been asleep. Embarrassment and hopelessness were an ugly, dark mixture inside me. Seeing him would break me, and I was barely holding it together. I knew I had disappointed my family. Severely. And even though Syd said she was proud of me, I knew she was also dismayed.

Syd smiled weakly. "Okay. I can respect that. I know he will."

And he would. Tanner was a good guy. He wouldn't push it. If Syd told him I didn't want to see him, he wouldn't show. Now more than ever I knew I wasn't…I wasn't worthy of someone like him. I was pretty sure my actions put me in the lowest of the low, like pond scum. Except pond scum probably had a purpose, and what was my purpose? To screw stuff up?

If so, I was exceeding expectations.

The morning I was discharged from the hospital, it was so hot that I swore I saw steam wafting off the asphalt. It was a typical August morning, except nothing was normal about that day.

I wasn't sure if anything would be normal again.

Only my dad and mom were present as I was wheeled out. No balloons or smiling faces. There really wasn't anything to celebrate, and I wasn't going home. I guessed it was a good thing I hadn't gotten a pet.

Getting into the backseat was harder than I thought since my tummy was still sore. On the seat beside me was my suitcase. Mom had packed for me. We wouldn't even be stopping at my apartment.

The ride to the treatment center was quiet, and I was okay with that. I didn't want to make small talk, to pretend that everything was okay. And I don't think my parents wanted to pretend either.

The center was outside the city, near Frederick, and in the middle of a long stretch of nothing. We took an exit I'd never even paid attention to before in any of my travels, and it took a good twenty minutes before the car hung a right. We passed a large sign with the words THE BROOK inscribed in the stone.

My first impression of the treatment center when we crested a hill was that my dad got the place wrong. This didn't look like a rehab. Oh hell no. With the rolling, manicured hills surrounding a massive, rancher-style complex, the visible tennis court, and what appeared to be a pool the size of a house, it screamed *country club* and not *rock bottom*.

Dad followed the road up and under a large awning. The entry reminded me of a hotel. Taking a deep breath, I glanced at my dad. His gaze met mine in the rearview mirror. He nodded, and I suddenly wanted to cry—wanted to throw myself on the seat and not move. But Mom climbed out of the car and opened the back door. There would be no throwing myself on the seat.

I eased out of the car, my wide eyes focused on the glass doors. My heart was pounding. Mom reached between us, threading her fingers through mine. I shuffled forward, my steps slow as my father joined us, my suitcase in his hand.

Cool air greeted us as we stepped inside a large atrium. Up ahead was a reception desk, again reminding me of a hotel. My father walked forward, stopping to speak with the woman.

"It's going to be okay," my mom whispered.

Doubtful.

I dragged in a deep breath and dull pain flared across my bruised ribs. A tremor rolled through me, and my knees shook as Dad wheeled around. His eyes met mine. To the left of the reception area, a door opened and a man stepped out.

He looked like he was in his mid-thirties, and he was rocking a mad pair of hipster, black-rimmed glasses that were as dark as his hair. He wasn't dressed like someone who worked here, not with his khaki shorts and sandaled feet.

"Andrea Walters?" He smiled at me in a pleasant way.

I jerked and glanced at my dad, then my mom. "Yeah." I cleared my throat. "Yes."

"My name is Dave Proby. Please follow me." He glanced at my parents. "You may also come."

My fingers were numb and tingly as we followed him into a small room beyond the door. There was another exit

on the other side, the window glazed over. We weren't alone. A nurse was waiting. In her hands was a blood pressure cuff.

Holy crap, this was like an episode of *Intervention*.

"Sit." Dave gestured at the green upholstered chair next to the desk.

Nervous, I did as he requested. My parents remained just inside the room. The nurse approached me, smiling gently. "I just need to take your blood pressure, hon."

I had no idea if that was normal or not, but I stuck out my arm as she asked, "Do you take any medication?"

Mouth dry, I nodded as Mom spoke up. "I brought her purse. She has sleeping pills and anxiety medication." She opened the purse and rummaged around until she found the three bottles. The nurse took them while I sat there, feeling like…well, a thousand different things. "And there are the meds the hospital has her on."

I felt incredibly small as the nurse looked over the bottles. My skin was uncomfortable and itchy as she placed them on the desk, stacking them up like a three-person red-bottled army. I wanted to shoot out of my chair and grab the bottles, throwing them through the little window, even the antibiotics.

Dave didn't speak until the nurse scribbled down my results and then handed them over to him. He sat in a small desk chair and picked up a pen. Twirling it between his fingers, he glanced over a file. "Do you have a cellphone with you?"

"Yes."

Without looking at me, he extended his arm and wiggled his fingers. "Hand it over."

I stared at his hand for a moment.

He wiggled his fingers again. "Sorry. For the first two weeks, you will have absolutely no contact with the outside world—no internet, no phone."

My eyes widened. I was going to go stir crazy. "It's…it's in my purse."

A second later, Mom had it and dropped it in Dave's hand. I glanced up at her, seeing lines around her eyes I'd never noticed before. Dave put my phone next to the bottles. Then he swiveled his chair toward me. "Do you know why you're here, Andrea?" he asked finally.

I thought that was a pointless question. "I…" I closed my eyes briefly. My cheeks stung. "I have…a drinking problem."

He inclined his head. "Is that the only problem you have?"

Pressing my lips together, I shook my head no.

"Do you know why you drink?"

Mute, I shook my head again, but it felt like a lie.

Dave looked at me and then turned a pointed stare on the bottles lined up on the desk. "I think you do, Andrea, but you're not ready to say those words. That's okay. My job is to get you to not only say them, but to understand and accept them." He leaned forward, resting his hands on his knees. "Are you ready to do this? To accept help?"

I sucked in a shaky breath and my voice cracked when I spoke. "Yes."

"Perfect. That's all I need to hear," he said, his bespectacled stare holding mine. "You've fought bravely this entire time, but you've lost this fight, Andrea. The good news is that you haven't lost the war. And you'll no longer have to fight this war alone."

# Chapter 23

**Andrea**

As expected, things sucked at first.

With no phone, no internet, and limited access to TV, it was an immediate shock to my system. Heck, even my little room with its single bed and dresser was a huge change, but these things weren't the biggest differences in my life.

Crying. Dear sweet Lord, there were a lot of tears. I cried when my parents left. I cried when I had to take the inpatient survey and got to the question: *have you had thoughts of self-harm?* I cried when I was shown my room after the tour of the facility and the grounds. I cried myself to sleep that night, and that took *hours*, because the sleeping pills had been taken from me. I cried in the morning, because it was the first morning there, and I realized my life had spun completely out of control.

I was *in treatment*.

And I wasn't supposed to be there. I was supposed to be a doctor. No. Scratch that. I was supposed to be a teacher. I was supposed to be a daughter and a sister, a friend and maybe…maybe even a girlfriend, and now, I was none of these things.

A nurse served breakfast in my room after she took my blood pressure and temperature. The utensils were plastic. Plastic. As was the plate. What did they expect me to do? I ate some of the eggs and a piece of bacon, but it tasted like sawdust to me.

Dave showed up about half an hour later. "Walk with me."

I didn't really have a choice, so I pulled myself off the bed and followed him out into the wide hall. There were other doors that I guessed led to rooms like mine. As we passed them, a girl who appeared younger than me smiled at Dave, but looked away when her gaze met mine. She disappeared into one of the rooms, and all I could think was how thin she was—so thin that she appeared ill.

"How are you feeling this morning?" he asked.

Folding my arms across my chest, I shrugged a shoulder. "Okay. I guess."

"Okay? Today is your first day in treatment. You're going to be here for *at least* thirty days," he said, shooting me a look of disbelief. "And you're okay?"

I shuddered. Well, when he put it *that* way… "I'm a little freaked."

"That's completely understandable. You probably feel like your life is out of control. You're where you never thought you'd be." He stopped in front of a dark-colored door while I wondered if he was able to read my mind. "Most, if not all, feel that way at first. Come on in."

Dave led me into a small office with shelves overflowing with books. As I sat in a chair, I looked over the titles. None of them appeared to be medical tomes. I squinted. Upon closer inspection, they appeared to be…a slew of romance novels. *What the…?*

"You've noticed my books." He dropped into the chair behind the desk and shrugged unapologetically. "I love me a happily-ever-after."

Okay.

"You're welcome to borrow as many as you like," he offered.

With no television or internet, I would so be taking him up on that offer with a startling quickness.

"Alright, I'm going to give you a little background on who I am and what we do here." Leaning forward, he picked up a baseball. "I'm a clinical psychologist who specializes in addiction counseling and treatment. Sounds spiffy, huh? Now, The Brook treats a whole wide variety of things. After all, variety is the spice of life, or so they say." He tossed the ball up and caught it.

Okay. This guy was kind of weird. Cute. But weird.

"We have people who are addicted to drugs and alcohol. We also have people here due to eating disorders and some who have depression. We've even had some who have extreme phobias and some quite random addictions. But what does this all mean to you?"

He tossed the ball again, catching it. "Some just do drugs. Some people just drink. We treat the addiction in those cases. But in others, we treat the disorder *driving* those addictions. If we don't, then all we are doing is treating the symptoms, but never the cause." Catching the ball once more, he put it aside and then tapped a slip of paper on his desk. "Now, based on your answers to our generic-as-hell questionnaire, you say you don't drink all the time. Is that the truth?"

My fingers were digging into the skin of my arms. "Yes."

"Are you lying, Andrea?"

I blinked. "No."

"But you drove drunk. Most people who drink occasionally do not drink and drive."

"I…I drink—"

"Don't answer that question yet," he cut in, and I frowned. "Answer this. Was that the first time you drove while under the influence or have you done it before, but were not that drunk?"

I shook my head a little. "I've never driven…" Pausing, I wetted my lips as my gaze shifted to the window behind him. "I might have done it before, after one or two beers, but I normally wait at least an hour or so."

"Normally? What made you not wait this time?"

My muscles were tensing up as my face heated. "There was this guy there, at the bar, who I didn't recognize at first, but he knew me. We must've hooked up, and I wanted to get out of there."

"Did you do that all the time, hooking up while drinking?" he asked.

I shrugged again as my face continued to burn.

"Andrea, I need your answers. Your *real* answers. Or this is an absolute waste of time." His stare met mine. "I need you to be honest. Sometimes painfully and embarrassingly honest. It's the only way I'm going to help you. In a way, I'm going to break you, because that's the only way I can really help you."

Wow. This sounded like fun.

"Do you want to change?" he asked.

I suddenly thought back to those moments before I left the bar, when I realized that the change I needed wasn't something external but all inside me. I'd recognized that before I'd gotten in the car.

Lifting my gaze, it was hard to hold his. "Yes. I want to change."

Dave smiled.

I didn't feel like smiling. "I've hooked up with guys when I've been drunk. There are times that I…" My face was seriously on fire. "That I don't remember the details. I don't even know what I've done or didn't do." Once I started speaking, the words kept pouring out. "I don't even know if I wanted to be with them or if I thought it was expected. Or because I'd been drinking. I've done it a lot."

"It doesn't matter if it's been two or two thousand, Andrea." He spread his arms wide. "There's no judgment here."

"That's…"

He waited. "What?"

It was hard to get the words out. "No judging? That's a… unique concept."

"Get used to it," he replied, flashing a quick grin. "Is that the only time you've had sexual relations?"

Goodness, this conversation got awkward quick. Totally no breaking me in, but I wanted…I wanted to change more than I cared about being embarrassed.

"No. Not every time," I whispered, staring at the front of his desk. There was a Baltimore Orioles sticker plastered across the center. "There was this one guy. He didn't like that I drank like…like I did, and I think…he really liked me."

Over the next couple of weeks, Dave became a magician when it came to getting me to put a voice to all my thoughts and fears and the random crap that sort of just came out of my mouth. There was a lot of talking and a lot of listening.

Sometimes we walked. Sometimes we talked in his office. Other times he made me talk in the art studio while I sat in front of a blank canvas. I had no idea what in the hell that was supposed to symbolize, but Dave…yeah, he was weird in a really effective way.

I didn't have withdrawal symptoms from alcohol, something that didn't seem to surprise Dave or the staff, but I did have a problem. I was a binge drinker, possibly one of the most dangerous forms of alcohol abuse. Where some…some alcoholics drank every day, a little here and a little more there, I drank until I was so drunk I couldn't say my name. I drank to the point that the alcohol in my blood could kill me. I drank until I was unable to think, every single time. I didn't have whatever people had in their heads that made them stop.

I couldn't.

That wasn't the only diagnosis. There were a couple more. An understanding that came two days after I'd told Dave how I had a habit of rearranging my furniture and painting the walls during those quiet moments. Of course, it wasn't the only thing that led to the diagnosis. Years worth of stuff had led to it.

Depression and Anxiety.

The…the diagnosis didn't surprise me either, not if I were being truthful. Maybe part of me had always known. Interesting enough, it would be a while before the role that alcohol played in my…my illness was known.

There was also an emphasis on physical activity. Besides the fact I was a little weak and a lot sore from surgery, there was a stress on staying healthy. I was lucky, though. I didn't need physical therapy.

After the third week, I was allowed visitors twice a week for an hour each time. My parents came the first time, along with my brother, and that was hard. Syd came the second time, and that had been even harder.

Syd had told me that Tanner wanted to visit me. I wasn't sure if I was ready for that, but I couldn't avoid him forever. He hadn't done anything wrong. For the most part, he'd done everything right, and I agreed to see him.

Tanner came on a Thursday afternoon, in the fifth week. Without makeup, I felt exposed as I waited for him in one of the visitation rooms. The whole makeup thing felt silly, but there was nothing between us now. Not even a layer of foundation. No pretenses.

The room wasn't bad. It had a couch and two chairs, a table in the corner, and it was painted a pretty robin-egg blue, but I figured the room was monitored. Made sense. No one who worked here wanted people passing drugs or something to the patients.

I'd been waiting for about five minutes when the door opened. I looked up and my tummy dropped as I saw him. Goodness, it felt like forever since I'd last seen him.

Tanner walked into the room and then stopped. The door shut behind him, and he didn't move as he stared at me. His brown hair appeared freshly cut, buzzed on the sides, and his jaw bare of stubble. Those electric-blue eyes burned bright from behind a fringe of dark lashes. His striking face was pale. For a long moment, neither of us moved, and then I stood on shaky knees.

He came forward, his long-legged pace eating up the distance between us, and then I was in his arms. I let out a soft gasp as I squeezed my eyes shut as he held me close to his chest, and I soaked up the warmth of his body, breathed in the fresh clean scent of his cologne.

"I had no idea if I'd ever get to do this again," he said, his voice gruff as his chin grazed the top of my head. "The last time I saw you…" He pulled back, sliding his hands to my arms. Despite everything, a tight shiver coiled down my spine. "I didn't hurt you, did I? I wasn't thinking—"

"No. I'm fine. Nothing really hurts anymore." My gaze drifted to his and caught. I didn't know what to say.

It seemed like Tanner didn't know either, but after a few seconds, he took my hand and guided me over to the couch. We sat side by side. I expected him to let go of my hand, but he didn't. "You look a thousand times better than last time."

"I can imagine." I laughed, but it was without humor. I studied our hands. "I wish you hadn't seen me like that."

"I wish that had never happened."

"Me too."

He was quiet for a moment. "I don't know what to say. We only have an hour and I don't want to waste a second, but all I can do is sit here and stare at you."

Oh gosh, why did he always have to say the right stuff?

"I guess I'll start with saying I'm happy that you were okay with seeing me. I knew you were okay, but I…I just needed to see it with my own eyes."

"I know…you heard the call go out and that you came straight to the hospital," I told him. "I'm sorry you had to go through any of that. I just wasn't ready to…to see you."

"You don't need to apologize." He squeezed my hand. "What's been going on in here?"

I raised a shoulder and then became aware of what I was doing. I wasn't being honest. I was hiding, and damn, if

Tanner deserved anything from me, it wasn't to sit here and act like a tool.

Taking a deep breath, I slipped my hand free. I couldn't be touching him when I had to be honest. Weird, but true. "I've spent a lot of time talking."

"About?"

I smiled wanly. "Everything."

"Would you...would you tell me?" he asked.

This was hard. Putting voice to this stuff, especially to someone like Tanner, who probably had only ever seen one side of me, but it was something we focused on during my sessions with Dave. To put a voice to what I was feeling, to cope that way instead of bottling it up...and turning to a bottle.

So I told him.

I talked about always rushing toward tomorrow, my restlessness and all those quiet moments. I confided in my fear of letting my parents down and how I couldn't settle on a future. I even told him about when I'd taken my first drink and how it felt to not care about anything, to feel like I was free, and I told him about the crash, because that feeling never lasted.

When I was done, I was exhausted. It was like shedding skin, but all of these things I spoke to Tanner about, it wasn't the first time I gave them a voice. These were all things that Dave had snaked out of me, one meeting after another.

I exhaled loudly. "So that's...that's everything."

"Yeah," he said quietly, and I peeked at him. He was staring at the wall. "That is everything. I..."

My cheeks heated. "You're probably wishing you hadn't asked."

"No. Not at all," he replied quickly. "I just didn't know. I mean, I knew you...I thought that there was something going on, but you're getting help."

I shifted. "Sometimes I wonder if I would've changed on my own. If I hadn't gotten in that car and had the accident, if I would still be doing what I was doing," I admitted.

Tanner nodded slowly. "I don't think you'll ever know, but you know what, it doesn't matter. You're doing something about all this now, and that's what counts."

I glanced over at him. "Really? That's what counts?"

His brows knitted. "Yes."

"I don't know. I think it has to be more than that. I messed up, Tanner. I drove drunk and could've killed someone. I think that counts."

"It does." He twisted toward me. "But you didn't. You only hurt yourself. And you're getting help. The fact that you are facing this is a big deal. And Syd told me you didn't fight it when your dad said you were going to treatment. Facing this takes real courage."

Courage? I wasn't sure about that.

His gaze searched mine. "Just in case you're wondering, I'm not looking at you any differently, and I'm still waiting for you to come to me."

My jaw nearly hit the floor. "What?"

He grinned a little. "Andrea, I really care about you. What I feel…" He moved his hand to his chest, above his heart. "I—"

"I've been diagnosed with depression. They think it's a chemical imbalance, since I haven't had any major life changes that would cause this, but that's not something that is as easy to diagnose as people think it is. I have anxiety too, and it could be coming from the depression or the drinking. Or it could be a whole different set of issues. It could take months to really give a definitive diagnosis, but I've been self-medicating," I rushed on, getting it out there. "With alcohol, and God knows what else."

Tanner blinked. "Okay."

A knot crept into my throat. "I think I've always known. I mean, I knew my head—my thoughts sometimes just didn't make sense. Like it always went to the worst-case scenario and I...I don't think I'm good enough or worthy enough, and those quiet moments, God, they're killer. That's what's really going on with me, so please—please don't say anything you really don't mean."

He didn't say anything for a moment and then, "First off, you *are* fucking good enough and you *are* worthy. Okay? Yeah, you made a shit choice when you got behind the wheel of that car, but that's not going to define who you are from this point on. You know why?"

My eyes widened. "Why?"

"Because you learned from your shit choice. You are still learning. You are doing everything to not make a shit choice like that again. And secondly? You have depression. So do how many million other people? I'm not trying to downplay it. I know it's serious shit, but do you think that makes me think less of you? Depression isn't a villain in this. The way you were trying to cope with it was. Depression isn't the bad guy and neither are you. Not when you recognize what you've done."

Tears rushed my eyes.

"And finally?" he continued. "I love you, Andrea."

My lips parted. "Come again?"

He barked out a short laugh. "I love you. Okay? I'm not quite sure when I realized it or how long I've felt it, but I know that's what I feel. Trust me. When I thought you were going to die, the panic and horror I felt? Yeah, I know how I feel."

All I could do was stare at him.

"I'm not expecting you to say it back to me." He gently cupped my cheeks and tilted my head back. "I don't want you to say it back to me now, because when I hear those words, I want you to be sure. I want you to say them with only happiness in your eyes. I can wait for that. I *will* wait for that."

As I stared into his eyes, in that moment, I knew that I still loved him, but I could not shake the feeling, the realization that I *so* did not deserve him.

I did not deserve the happy ending Dave loved so much.

# Chapter 24

**Andrea**

"Do you really believe in happy endings?" I asked.

Dave arched a brow as he sat behind the desk. "Of course I do. Without them, what's the point of all of this?"

It had been two weeks since I'd seen Tanner, two weeks since he'd said that he loved me and he'd wait to hear me say it with only happiness in my eyes. Two weeks where I had a hard time accepting that I deserved a happy ending.

"It's a strange question to ask," he commented. "May I ask why?"

The last thing I wanted to do was talk about Tanner with some oddly attractive guy. Why, oh why, did my counselor have to be a dude? "Tanner said—"

"Oh, the dreamy Tanner?" He grinned when I narrowed my eyes on him. "Continue."

"He said that he loved me," I told him.

Dave picked up the baseball. It was like he had a special relationship with the damn thing. "Is this a bad thing? From what you've said, he's a good guy." He threw the ball up and caught it. "Or do you not feel the same?"

My heart did a little jump. Answer enough. "I…I love him."

"Does he suck at kissing?"

I rolled my eyes.

He chuckled and then quickly sobered as he clenched the ball. "Do you think you don't really deserve it—the happily ever after?"

I pulled my legs up and wrapped my arms around my knees. A moment passed and Dave waited, and from prior experience, I knew he literally would sit there and wait until I opened my mouth. "I don't know," I said, shrugging one shoulder. "I mean, I'm a fuck-up and I'm a shitty person. I could've killed someone, and he…he deserves someone better than that, you know?"

"Having depression does not make you a fuck-up, Andrea."

I frowned. "That's not what I mean." Or was it? I was still coming to terms with what it meant to have something that was shaping my life.

"We obviously haven't gotten through your skull yet. Not completely. I see I still have lots of work to do," he said, placing the ball on the desk. It rolled to a stop against a large binder. "That's good. I like job security."

"Ha. Ha." My lips twitched, though. "Seriously. I just…I just want to be normal."

"You *are* normal," he replied. "Depression does *not* make you abnormal. Neither does anxiety, but the way you cope with it, the way you treat it, is what can make you abnormal."

I nibbled on my lower lip, mulling that over.

"Let me ask you a question. When you volunteer at the suicide call center, do you think the people you talk to are fuck-ups?"

"God." I scrunched up my face. "No."

"Do you think they're abnormal?"

"No. I think…I think they just need…" *They just need help.* God, I closed my eyes, exhaling softly. A few minutes passed before I reopened my eyes. "I think that's why I volunteered there. Maybe in a way I related to them. Maybe I was coping…"

"And that would be a good coping mechanism as long as you're not bringing that home with you."

I hadn't. At least as far as I knew. We'd talked about my volunteering before. Dave thought it would be a good idea if I backed off from that until I had a better grip on everything.

"I'm going to ask you another question." Dave inclined his head. "Do you think I'm a terrible person?"

Odd question. I looked around the room. "Um, no?"

He sat back, resting his ankle on his knee as he studied me. "When I was close to your age, maybe two years older, we had a lot of things in common. I didn't drink a lot." He smiled. "Or at least I didn't think I did. I just liked to relax on the weekends or whenever I was out with friends or when the day was stressing me out."

Yeah, that sounded familiar.

"One night I was at the bar with a couple of friends and it was getting late. I had what I thought was a couple of drinks. I didn't think I was drunk, and no one stopped me. No one was like, 'hey, drunk guy shouldn't be driving.' I left. I got in my car and I started to drive home. I didn't make it. I wrecked, but right there is where our similarities ended."

I couldn't look away.

"I totaled my car, but I was basically uninjured. Sure, I was bruised a bit, but I walked away from the accident with nary a scratch." The smile faded from his lips. "But I didn't hit a barrier wall, Andrea. I hit another car."

At that moment, I wanted to look away, but I couldn't.

"His name was Glenn Dixon. He was thirty-six years old and he was getting off from his shift at one of the warehouses in the city," he continued quietly. "He was married and had two children. One was four and the other was seven." Pausing, he drew in a deep breath. "I didn't realize I'd crossed the center line until it was too late. I tried to swerve, but it was virtually a head-on collision. He died on the scene."

I closed my eyes then. "Oh my God…"

"My actions took his life. One decision. One choice. I got behind the wheel of a car, and although I spent time in jail for it and I'll spend the rest of my life making damn sure I try to stop another person from making that one choice, I will never fully pay for what I did."

Horror filled me—horror for the deceased man's family and even for Dave, because I couldn't imagine living with something like that. But that horror—God, that horror—was also for how close I'd come to becoming Dave.

"So, let me ask you again, Andrea," he said, and I opened my eyes. "Am I a terrible person?"

I never answered Dave's question. I tried to give him an answer, but I never found the right words, and it wasn't until later that I realized there was no right or wrong answer to that.

At first, I did look at him differently. I hated to admit that about myself, but I couldn't help it. He'd killed someone. Accidentally, a dozen or so years ago, but he'd made a choice that had ended with someone losing his life.

And his story, what he confided, hit close to home. That could've been me, but it wasn't. Not because I did anything different or better than Dave. I had luck on my side that night. Just damn luck.

Did I think Dave was a terrible person? That was a stone I wasn't ready to cast, and there was a good chance I would never be able to, but something about his story not only hit home for me, but shook things up hardcore.

I wasn't Dave. Whether it was due to luck or what, I wasn't him. I, for the most part, could walk away from all of this and move forward without major baggage. I could get to that happily ever after, but I was going to have to work hard.

So I stayed in treatment longer than was required. Not because I was hiding, but because I knew, deep down, I knew that I still needed help. I needed to learn to recognize when I was feeling depressed and what those quiet moments signified. I needed to develop better coping mechanisms, and that's what Dave and the staff helped with. When I started to become restless, it was time to pick up a book, go watch a movie or take a walk, call a friend or visit family. I learned that I needed to open myself up. I had an amazing support system right at my fingertips. I just needed to allow myself to use them.

But I was leaving, after all that.

My suitcase was packed up and my parents would be arriving soon to pick me up. I'd briefly considered moving back in with them, but right then, I was sure I could handle being on my own.

I would be attending therapy sessions once a week and Dave was hooking me up with local AA meetings. Even though my addiction to alcohol was not as severe, it was still an addiction. The outpatient therapist would determine if I needed medication to help keep balance or if I could continue without meds.

When I left my little room for the last time, I went and saw Dave. He was in his office, with that damn baseball in his hand. I didn't say anything as I placed my suitcase down and walked to where he stood by his desk.

I stretched out, wrapped my arms around him, and gave him a quick, tight hug. Settling back, I exhaled softly. "Thank you. For everything."

A quirky grin appeared. "You're going to be okay."

"I know," I said, without hesitation. "And even if I'm not okay, I'm going to be okay."

"Right."

I nodded and then turned, heading back to my suitcase. "Goodbye, Dave."

"Make yourself proud," he called as I walked out. "Don't forget, Andrea, make *yourself* proud."

That was something I wouldn't forget as I walked down the wide hall, toward the doors leading to the reception area. *Make yourself proud.* That's what mattered, because I could still be a daughter, a sister, a friend, and maybe even a girlfriend one day. I could be a teacher or I could be whatever I wanted. I could be all these things.

This was the new normal—*my* new normal, and I was going to be brave. I was going to use that courage some had seen in me long before I ever had.

### Tanner

My legs burned and my heart thundered as my sneakers pounded on the treadmill. The whole damn thing was shaking, but I didn't slow down. It was early, way too damn early to be up and running, but once I woke up, I couldn't go back to sleep.

Forty-two days.

It had been forty-two days since I'd last seen Andrea in the treatment facility. And those forty-two days felt like a lifetime ago.

I knew she was out. She'd been out for the last week and a half, according to Sydney, and I hadn't heard from her. There was an ache in my chest, but I'd meant what I'd said to her that day. I would wait as long as she needed me to and I wanted her to come to me when she was ready.

I was not and could not be her first priority right then. I understood that and believed in that a hundred percent. She needed to take care of herself first, and if that required another forty-two days, then so be it.

But I missed her. Fuck. I missed her.

I missed her snappy comebacks and the way she gave as good as she got. I missed the sound of her husky, throaty laugh and the way her brown eyes reminded me of aged whiskey. I missed those tiny, feminine sounds she made, and I missed the way she said my name.

I simply just missed her.

And truthfully, I didn't think of her differently. Yeah, I'd wanted to yell at her when I found out she'd been drinking and driving—she could've killed someone or herself. I was pissed, fucking in a rage, but the fact that she'd immediately gotten treatment and held herself responsible for her actions lessened that anger pretty quickly.

I was just happy that she finally had an answer for why she turned to alcohol—that we all had an answer to why. Knowledge was everything, the only way she could get better. Having depression didn't make me think less of her. Honestly, if anyone thought less of someone because of that, they could go fuck themselves.

A huge part of me wanted to be there for her right then— wanted to help her in any way possible, to take care of her. But I knew she didn't need that. Andrea didn't need me to swoop in and save her. I knew damn well she could save herself.

She *would* save herself.

A beep intruded on the music blasting from my phone.

Slowing down, I pulled my phone out of my pocket and hit the screen, revealing the text message.

I straightened and almost fell off the damn machine. Smacking the stop button, I stared at the message, no longer feeling the burn in my calves or my lungs as my lips spread into a wide smile.

# Chapter 25

**Andrea**

A breeze rolled across campus, stirring the loose curls around my face. An hour had passed since Syd had dropped me off and I'd texted Tanner. My phone was in my purse beside me, and I hadn't obsessively checked it. I didn't know if he would come or not. It had been a while since he'd visited me in rehab and I'd gotten out. For all I knew, he could've moved on. It wasn't like I expected him to seriously wait for me. People's lives changed in a matter of minutes. That was the way life was, and he'd said he loved me, but while love was strong, things...things could change.

It would suck if they had. Admittedly, there were many moments while in treatment that I did cling to the idea of him and me, the promise of a sweet future, and that dream had helped get me through the roughest of the moments, but if there wasn't going to be us...I was going to be okay in the end. I'd be sad. I'd cry. And I'd want to take a drink, but I wouldn't.

Today, I was ready to face the future with or without him.

Moving my hand to my wrist, I toyed with my newest fashion accessory. My über-chic medical-alert bracelet that made people aware of the fact I was spleen-less. It wasn't like I'd drop at any given moment without a spleen, but I was more susceptible to infectious diseases. Good news was I didn't have to take antibiotics every day, but one of the first things I'd done when I'd left rehab was get all kinds of immunizations.

It was just another way my life...my life had changed.

While I'd been in rehab, I hadn't been on medication to treat the chemical imbalance. At first, they had wanted to try a more…holistic approach, considering I had addictive tendencies—talking, developing coping skills, and all that jazz. After a few weeks, though, they knew I needed more. So, another thing I had done within the last couple of days was pick up my prescription. It was strange thinking that I might have to be on the medication for the rest of my life, but it was far better than the alternative.

I watched a bird hop across the grass as it twitched its wings. The little guy stopped, glanced in my direction and then took flight. It flew to a nearby branch and landed, rattling the leaves. I'd watched the leaves changing color while I was in rehab. No longer green, a few that remained on the branches dropped to the ground in lazy spirals. A shadow fell over me.

My breath hitched in my throat as I lifted my gaze.

Tanner stood at the other end of the bench, his hands shoved into the pockets of his dark denim jeans. He had a dark blue baseball cap on, and it was pulled low, shielding his eyes.

For a moment, neither of us moved or said a word, but then one side of his lips quirked up in a lopsided grin. "Hey," he said.

My heart was pounding fast and that hope was a wildfire burning in my chest. "You came."

"Of course I did." He sat beside me, so close his thigh pressed against mine. His eyes never left my face. He stared at me so long I felt my cheeks start to heat.

"What?" I whispered. "Why are you staring at me like that?"

His grin spread. "You just look different. I don't know what it is. Maybe because it's been forty-two days since I last saw you."

My brows flew up. "You've been keeping track of the days?"

"Hell yeah, I have been." He angled his body toward me, dropping his arm along the back of the bench. "I've missed you, Andy. You look good—great. Beautiful."

"I've missed you, too," I admitted.

His shoulders loosened as if some unseen tension bled out of him. "So…did you talk to your advisor?"

I blinked, surprised. "How did you know about that?"

Tanner grinned. "Not to sound creepy, but I've been keeping myself updated on what you've been doing." When I arched a brow, he looked sheepish. "I've asked Sydney. I know I could've asked you, but I wanted—no, I knew I needed to give you time."

Syd hadn't said anything to me about it. Part of me could understand why. The other half wanted to throttle her. "I did talk to my advisor. I was…I was honest about why I missed virtually half the semester. There's no making up lost time at this point, but they're going to work with me. He's checking to see how tuition can be moved to next semester, and we're checking to see how having a DUI on my record may affect future employment." Saying DUI out loud was still hard, but I needed to speak it, because that made it real. "It could be tricky with teaching."

"What will you do then, if it does impact that?"

That was an important question. Good thing I'd spent a lot of time thinking about it. "You remember how you kept asking why I wasn't going to become a therapist? Turns out that might be a good option."

His smile was back, spreading across his face. "I like the sound of that."

I grinned as I shrugged. "Obviously, I have firsthand experience with some of these things, and I think…I think I could help other people. I don't know. It's something I'm considering. I have time to decide and I can change my mind. I'm okay with that—with either one. Nothing is written in stone."

"You're right," he agreed, lightly knocking his knee against mine. "You can do whatever you want."

"It's such a...a relief knowing that," I said, and I could tell that he was surprised by the fact I'd spoken that out loud. I was even a little bit surprised, but I'd been surprising myself every day recently. I drew in a deep breath as I glanced out over the grassy knoll. "When you visited me, you said—"

"I told you that I loved you," he cut in, and my heart jumped a little. "That hasn't changed, Andy. I love you."

I sucked in a sharp breath. "I didn't know if you'd still feel that way."

"Why? Did you think how I felt would change because you have depression?" he asked, his gaze unwavering as he reached up and twisted his cap backward. "Andy, I really hope you don't think that badly of me."

"No," I immediately replied. "You're a wonderful person."

"And so are you. You are an amazing person, Andrea. Frankly, you did something so many people never do. You realized you had a problem and willingly got help for it. Yeah, it took something drastic and it could've been worse, but you did it. You turned your life around and you're still turning your life around."

I blinked back sudden tears. Oh gosh, he was going to make me ugly cry.

"Like I told you before, you made a shitty decision that could've been so much worse. You could've died. You could've killed someone else. You're lucky that those two things didn't happen, but you didn't wallow in that and make more mistakes. You *owned* what you did and what could've happened. I saw your heart break when you told me. You had already realized how badly that night could've gone. You didn't fight what your family wanted. You willingly went into rehab and stayed longer than the minimum. You got help, and Andrea, you have my upmost respect for that. Seriously."

Tanner smiled at me. "You are incredibly courageous and you're remarkably strong. You're beautiful and you're funny. And you are kind," he continued. "Why wouldn't I feel the same way about you?"

"But I…" I almost stopped right there, kept what I wanted and needed to say to myself. Almost. Part of healing and getting better was to be honest. To speak. To not bottle everything up. "I have baggage. Real baggage. I'm working on it, but I know there are going to be moments when I'm annoying and it's going to be hard. So hard. That's a lot to want to be a part of."

"You don't see me running, do you?"

I shook my head.

"And I want you to know something else, okay? I hear you."

My throat closed up. "Tanner…"

"I *hear* you. Okay? I'm always going to hear you," he said, and my heart broke and was stitched back together in the same moment. He'd remembered what I'd told him about the people who called the hotline, just needing someone to hear them. He tipped his chin to the side. "I just have one question for you, Andy."

"What?" I whispered, still desperately trying to prevent the tears from falling.

"Why in the world did you have paint and summer sausage in your car?"

His words took a moment to sink in and when they did, a shaky laugh escaped me, and that laugh…it turned into a longer, deeper one that lasted. And goodness, it felt good, that full-body laugh. Tears snuck out the corners of my eyes, and I wiped them away, still chuckling. "Yeah, I bet…I bet that was a weird combo for everyone to see."

"It was." He lifted his hand, carefully swiping away a tear. "I missed your laugh."

Blinking my eyes, I met his stare. "So have I."

"I have something to tell you." He leaned in so close I could almost taste his kiss. "You've ruined me," he said against my mouth, his breath hot. "You've ruined me for anyone else. You know that, right?"

My heart was pounding again, but this time for a very good reason. "I'm not sure if that's a good thing."

He rested his forehead against mine. "Ruined me in the best possible way. So yeah, it's a good thing."

"You really want to do this?" I asked.

Tanner stared into my eyes as he cupped my jaw, gently smoothing his thumb along my cheek. A naked Santa Claus could come prancing out from behind the trees, and I wouldn't look away from those beautiful, brilliant blue eyes.

"I love you, Andrea. I'm in love with you," he said, voice firm. "And I'm going to be right here with you, through all of it. That's what love makes you do."

Tilting my head, I brushed my lips over his in the lightest touch, but I felt it all the way through me, invading every cell with its warmth, and I made sure when he stared into my eyes, all he saw was happiness. "I love you, Tanner. I love you," I said. "Do you see it?"

Tanner made a deep sound in his chest, and it rumbled through me. His hands trembled as he said, "I see it. I see the happiness."

Hope that had sparked in my chest now lit a fire, and I fanned it, wanting it to burn hot and bright, because hope… hope was not the enemy. It was a friend, a savior. Hope was more than a new beginning. Hope was tomorrow, and hope was the symbol that I would get better, that I would undo the bad choices that I'd made, and that I would never make them again. Hope was more than a chance of redemption. It was the promise of one day finding absolution, of forgiving myself.

But it was more than that. Hope was also today, and today was so very important. There would be no more rushing through seconds and minutes. I promised myself that. I was going to live, and it was going to be hard at times. There would be setbacks and days when everything would feel dull and tarnished somehow, but I had *hope* and I had the *knowledge* to face what was causing me to suffer. I had my *friends*. I had *Tanner*.

And most importantly, I had *myself*.

# Two months later...

**Andrea**

"Your parents like me."

I grinned as I glanced over to where Tanner stood in the doorway of my bedroom, watching me tug the rings off my fingers and drop them in the little jewelry box on my dresser. "I think they like you too."

He folded his arms across his broad chest, stretching the plain white T-shirt he'd worn under the button-down. His dress shirt had come off the moment we'd entered my apartment and now hung over the back of a chair. "Everyone likes me."

Laughing, I rolled my eyes, but truthfully, the fact my parents had openly welcomed Tanner had me giddy with relief. I'd held off on formally introducing them to Tanner, waiting until now, a few days before Christmas, before bringing him to Sunday dinner.

Once the rings were off, I kicked off my heels and moved to the center of the bedroom. "Seriously, though, they really do like you. I think Mom wants to adopt you."

He grinned. "I'm all about being adopted by rich doctors, except that would make things a bit awkward between you and me."

"Just a little." I walked toward him, my heart fluttering as he pushed off the doorframe and met me halfway. I slipped my arms around his waist. Hugging him tight, I pressed my cheek against his chest.

One of his hands curved around the back of my head and the other landed on the small of my back. He didn't speak as we held each other, and that was okay. I was…content with the quiet moment, with me just listening to his heart beat steadily.

It was peaceful.

The last couple of months had been a mixture of failure and triumph, of peace and chaos as Tanner and I had navigated my sobriety and treatment together. It hadn't been all easy. There had been times when I'd wanted nothing more than to take a drink, like when I thought about Tanner leaving for the academy or when the seemingly never-ending consequences of my actions resurfaced to give me a nice smack in the face, reality style.

Dave had suggested that I take some time away from volunteering at the hotline and the hospitals. The admins in charge had agreed, feeling it would be best for me to take a break. It was a nice way of them saying they weren't confident I could handle the pressure, and I understood that. As much as it sucked, I really did understand. And I also understood that while the depression wasn't my fault, the way I had coped with it had been a terrible decision, and I was going to have to prove that I was capable of handling my illness and stress.

I still worried about the long-term consequences—what having a DUI on my record would mean for employment and the fact I was still adapting to living without a spleen. I still dealt with the guilt over my parents stepping forward and paying the assload of fines associated with my DUI and the lawyer fees that had enabled me to avoid jail time. I'd been lucky, with no previous record, and the fact that I had willingly entered rehab and had stayed beyond the required minimum had helped.

But some days it was hard to look in the mirror, and every so often, I wondered how Dave did it every day.

Over the last couple of months there had been times when I'd come really close to picking up a beer, telling myself it was just one beer and one beer wasn't going to hurt me. But

I'd been able to catch myself and stop that line of thinking. Because one beer *would* hurt me. I was a binge drinker. One beer would not be enough. I wouldn't stop after it touched my tongue. And the times when the desire was too great for common sense to make a difference, I had my friends. I had Tanner.

The thing about alcoholism and depression, I was learning, was that it wasn't a one-person problem. It affected everyone you came into contact with, sometimes in ways you didn't even know, and not necessarily negatively either. People wanted to help you. They wanted to understand. You just had to let them.

And one of the most important things I kept forcing myself to remember was that I wasn't alone in this. Through the ups and downs since I'd gotten out of rehab, Syd and Kyler had been there. *Tanner* had been there, a constant source of love, acceptance, and support.

Even when I was sure he wanted to strangle me.

"Hey," Tanner murmured, his fingers sifting through my hair. "Where'd you go?"

Lifting my head, I smiled up at him and felt my chest swell with all the love I felt for him. Sometimes that was scary, holding on so tightly to those feelings, but it was also exhilarating, downright magical, and I knew now I would never trade what I was feeling for a beer.

"I'm here," I told him.

Tanner's hand slid out from my hair to cup my cheek. Those blue eyes, filled with tenderness, met mine. I stretched up on the tips of my toes and looped my arms around his neck. I didn't have to ask. He lowered his mouth to mine. The kiss was gentle at first, a soft exploration that sent a pleasant hum though my veins, and then, when his tongue touched mine, raw passion exploded.

My fingers tightened along the back of his neck as I pressed my hips against him. He groaned into my mouth, and I felt his reaction swell against my belly. I slid my other hand down his chest and pulled on his shirt, a silent plea that was answered by Tanner pulling back, his eyes glazed over with pent-up desire.

"Are you sure?" he asked, his gaze searching mine. "Are you ready for this?"

Tanner and I had held off on taking our relationship back to what we'd shared while we were at the cabin. My counselor had recommended against having sex, because it was quite possible that I would substitute one addiction for the other to cope with the depression. At first, that didn't make a damn bit of sense to me, because I'd never used sex as a way to not deal with things.

Until I realized through the weekly sessions that yes, I *had* used sex to not deal with things. That had also sucked, understanding just how deeply my illness had penetrated every facet of my life, but I wanted to get better. I wanted to be better, so I followed the rules, and even though I'd been more or less cleared for sexual fun stuff weeks ago, I had held off. Tanner had understood. He was patient. He waited.

But damn, it had been hard. The tension, the chemistry was always there between us, and denying it was torture even though I hadn't been ready to go there.

I was ready now.

"Yes." And to prove my word, I reached down and cupped him through his trousers. He was hard and thick, straining the material. "I'm ready. Like, way past ready."

His eyes closed as he shuddered and when he spoke, his voice was rough. "We can wait—"

I squeezed him through his pants and arched a brow.

"Fuck. Okay. You're ready."

His mouth smothered my giggle. The kiss that time was not sweet or slow. His mouth dominated mine and set fire to my blood. He backed me up as his hands coasted down my sides, balling around the material of my blouse. Not having time for buttons, he pulled the thin material up over my head while I started to pull off his shirt. We broke

Scorched

apart long enough for him to strip, and dear Lord, I'd never seen someone get their clothes off that fast, even though he'd forgotten to take his shoes off first and got hung up on that for a moment. I didn't waste time as he undressed. With trembling hands, I undid the zipper on my pants and dragged them down, taking my panties along with them. By the time I straightened, Tanner's fingers had already found the clasp of my bra.

There would be time later for a slow seduction, because I was really looking forward to Tanner undressing me, piece by piece of clothing, but I was aching and I knew he was too.

Then his hands and mouth were all over me, kissing and licking, nipping and tasting. I grew impossibly damp and he became so much harder. We stopped long enough for him to grab protection, and then he shoved his hands under my arms, lifting me up and tossing me on the bed.

I laughed as I bounced, and he came up and over me, his mouth claiming mine as he reached between us, guiding his erection. His hips thrust forward and I nearly exploded right then. He started moving, pumping in and out, and I tilted my hips up, wrapping my legs around his waist, taking him in as far as he could go.

Our mouths were greedy for one another, our bodies not easily sated. We clamored for one another, oblivious to the rattle of the headboard against the wall, fully focused on each other's sighs and groans.

Tension coiled tight when his large hand curved around my cheek in such a tender, gentle grip completely at odds with the surges of his hips. "I love you," he gasped out, his voice guttural. "I fucking love you."

I tightened all around him, breaking apart as I said those words back to him, over and over, until his hips grinding against mine stilled and he gave a hoarse shout as he came. I was spinning and spinning, tossed up so high that when I came back down, I was shocked to find that I was still in one piece.

Afterward, we lay together, our arms and legs tangled, my cheek resting on his chest. There was no need for words, not when his hand trailed up and down my back lazily. Not when the last words we'd spoken to one another were ones of love.

Quiet moments could still be really tough, but they weren't all bad. A sleepy smile stretched my lips. Nope. Sometimes those quiet moments could be heaven.

THE FATES ARE CACKLING THEIR BONY
ASSES OFF, BECAUSE HISTORY HAS ONCE
AGAIN BEEN FLIPPED TO REPEAT...

*The* A TITAN NOVEL

RETURN

#1 *New York Times* and International Bestselling Author
JENNIFER L. ARMENTROUT

# Acknowledgments

Andrea's story wasn't an easy one to tell, but I felt that it needed to be, and that by the time you've reached the end, you can see that no matter what you're facing or the mistakes you have made, there is always a happily ever after waiting for you.

First and foremost, a major thank you to the team at Spencer Hill Press—Kate Kaynak, Jessica Porteous, Rachel Rothman-Cohen, and Cindy Thomas for bringing *Scorched* to life, and to my awesomely awesome agent Kevan Lyon for always having my back, and major thanks to K.P. Simmons and the Inkslinger PR team.

Thank you Stacey Morgan for not only being an epic friend, but a wonderful assistant who helps keep me sane. Another big thank you to Laura Kaye, Sophie Jordan, Tiffany King, Chelsea Cameron, Jen Fisher, Damaris Cardinali, Jay Crownover, and Cora Carmack (to name a few) who help me procrastinate on a near daily basis.

This book wouldn't have happened if it had not been for you, the reader. Thank you so much for supporting this story and me. There can never be enough thank yous in the world.

Photo by Vania Stoyanova

#1 New York Times and USA Today Bestselling Author Jennifer L. Armentrout lives in West Virginia. All the rumors you've heard about her state aren't true. Well, mostly. When she's not hard at work writing, she spends her time reading, working out, watching zombie movies, and pretending to write. She shares her home with her husband, his K-9 partner named Diesel, and her hyper Jack Russell, Loki. Her dreams of becoming an author started in algebra class, where she spent her time writing short stories...therefore explaining her dismal grades in math. Jennifer writes Adult and Young Adult Urban Fantasy and Romance.

Come find out more at: **www.jenniferarmentrout.com**